_____ *Close to Home* _____

She also thought about the dress showing the freckles on her shoulders. No one had ever noticed before.

He asked: 'What's the solution, you frustrated one?'

They talked about solutions; none of them workable, but still, it was nice to discuss them. They talked about Samuel's book.

'Have no qualms, I can talk about *my* work for hours.' He plucked a stalk of grass and twirled it in his fingers like a dandy. 'Till you pass out, crushed by the sheer weight of my egocentricity.'

'Go on then.'

And he told her how it was a high-class spy thriller, lots of pace, lots of sex, three deaths so far, two of them violent, all the right ingredients. 'Bound to be a blockbuster,' he said. 'Once I've figured out the end.'

The sun glinted on the water. Up the towpath they sauntered, beside them the cow-parsley, masses of it, white and filigree-fine. It was quiet here, a tranced place with its motionless, floating slices of bread. Up above in the streets the world rumbled on and in Brussels James was sitting at his desk on the tenth floor – or was it the eleventh? She had never known.

One of four daughters in a family of writers, Deborah Moggach has written ten novels including the bestseller *Stolen* (subject of the high-rating television series starring Art Malik), *Porky*, *Hot Water Man*, *You Must Be Sisters*, *To Have and to Hold* and *The Stand-In*, which she is adapting as a Hollywood screenplay. She has also written a book of short stories, *Smile*, and a stage play, *Double-Take*. She lives in Camden Town, London, with her two teenage children.

DEBORAH MOGGACH

Close to Home

Mandarin

A Mandarin Paperback

CLOSE TO HOME

First published in Great Britain 1979
by William Collins Sons & Co. Ltd
This edition published 1993
by Mandarin Paperbacks
an imprint of Reed Consumer Books Ltd
Michelin House, 81 Fulham Road, London SW3 6RB
and Auckland, Melbourne, Singapore and Toronto

Copyright © Deborah Moggach 1979

This is a work of fiction.
All the characters are imaginary.

'The Man I Love', music by George Gershwin,
words by Ira Gershwin
© 1924 Harms Inc. (Warner Bros.)
reproduced by kind permission of Chappell & Co. Ltd

A CIP catalogue record for this title
is available from the British Library

ISBN 0 7493 1229 7

Printed and bound in Great Britain
by Cox & Wyman Ltd, Reading, Berks

_____ *Close to Home* _____

'Sorry about this.' Kate's carry-cot bumped into someone's legs. 'It's all the handles,' she said, as a body pressed against the wall. Motherhood had turned her into a woman who was always apologizing.

Here in the ladies it should be better. Beyond the doors she could hear the loudspeaker booming. Flight arrivals, flight departures. Here, off stage, amongst these hygienic tiles one could draw breath. Fewer bodies to bump into; in this room of clicking powder compacts and small repairs one could relax. The carry-cot, resting amongst purely female legs, seemed less of an embarrassment.

Could even be an asset. 'Gorgeous isn't he, and only four months?' Women would bend down and inspect Ollie. 'Isn't he big,' they would say, or 'Isn't he tiny.' 'He's just like you,' friends would declare, or 'Isn't he the picture of James.' Baby comments, though kind, always struck Kate as arbitrary.

Today though, Ollie was grunting irritably. Today he would be. Squirmy he was, tetchy. A mottled leg had escaped from the blanket, it jerked up and down. In the mirror Kate could see, sitting in a chair, an Indian attendant. She was wearing an orange sari covered in little sequins. Always Indian attendants at Heathrow; their strangeness never failed to startle her, like finding jewels in a fridge.

Ollie let out a yell. She could see his purple hands, fretful,

1

clasping and unclasping themselves. Tax demands, union confrontations – his face wore its crumpled businessman's look, comic on one so young. Kate tried to meet the attendant's eye in a rueful, us-women look, but the Indian lady stared at the white wall. Kate gave up and turned back to the mirror. She was wearing a new blouse. Already its buttonholes were grubby. Hungry baby, was there no end to the buttoning and unbuttoning? She wondered if James would notice the buttonholes; he was the sort who would. And today she was trying to look cool, intriguing, a wife to be reassessed. When he returned from Brussels she liked to present him with a small shock, a new appraisal of herself and their marriage. This time it was a crisp-bloused, efficient look, most unlike her. For a moment standing at Terminal 2 Arrivals she would be no longer the messy wife but the woman he had once married, the secretary with her own extension on the office phone and her wallet full of Luncheon Vouchers. Except, she thought, staggering towards the swinging doors, secretaries don't lug carry-cots. As a general apology to James, to the legs she had bumped, to something superior about that Indian lady, she clattered 10ps into the saucer.

'*Flight SN 607 from Brussels . . .*' Kate liked standing here at Arrivals, sharing the return of strangers, watching the smudges behind the frosted doors marked *HM Customs: No Entry*. Then the doors swinging open and faces appearing with that momentary hesitation, that expectant look that they wear even though they know they are not going to be met. It touched her, that. Some of them wheeled luggage; some held children; some – must be *IB 894 from Palma* – had suntans. Before the doors swung open each of the taller smudges could be James. She tensed.

She always tensed. Silly, after six years of marriage, but waiting made her nervous. Each time James returned she had to get used to him again. Two weeks away in the corridors of the Common Market returned him to her changed – a tall man with a slimline briefcase, a sleek airport stranger. Do all wives feel this? she thought, stiffening as each smudge darkened and the doors swung open. These occasions made her shy.

'Yes, shy,' she said, as he walked up to her. 'I shouldn't be.'

He put down his briefcase and smiled; she embraced him and smelt his aftershave, the James that commerce had given her. He picked up the carry-cot and they walked towards the Exit. She looked down at his polished shoes walking beside her own and was flattered, as always, by his obedient homing, by everyone's obedient homing. All those businessmen, all those thundering networks of buses and taxis and planes, all to return to one particular front door, one bed. She looked at James: was she worth it, so thoroughly explored, so grubby-buttonholed? So many other front doors, other beds.

She did not tell him these thoughts; he would consider them fey. Instead she asked:

'Lots of meetings? How did the agriculture committee go?'

She used to ask 'Did you have a nice time?' and silly questions like that; the messy wife might ask them but for the moment she was trying not to be this particular person. For the same reason she refrained from asking him what he thought of her blouse. Why indeed should he notice that it was new?

'*Alitalia flight 232 from Naples* . . .'

3

James's answer was drowned by the loudspeaker.

'*L 07 Polish from Airlines Warsaw . . .*'

Kate felt expanded. Naples . . . Warsaw . . . the airport made her feel larger, through its keyhole she peered beyond into space and distance. Coming from a house of children, of things pressed up close, needing her, it was a relief to wander through these polished halls that echoed with the names of far cities.

'I shall carry your briefcase,' she said.

As always, this expanded feeling lasted all the way back along the motorway and enabled her to converse with James about large, impersonal things. Ignoring the whimpers from the back seat, they talked in the way she suspected he would like them to talk more often in their married life: about politics, and the government's attitude to the particular section of Britain's EEC policy with which James was concerned. Ahead the wide motorway; on the horizon, glinting, the fins of planes. These drives home were drives through limbo, as yet uncluttered by the domesticity that lay ahead in the tall narrow house. Views were passed from Kate to James, from James to Kate, in the clear courteous manner of two people who have just met at a cocktail party. There might be the occasional silence, but Kate knew better than to fill it with the blocked drain and collapsed TV aerial that James, all too soon, would discover for himself.

'So that's what the Dutch,' he said, 'are planning to do.'

'But don't the French object?' She tilted her head intelligently.

He changed gear as they swung off the motorway. 'The French can't, can they; not the way things stand . . .'

As he answered she looked down at his trousered

thigh. In its businessman's charcoal flannel it looked the limb of an unknown man. There was no doubt that this was exciting; soon this unknown man would be taking her to bed. Nevertheless it also rebuffed; she found it disconcerting that six years of marriage and all her caresses could leave no visible change on a body which, like all men's, remained his, complete and contained within itself in a way that hers, belly softened by childbearing, breasts achingly full, could never be.

'And then,' he went on, 'we had to have another meeting about the tomatoes.'

'Oh yes! Tell me about the tomatoes.' Secretly she found the intricacies of EEC policies on the boring side; the mention of something as friendly and juicy as tomatoes always enlivened her. James's job was concerned with marketing restrictions, how many Golden Delicious one should be allowed to pack into a box, how much water should be contained inside a chicken. Mention would be made of milligrams and cubic metres. In the more abstract parts of these conversations she had been known to drift off, only to be jolted into life by the sound of something homely like a plum.

'And how's Joe?' asked James.

'Strapping and busy. I left him at home. Marion from next door said she'd sit with him. Too bothering to bring him to the airport.'

'Elly, Joe. Joe joggle the elly. Look.'

With one hand Marion was bouncing the rubber elephant up and down. With the other she was turning the pages of *Honey*. Each hand moved independently, like an automatic motor; she could run them both concurrently.

And she was thinking neither of Joe nor of *Honey*, with its printed confidences and glossy girls. Lying on the scratchy wool of the Coopers' sitting-room rug, she was thinking about Ron.

'A useful girl,' said Kate. 'That Marion.'

They were driving now through the London streets. Shiny in the sun, parked cars slid past the window. It was a bright Saturday in May, the pavements were crowded with shoppers. They drove down the Marylebone Road, nearing home.

They turned into the High Street. Passing the familiar shops, Tesco plastered with luminous offers, baskets of cut-price plastic sandals outside Philips Footwear, Kate experienced the draining away of that large, expanded feeling. She fell silent. Should she tell him about the aerial first, or wait until he turned on the TV and puzzled over the snowstorms? And what about the boiler?

'Any catastrophes,' asked James, 'while I've been away?'

Only about fifty. 'None,' she replied, smiling at him, 'that I can think of.'

'Committees,' he said. 'All those committees. It's nice to be home. To actually relax.'

When should she tell him about the drains? And Joe's Biro squiggles: when would he notice those?

James said: 'Every time one sets foot in Brussels it seems they've invented a new department. The paperwork!'

The thing about the Biro squiggles, as with most of Joe's misdeeds, was less the damage in itself than the evidence it gave of her own neglect that must have led up

6

to it. Sooner or later James would go into the sitting-room; sooner or later he would open his precious desk diary and find the scrawls – not, however, just on one page which could be excused, but on every single page from 21 May, at which he had left the diary open, to 31 December when it finished. What would he say, the rest of his year in confusion? His desk was sacrosanct; what a brain is to a body, his desk was to the house, and Joe was forbidden anywhere near its shiny mahogany surface.

'One is fighting against chaos,' said James. 'Bumpf breeding bumpf.'

The fact that Joe had got all the way to December showed plain as plain that Kate had not been in the room at all – had actually been down in the kitchen, busy feeding Ollie with one arm, answering the telephone with the other and also deep in a particularly engrossing chapter of her library book where the husband was just climbing into bed with his *au pair*, an eighteen-year-old Nicaraguan nymphet. How could she move? And as usual, James's exasperation with Joe would be as nothing compared to his unspoken disappointment with Kate, the neglectful mother. James was much more watchful with his babies. But then he could afford to be, couldn't he? He was not with them all day.

They turned down towards Brinsley Street. It was an ordinary terraced street of four-storey houses, some neglected with yellowing lace curtains, some smartened up with venetian blinds and William Morris prints. Though the fronts were unremarkable, the backs of the houses led into secret and surprisingly rural gardens, long and narrow and shadowed by sooty sycamores.

James parked outside number twenty-three. Kate

realized that there was no longer any chance of his noticing her new blouse, for he was gazing past her with a frown.

'Why are all the rubbish bags still out?'

'Oh, some dustmen's go-slow. They haven't collected for two weeks.' Seeing his continued frown, she added brightly: 'Don't you think it's instructive? We can see what all our neighbours have been throwing away.'

He received this remark in the silence it deserved and started getting the things out of the car. At the same moment Ollie, who had been lulled asleep, woke with a yell. Kate bundled him out. It was true that the street did look messy with all its bulging bags and overflowing cardboard boxes, but why did James have to notice those before noticing either her new blouse or the row of red geraniums she had planted in their window box? Why the rubbish first?

But then he straightened up and smiled. 'Never mind, it's nice to be back.' She smiled, warmly. It was, of course, nice. It was just that her pleasure at his homecomings was inclined to be mixed with anxieties, more and more of them lately. So often she was nervous of her husband.

Searching for the door keys, she whispered: 'Look. Next door's in full spate.'

James turned to look on the steps of number twenty-one, where a transparent rubbish bag bulged with paper. All of it was typewritten, most of it crossed out. It was well known that Samuel Green, their next door neighbour, was engaged on the definitive novel.

'There seems an awful lot of it,' said James. 'Perhaps he's given it up in despair.'

Kate laughed and squeezed his arm. They were confederates. Then he added: 'Good thing too. Then perhaps he might exert himself to support his family.'

Kate let go of his arm then, as that sounded pompous. She could not bear him when he was like that.

They opened the front door. Kate wondered how Joe would greet him. She longed for him to totter forward crying 'Daddy!' But usually he just looked elaborately unconcerned and went on playing, though with more studied concentration. It took him a while to get used to his father after these absences.

Joe was sitting on the floor with Marion. He glanced up and clambered to his feet. Kate brightened. He went up to his father and pulled up his jumper. 'Tummy,' he said. He walked over to Kate and showed it to her, his proud pale globe.

'He's got a thing about it lately,' Kate said. 'He's always showing it to people.'

James picked up Joe; Joe politely put his arms round James's shoulders but looked across at Kate. Kate felt a pang; so many stages Joe passed through – tummy stages, other stages. So many of these stages his father missed.

She said: 'When Joe shows it to him, the man at the dry cleaners . . .'

Her words trailed away for two reasons – the sudden thought that Marion must be paid, but how much? And the realization that James, the progenitor, had shared less in Joe's current unveilings than the small bald man behind the counter of Sunlight Same Day Service.

Two

Ron. Ron Blashford. It was an awful name but Marion could get over that. Ron . . . in her thoughts she could make him a bit more glamorous. Once he was not there her imagination could colour him up, fill him out, make him altogether dishier. In fact, when she had had a lengthy session of thinking about Ron it could be quite a shock actually coming face to face with him again. He seemed suddenly narrower, pastier, there seemed less of him.

The Coopers would not be back from the airport for a while. Marion shifted herself more comfortably on the rug. It was easier thinking in this house, instead of next door. No Mum or Dad to disturb her here.

The question was: should she ask Ron home? Would he think it too come-on-ish if she very casually dropped an invitation into the conversation? More to the point, did she actually want to drop an invitation into the conversation at all?

She turned the pages of *Honey*. An ad said: '*Get Ahead with Wella Hairspray.*' Tanned girls stared up from the pages, challengingly. All of them would know what to do. Marion's usual helplessness swept over her. The thing was, all the girls at school – well, all the girls that mattered – by now possessed a boyfriend. Proper ones – they had got past the stage of going to the cinema and giggling next day about the moist hand-holdings. There were no giggles now; in their superior, casual way they now had

Kevin and Rick and Tony in and out of their houses all the time, part of the fixtures and fittings. The chosen one accompanied them down the High Street to Woollies; at unscheduled moments of the day he would be occupying the sofa when Marion came to visit; he was *around*. She, Marion, could no longer ring up any of her friends without knowing that Kevin or Rick or Tony would not be sitting next to them, making them inhibited in what they said – duller really, guarded, with carefully carefree little laughs. Their boyfriends made them stodgier, proprietorial: 'Oh, Kev and I . . .'

She pushed *Honey* aside and turned to her next magazine. '*Adam says he loves me, but since he's moved in he's starting to take me for granted.*' They all had them. '*Damon is jealous of Mark, but I haven't dared tell him about Jim.*'

'Tummy.' Joe was standing in front of her.

Marion jumped. 'Joe's tummy. That's right.'

'*The problem is, Mark and I are marvellous in bed, but I'm feeling so guilty about Damon.*'

'Tummy.'

'Yes Joe. Joe put the rabbit in the jigsaw.'

'*Sex with Damon is –* '

'Rabbit? Rabbit?'

'The rabbit. Here.'

And it was not just Sharon and that lot at school. It was her parents too. There was something about her mother's elaborately casual questions, her artificial unconcern, that made Marion know she ought to be getting a move on. Dad was all right; he just sat typing away in the attic. Perhaps it was because her mother was a psychiatrist and knew precisely at what stage Marion ought to be arriving.

There was no doubt that someone must be produced,

11

and there were several points in Ron's favour. The main one was that he looked unsuitable. Marion knew in a flash that her mother would approve of that. Ron's earring and his funny leather trousers would produce in her mother that pleased and tolerant smile that made Marion lower her eyes and concentrate on the carpet.

Do I like my mother? she suddenly thought, staring at a page of her magazine. No, think about Ron. Do I like him?

Of course she did. Anyway there wasn't much choice, was there? They weren't exactly queueing up in the aisles. She looked around the sitting-room, at its little heap of sewing beside the sofa, its flowery curtains, its contentment. How nice to get over all this business and just be married: upstairs children sleeping, downstairs just the two of them, herself and an indistinct male, watching telly perhaps, leafing through books perhaps, she pouring out the Nescafé for him, no need to go through the agonies of thinking of something to say because they'd be married, wouldn't they?

A key rattled in the front door. Marion stiffened. A banging of suitcases and Mr Cooper was in the sitting-room. 'How's my Joe?' he said, picking him up.

Marion blushed; always, for everything, infuriatingly she blushed. This time she blushed simply because she was there in their sitting-room, bulky, taking up space, her magazines suddenly looking so trivial. Silly to be embarrassed about being there when Mrs Cooper had asked her, when in fact she was doing them a favour. She could see this, but in a grey, theoretical sort of way. Here on the scratchy orange rug, in hot, breathing reality – here, stupidly, she blushed. She blushed, too, because Mr Cooper was standing quite near; she had never been so close to him before. She could see the tiny lines on each side of his mouth. He was so tall, so slim, brown hair, brown eyes, lovely handsome face, but pale from all those executive decisions.

Even Mrs Cooper, her blonde hair brushed, looked quite tidy for once. They seemed such a couple. Marion felt cut off – worse, squatting on the floor like this meant that in her jeans her thighs were squashed out and looked, if that were possible, even fatter than usual. She struggled to her feet.

'You must take this, Marion.'

Heavens – Mrs Cooper was searching in her handbag. Was she going to pay her? To refuse seemed too complicated but Marion could not thank her properly either; only a mumble came out. How very much easier it was, being with children. Joe didn't notice her fat thighs or confuse her with money. Actually, they were the only people who didn't confuse her nowadays – children and Alf, the old man she visited down beyond the High Street.

Back home she met her father coming down the stairs.

'Been seeing Jock then?' he asked. Obviously he did not know where she had been. 'How is the old bugger?'

'He's not called Jock, he's called Alf.' She frowned at him; why didn't he remember anything she told him, ever? 'You always get his name wrong.'

'I forget. Anyway, he sounds like a Jock.'

'Well he's not.'

Her father put his arm round her as they walked down the hall. Part of her was annoyed that he could not get her old man's name right; part was pleased by his arm around her; yet a third part embarrassed by it, wanting to wriggle away. 'Anyway,' she added, 'I wasn't visiting him. I was baby-sitting next door.'

'Aha.'

She looked at him; he was in high spirits, his eyes twinkling but sort of twinkling beyond her, over her shoulder. Did he never notice what she was doing?

'Tell me about next door then,' he said. 'Back from Brussels is he, our faceless Eurocrat?'

'He's not faceless.' She looked at her father's woolly waistcoat matted with darns; he always wore it when he was writing. Never, ever would she admit to him how keen she was on Mr Cooper. All she said was: 'His suit is so nicely cut. You can tell.'

'Smarter than me, is he?' Her father lifted one foot and wriggled his toes in their battered sandals.

'Ugh.' Marion had to smile.

They clattered downstairs into the basement kitchen. He charmed her, Dad. Sometimes, anyway. In fact, he charmed a lot of people, with his fuzzy black hair and laughing eyes and complete unconcern about his appearance. Sometimes she could even forgive his bequeathing to her his large Jewish nose. Why did it look so much nicer on him than on her?

'They intrigue me, those two,' he went on. 'What does she do all the time he's away? I bet she gets lots of propositions.'

'Why should she?'

'She's so lovely. That breathless, expectant look, as if there's something just around the corner. That earth-mother's body.'

'You mean she's fat,' said Marion coldly. 'She's not that wonderful.'

'I like the way that when she puts up her hair bits of it are always falling down.' They were in the kitchen now. 'Yours, darling,' he said to his wife, 'always stays up.'

Marion's mother was putting out the lunch. It was true: her hair, a sleek brown roll, was pinned firmly on top of her head and there was no possibility of any of it coming down. A busy woman with a career, she looked out of place in the kitchen; as a politician might wear an overall to visit a factory, so she wore an apron to visit her kitchen – each garment had the same well-pressed, transitory air about it.

'What did you say, Sam?' She looked at her watch.

'That you're gorgeous, sweetheart.' He left Marion and went up to her, nuzzling her neck. 'You're looking delectably head-girlish today.'

'Careful of these glasses.'

'So severe. I love it.'

He was shorter than Jetta; impish, he looked beside her. An attendant satyr. Jetta was long, narrow and intelligent; she had slender tanned hands, slender legs with neat chiselled knees. Marion thought: how could they have produced a gross heap like me?

Her father, his head on one side, said: 'I'd love to see you in uniform. You should wear one at the clinic; give 'em something to *really* fantasize about.'

Marion sat down at the table. In this mood her father produced mixed feelings in her. Embarrassment was in the mixture of course, but in what mixture was it absent? Other things too. She could see that even at forty her father was sexy.

'I gather from this,' said Jetta, 'that your book's going well.' But she smiled and did not shake him off. 'Let's sit down, shall we?' She put the glasses on the table. 'I've got a meeting this afternoon and I'm sure Marion wants to be off, don't you, darling, after being stuck next door all morning.'

Off where? thought Marion. Of course she ought to be off, doing jolly Saturday things with her friends. The pressure was there, she could hear it in her mother's tap-tapping heels as she crossed the kitchen to the oven – the pressure was there to be off doing these nameless activities, but actually nobody had asked her to do anything and all she had planned was to go down the High Street and buy some shampoo and then take her magazines into the garden and finish that story about Tina and Luke, substituting herself for Tina and Mr Cooper for Luke. It had seemed a nice idea; so had the prospect of lying in front of the television all evening and wondering what to do about Ron. But she could just imagine her mother's hesitation, her faint surprise when she came back from the clinic and found her, *in* on a Saturday night. No, she must decide about Ron. Now.

They sat down to lunch. She took a breath.

'Er, I was thinking of – well, I thought I might . . .' she hesitated. 'You know, ask a friend round to supper next week. Would that be all right?'

Her mother smiled. 'Of course, darling. I wish you'd do it more often.'

'He's just, well, a vague friend.'

Her mother smiled her understanding smile, a smile that showed she knew what 'vague' meant. 'I see. Well, sweetheart, let us know the day, won't you. Your Dad and I have been dying to see that Russian film at the Academy, haven't we, Sam.'

Marion stared at her. 'What?'

16

'*Battleship Potemkin*. It's a classic. Extraordinary that I've never seen it before.'

'No, I mean what do you mean, you're going to a film?' Realization was slowly dawning. 'You mean, on that night?'

Her mother smiled. 'Don't worry, darling. We'll be sure to treat ourselves to a pizza after that.' She turned to Sam. 'Won't we.'

Marion gazed at her, open-mouthed. She had not antici-pated this. A whole evening alone with Ron? Her mother had got it all wrong. 'But you can't go out!' she gasped.

Her mother raised her eyebrows. 'Darling, it's a treat for us. Don't worry.'

'No, I mean . . .' I mean, what on earth shall I say to him for a *whole evening*? She glanced furtively at her mother. How could she explain this? The whole point was for her parents to be there – Jetta and Sam, so talkative and sophisticated and adept at carrying an evening along on a flood of conversation. She, Marion, could never think of anything to say to Ron; once she'd been alone with him for at least an hour – in that pub, when his friends kept on not showing up – and never had an hour seemed more like a century. Marion stared hopelessly into her plate: fat, complacent carrots. She must think of something quickly. Never, ever must her mother have an inkling of the real reason. Not that she ever would, of course – never in a million years would she understand that. But if she did guess – imagine the deep, deep pity, the slow unbelieving realization . . . Marion's stomach shifted inside her.

She swallowed. 'But Ron specially wanted to meet you. You see, he's, well, interested in novels and things. Awfully interested. He wants to talk to Dad about it.'

That did the trick. Marion subsided. The conversation turned to what they should eat and Marion was so relieved she could actually smile at them and say: 'Ron'll like you.' Too embarrassed to add: because you don't seem like parents at all.

Even in Brinsley Street a slight hush fell at lunch-time. Only a slight one; it was a noisy road, a through route, part of a complicated traffic system that led towards King's Cross and the City. Day and night lorries rumbled past, coming from the south coast, from the M1, from everywhere. They shook the old terraced houses. The noise reached its crescendo at rush hour when bursts of lorries and cars, released from the traffic lights at one end of the road, raced up the street only to be halted by the traffic lights at the top, there to rev their engines impatiently and fill the air with fumes.

This had an inhibiting effect on those who lived there. Chatting to each other on the pavement they felt on public display, especially on weekdays when the traffic was at its heaviest. Then the lights turned red, the cars queued up and the drivers, tapping their fingers to the music on their radios, would turn to stare at whoever was standing on the pavement, making them feel shy, making them feel they had come out in their curlers even when they had not. Then the lights would change and the traffic start moving, working up speed until the street shuddered and mothers, clothes whipped up by passing pantechnicons, would clutch their infants with one hand and their skirts with the other.

At weekends however the traffic thinned, and at Saturday lunch-time it almost ceased. A hush fell. Doors slammed shut, children jammed their trikes sideways in halls and ran downstairs to kitchens; far clatters could be heard in basements or, in those houses that were divided into flats, in upstairs rooms.

Down in the basement of number twenty-three they were having lunch.

'Poor Marion,' Kate was saying, to divert James's attention from Joe who was eating his mince with his hands. 'How awful to be adolescent. That shy aggressiveness. Such a relief to grow up.'

James said: 'She's a bit on the lumpy side.' He paused. 'I say, Kate, shouldn't we be teaching Joe about spoons?'

By the considerate way he said 'we', it meant 'you'. Kate struggled to her feet. 'Look, Joe.' She picked up his spoon from the floor. 'Look, lovely meat.' She scooped up a spoonful. Joe ducked his head and with one hand, the meaty one, rubbed his face. He gazed back, mince-bearded.

Kate looked at James. She wished he were not still wearing his Brussels suit. He looked out of place in the kitchen; his career still clung to him, off-puttingly.

James looked at Joe. 'He doesn't seem to get the hang of it, does he.' In his weekend clothes such a remark would have seemed rueful and companionable. In his suit it seemed censorious; he appeared less the father of his family than its visiting inspector.

This added to the odd politeness with which they always treated each other until they had slept together. She never felt he had arrived home until then; lovemaking was the first step but it was the ensuing shared slumber that finally did it. Before the advent of Joe and Ollie they might have hastened this process and gone to bed after lunch, rumpling up the afternoon. It was nice, that.

Kate's thoughts were broken by James asking: 'How do you like this *pâtisserie*?'

'Lovely,' said Kate without thinking.

James had a nice habit of bringing home, if he had time, groceries from some Belgian supermarket. Today it was a sort of custard tart. No doubt James knew its proper name; Kate could not understand French. She looked at her plate; a piece of it lay there, apparently half-eaten. Had she tasted it? There had been so many other things to think about first. Was that a whimper from Ollie upstairs? Would James notice – *one* – the bleached, scrubbed patch on the floor, the result of Joe's first bungled attempt at potty training – *two* – exactly what Joe was doing with that piece of soggy bread – *three* – the fact that the cat had been licking the butter again – with sinking heart Kate gazed at its rounded, fuzzy edges. How on earth could she have space to actually notice what she was eating, for heaven's sake, let alone pause to consider whether she was enjoying it? That was the very bottom of her list. She thought: I scarcely possess my body; it belongs to everyone else.

This was ridiculous. She speared a mouthful; she sank her teeth into it, sank through its crunchy crust to the sweet softness within. Her eyes closed. 'Delicious,' she said. How nearly she was becoming the tense, dreary little wife. Why should James struggle his way through Customs to get to her? She must not be like this; and would she not like to enjoy her custard whatever-it-was?

And she did, even though out of the corner of her eye she could see Joe. He had now picked up his spoon, but with it he was tackling a biscuit.

'Perverse child,' said James, but he was smiling.

It got better after that. Lunch over, James changed out

of his suit and at last became accepted by the house. Also, such is anyone's unpredictability, he was taken aback by the Biro marks but managed to remark 'Quite the little Leonardo'. So often Kate miscalculated; how often was she unfair? His trips abroad must be partly to blame; in his absences he became frozen like a snapshot – tall, thin, pale, a kind man, irritable over small things but good over the large ones, a man too masculine to examine himself, a man who seldom unbuttoned his feelings . . . thus she could start to label him, but really it would not do. Her mind, like most, neatened things once they were out of sight, put them in boxes the more conveniently to be stored. Poor James, boxed.

Brinsley Street was all fumes and noise; passers-by could scarcely guess at the sweet green release that lay behind the houses, the shade and silence and dappled patches of grass, the flowers and sleeping cats.

The residents, sharing over honeysuckled walls their rural secret, behaved differently here from the way they did in the street. In the street they had to shout to be heard, their eyes flickered always to their children, they had to press against the railings for the passers-by. Here in the gardens, their own countryside, they felt private and sufficient unto themselves. Kate, leaving the kitchen, sat on the lawn, unbuttoned her blouse and started feeding Ollie. Joe wandered off and prodded at the flowerbeds with a stick, bees murmured, pansies lifted towards the sun their sweet, anxious faces.

Through the foliage came the familiar sounds. On her left she heard the mutterings of old Mrs Forsythe, who kept her curtains drawn all day and whose garden was lost

21

and tangled. She liked standing amongst her bushes going over an ancient quarrel. Kate could hear her now. It was always the same quarrel; her mutterings, rising and falling, were never quite loud enough for Kate to hear the actual words, they had the mesmerized rhythm of a chant.

To her right she had seen, on entering the garden, that Marion lay drying her hair in the sun. Silence from there.

Silence, because Marion was reading.

'*Luke was sliding his hands round me and caressing me as only he knew how. His lips came down on mine and I felt warm waves of pleasure licking through my body. "Luke," I whispered. "Yes, yes!" Luke's hands were over my breasts, his lovely tanned hands, so strong, so gentle. "I love you, Tina. You know that, don't you." I gazed into his eyes; against his tanned skin they looked so blue . . .*'

Marion's wet hair was tickling her chin; she pushed it back and shifted her position on the grass.

'*. . . blue and urgent, yet strangely tender. Gently I traced round his lips with my fingertips. "I know." I could feel his hands undoing my blouse. "Oh yes," I whispered. Turn to page 71.*'

From the window high above her Kate could hear the tapping of a typewriter. If she looked up, no doubt she would see Samuel Green's profile at his attic window. Kate did not look up; she felt shy. Coming face to face with Samuel Green, even across a garden, she always had the same sensation; she was conscious of the skin beneath her clothes.

This only added to the intimacy she already felt with

him through his book. She had lived in Brinsley Street for six months; by now she was familiar with it, the rattling typewriter keys had merged into the background murmur of her garden along with the rustle of leaves on the apple tree and the far rumble of traffic. What was the book about? When she was up in Joe's bedroom she could hear the tapping through the wall. It had become as much a part of the room as the row of Peter Rabbits on the Beatrix Potter frieze; it had seeped into those times when she tiptoed upstairs to gaze at Joe asleep in his cot, fragrantly breathing. Samuel's novel had shared those moments, its unknown contents were part of the closed and secret life she lived with her children. The inspired bursts of tapping, the rattle of his thoughts, the poised hesitations were part of her day. This made her feel strange when she met Samuel Green in the street, as if they had spent the night together and only she could remember it.

Tap tap. Sam was busy, but to tell the truth he was busy with x's. Tap tap – a smug black row of x's, briskly they marched across his sentences, engulfing them.

Was it any good? He bent over the typewriter; he concentrated. Anyway, he tried. He knew that down in her garden Kate Cooper was feeding her baby.

These houses had brick extensions. Once they had been sculleries; Mrs Forsythe's probably still was. The Greens', judging from the prolonged rumbles heard from it during the day, must have been modernized to house a washing machine. The Coopers' own outhouse simply contained James's tools.

He was in his toolshed now. Kate could hear clatters

23

and bangs and the radio murmuring. James must be sorting things out, but cheerfully. The timbre of the clatters told her they were cheerful ones. She had attuned ears, wifely hearing.

Down the opposite end of the garden, through the trees, stood a tall block of half-derelict flats. This area was full of old tenements. Most of them were due for demolition and had their windows boarded up, but in this particular building some people still clung on behind ragged curtains, growing tomato plants on their windowsills in plastic buckets, switching on bare light bulbs at night. Kate was ashamed of the twinge these flats gave her, the thankfulness. Their glinting windows were the spectre at her feast; turning back from them, around her the garden grew greener and more precious. She might be selfish but was she not grateful?

The sun shone; happiness swept over her – happiness because she did not live in those flats, that she had two children, one at her breast and the other standing on sturdy pink legs, that James was home and because at that moment the tortoise emerged from the bushes. So dry and prehistoric, he filled her with awe, he walked across the grass as if walking across the centuries.

The toolshed door opened; James appeared to inspect something in the daylight.

'So lucky, we are,' Kate called out in her vague way, meaning everything.

'I know,' answered James, meaning the weather. 'And the paper did mention rain.'

He is so masculine, thought Kate, but fondly.

James was cheerful enough. Busy, anyway. Unlike his wife he was not a soaker in baths, a lounger on lawns.

For him to be active meant an up-tempo in his spirits. He had to be doing things. Not an introspective man, he did not examine why upon his returns from Brussels he felt impelled to retire to his toolshed.

'England 110 for 4, Greig not out 32 . . .'

He certainly did not consider himself a potting-shed husband. That was too much of a cliché. They were just soothing, these hooks, each one occupied; that row of chisels, largest tapering to the most slender; those labelled containers, containing exactly what they said they did. Solid tools, workmanlike and shapely. He could finger them lovingly. Everything ordered.

'England 113 for 4 . . . Hamid to bowl . . .'

Order there too. White figures, immobile; scoreboard waiting for its next number. Kate did not understand cricket; he considered her *faux naif* when watching it on the TV. 'Who's that one?' she would ask. 'What a perfect Greek nose.' Then she had been quiet for a while and he thought she was really getting to grips with the game, but do you know what she had done? Breathed a sigh and pronounced: 'Amazing to think of all those huge brawny bodies being once in nappies.' Pray what does one answer to that?

To his Black and Decker workbench James clamped a length of two-by-four. Parts of the window frame at the back of the house needed replacing; the bolts, too, should be reinforced. He was even speculating on a set of iron bars for the basement window. By nature a responsible man, the arrival of children had given shape to his responsibility. He had a strong impulse to seal in his little brood, make them safe. Nobody could call this area secure . . .

Those flats at the back, for instance. Once, walking past

their front entrance, he had put in his head and smelt the despair. Tramps, squatters, general misfits . . . they all haunted ruins like those. Stone stairs, broken glass, on the walls urine stains and *Fuck You*. Nightly from the basement tom cats crept out and climbed over the wall into his house; they got in through the cat flap. Once, going downstairs for a drink of water, he had met one face to face, sitting bold and smelly on the kitchen table.

Roaming tom cats, roaming men. *Fuck You* on a thousand walls. His sons were so young, so tender, with their fair heads of hair.

Kate was too casual. Old men in bedroom slippers came to the door; could they clean the windows? they asked. Blithely she let them in. 'He looked so pathetic,' she would confess when James came home in the evening. 'His hands all shaky.' James would not have minded so much – after all, it was something joyful and easy in her that he had first loved – he would not have minded so much if she had not then reproached him, less by words than by manner, for being the killjoy.

Somebody had to, hadn't they? His being the killjoy, the one who bolted and barred, enabled her to be free; within his safe circle she could dance. Just so long as she realized it was himself, hammering away here, who was making it secure. Give me credit for that. 'Daddy'll fix it,' she would say to his sons as they grew. 'Wait till Daddy gets home.'

'*Greig out for 54 . . .*'

Lord's Cricket Ground, how reassuring you are. The house might be a mess, the neighbourhood full of thieves, *UP THE IRA* scrawled huge and spidery over the misused old buildings, but over at Lord's everything is in order. One sane square – large, calm, green.

James picked up his Biro to mark the wood. Biros – he thought of his defaced diary. Also of Kate inking in her tights. Early on in their marriage he had caught her at it – bent over her leg, filling in a hole in her black tights with Biro. Yes, filling it in. She had laughed. 'How shocked you look!' Indeed he was.

At fond moments he could smile about this – this and other things, like returning home to dead radios because all their batteries had worn out. Yet he also felt an irritated despair. Visions of chaos and himself fighting through it.

James took the piece of wood outside to measure it in the light. He glanced down the garden. Kate lay beside Ollie on the grass; she looked up and smiled. She had a lovely face; at the airport he had felt a shock of pleasure, seeing that unknown woman in an unknown blouse.

He said nothing though. He had said nothing then. She knew she was pretty. Telling her things like that always made him feel awkward, as if he were being pushed into an overheated room. Anyway, he wanted to get a move on with these window frames, didn't he.

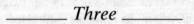

Three

Twenty minutes to go.

Throat dry, Marion sat in her den. Twenty minutes to zero hour: Ron hour. Her Mickey Mouse clock stood on the mantelpiece; it wore a stupid grin. What was there to smile about? Infantile clock.

It was called the den now, her room. Her mother, in her casual yet somehow pressing way had named it that, and had helped her to paint over the juvenile wallpaper and install the record player and dressing-table more appropriate to Marion's age. On the shelves a teddy or two remained, past companions, collecting dust like exhibits.

Marion was sitting on the edge of the bed. Her den was up the stairs at the front of the house; from this vantage point she could look down on the street, the passers-by and, when the dreaded moment arrived, Ron. It was ten past seven and still light outside; nevertheless she could see the glowing blue squares of televisions all down the street. She would give anything to be in one of those living-rooms, ensconced in front of the telly. Safe viewers – didn't know their luck, did they.

She ate another spoonful of chocolate mousse. They had made it for supper but she had left enough over for just this purpose. She was adept at this; she hid her scraped-out bowls under the bed as furtively as a secret toper would hide his empties. More furtively, actually: at the advanced age of sixteen her parents would expect her to swig the family sherry or smoke a crafty packet of Rothmans. She wished she liked either of these.

Better even than drinking or smoking, she should of course be taking drugs. Her mother had had a frank discussion just the other day about what she called 'dope'. She had explained how natural it was to try anything new at Marion's age. She, Jetta, respected this. At this point Marion had blushed and her mother, noticing it, had gone on to explain how she should not feel ashamed; most soft dope was relatively harmless, it was only the hard variety that one had to guard against. By this time Marion's face was burning: how she blushed for her hidden little packet, McVitie's Coconut Crunchies.

Drugs had another advantage: they did not give you spots. The more Marion ate the more spots she got, and the more spots she got the more she had to eat to cheer herself up. She examined her face in the mirror. Those who have never had spots cannot understand the peculiar relationship between spots and their owners, the dreadful closeness. Marion could spend hours in front of the mirror, examining hers with a horrified fascination that in its lingering care was almost lover-like. They never failed to surprise; as the days went by, like the constellations in the night sky old spots would disappear and new clusters appear, altering the map of her face into ever more gruesome combinations.

Ten minutes. Marion scraped out the chocolate mousse. Just occasionally her spots disappeared and migrated mysteriously to the portion of her back between the shoulder-blades. The next week, back they would return to their familiar roost on forehead and chin.

Mickey Mouse grinned. The only slight consolation was that Ron himself was fearfully spotty too. Would he try to kiss her soon, spot against spot?

So that she would not be seen at the window, Marion got up and wandered around the room, fidgeting with the things on the mantelpiece. To tell the truth, though it was a year since the room's transformation into the den she still did not feel quite comfortable in it. Her mother (Marion knew that nowadays she ought to call her Jetta) – her mother had not chosen the things, of course; she had just lightly suggested them, but there was something powerful about her lightness. Alternative suggestions would have met with that moment of hesitation, just a moment, that made the person suggesting it feel ashamed that they had thought of something so silly or irrelevant. Anyway Marion's ideas were never as interesting as her mother's. Jetta was kind; very kind, in fact, but bossy with it, and Marion felt as putty in her hands. Did Dad feel that too? Probably, but then Marion had been seeing Dad more clearly lately and she suspected that he liked being putty. He had announced one night: 'My dream woman has a D. Litt. and is wearing a nurse's uniform. It is starched but frilly. She is bending over me.'

It was off-putting, the way her mother was invariably right. She knew that Marion would like the privacy of a lock on her door and a subtle grey-green on her walls; the fact that she understood shrivelled things up in advance.

Silly, wasn't it, to complain that one's mother was too intelligent, too understanding! Sharon and that lot had mothers who were all the right things – stuffy, prim, ordering them to be home by eleven. 'No daughter of mine's going out in that dress,' they would say. Or 'Take that stuff off your eyes. You look like a tart.'

Five minutes. Marion slowly brushed her hair; the plastic handle felt damp. How would Ron behave? How would her parents behave? Could she trust any of them?

She wandered around the den, pushing her books straight. When she was younger the room was full of places to play – even the narrow strip of floorboard between carpet and wall was a lane down which she would push her Corgi cars. The room was limitless; it could become anything she wanted. But her childhood was gone; the floorboard was just normal floorboard again, rather awkward to clean. The magic of childhood had ebbed away, vanished, leaving it all as ordinary as it must be to anyone else. The table, no longer changeable into a fort or the counter of a grocer's shop, was just a table, the looking-glass just an object in which she could inspect her awful face.

Downstairs the doorbell rang. Marion stiffened. How uncool of Ron to be so punctual! She would linger here a bit and then go down the stairs all casually.

Lingering a bit, then sauntering down the stairs, lips pursed in a silent whistle, the thought struck her: poor Ron. I've never actually thought of him at all. Would *he* enjoy this evening?

'Can you remember it?' Kate was asking next door.
    'Remember what?' James passed her a glass of Cinzano.
    'You haven't been listening.'
    'Yes I have. Something about matchboxes.'

She could tell James was dying to read his *Evening Standard*. He was fidgeting with it on his lap.

She said mercilessly: 'I was thinking about the old days. When we were Marion's age. I watched her drying her hair in the garden and it took me back – you know, getting ready for Saturday night. Wonder where she was off to.'

'What's the matchbox business?'

'Well, I'd look in my handbag and find phone numbers scribbled on my matchbox or my cheque book. People I'd met at parties. It seems an age ago; I can hardly believe I'm the same person.'

'Let's not get too maudlin.'

'I'm not. I'm just remembering it all. You know, young and unattached, roaming about for a mate. Intense discussions in Indian restaurants at two in the morning. Bedsits and last buses.' She could still taste it, the lukewarm Sauternes at gate-crashed parties; unknown Earls Court flats, a press of bodies, glances flickering around the room.

Starved of company all day, Kate longed to talk. This happened every evening. James, returning from a busy office, needed a dormant armchair period, emptying his glass of whisky and filling himself with print. Kate, tired in body but unused in brain, needed to speak to this envoy fresh from the outside world, hear the events of his day. Offer him hers too, for what it was worth. ('Darling, the Hotpoint man came today. He told me all about the inside of Peter O'Toole's house.' What else? 'A woman in Sainsbury's spilt a whole box of eggs. Joe was mesmerized by the fuss, a man with a broom sweeping it up. I thought of the six straining hens.' Any more?

32

'Joe watched a beetle walking across his leg and then he squashed it. I burst into tears.') Three modest sagas. She had little more to offer. James knew her world so well, its four walls and its three principal characters; its furniture, its network of well-trodden pavements were familiar to him. Sometimes this struck her as unfair.

James listened patiently, not even sneaking a look down at his lap, but she could tell he would really rather be immersed in the overseas report. And who could blame him? Even as she said the words to this dark-suited figure, they sounded dull. I shall live off the stored fat of the past, she thought. I shall escape into housewife's fantasies. She said aloud: 'I shall watch Marion next door reliving my youth.'

She got to her feet. Nowadays they seldom went out in the evening; since the second baby the cumbersome apparatus that was now necessary, the complicated series of arrangements caused them not to bother. After James's hectic day this suited him.

She stopped in the hall to pick up Joe's letters. Joe, knowing that letters were found on doormats, had developed the habit of collecting up any that happened to be about the house – opened ones, unopened ones, a stack of bills ready for posting on James's desk. He then took them along the hall where, with the officious manner of a tiresome duty done, he would deposit them on the mat.

Kate bent down to collect the little pile; their lack of a postmark gave them a virginal look. She jumped: in her ear she heard the doorbell of number twenty-one. The two houses, being the centre couple of the terrace, had been constructed not as part of a repeated pattern but as a mirror image of each other; consequently their hallways were adjacent, the Coopers' hall to the right of their sitting-room, the Greens' to their left. This made the hallway noises sound very close.

Murmurs; the click of the Greens' front door. Guess who's coming to dinner? In the few months she had lived at number twenty-three she had become familiar with their comings and goings, though as yet she did not know the Greens well, their circumstances being so different from her own. They were neighbours, they were acquaintances. A descending creak; someone coming down the stairs. Who? A door closed; the murmurs grew muffled. They must be in their sitting-room. What were the murmurs saying – intense things like 'Tell me all about it?' Jetta Green looked as if she might be rather intense. Or polite things like 'Isn't it hot for May?' What were they going to eat?

An inoffensive little game; if Kate could not go out it was better than nothing. She liked imagining their lives as she stood in her own narrow hall. Daytime sounds, the typewriter tapping, music from the upper room that must belong to Marion, various voices, suddenly loud and clear – 'Brillo Pads', someone might say, or 'No!' Startling, that. Evening sounds – the doorbell, hellos and hallway laughter; then at midnight louder goodbyes, louder, boozier hallway laughter, the front door slamming, her own front door shuddering. She knew it all so well; ah, the thinness of walls, the paperiness of one's little box.

'James, you're not nosey like me, are you.' Kate brought in some more ice and put James's letters back on his desk.

'It's a feminine characteristic, I believe. More Cinzano?'

Kate looked out of the window at the houses opposite. Familiar, their rhythms, by sight if not by sound – the opening and closing of curtains, the switching on and off of tellies. Flickering windows, rectangles through which could be glimpsed fragments of lives. Round these rectangles she liked to construct the unglimpsed bulk, as an archaeologist, given some fragments of pottery, might construct around it the complete shape of the vase. She filled them out with her thoughts. But it was next door that intrigued. Was it that they lived the sort of life which at this childbearing period of her own was denied to her? Evidence of this she could see: on the Greens' doorstep the adult single bottle of milk compared to her own familified four, in their garden the chairs arranged for gin and tonics rather than disarranged for play. Every morning Jetta left in the car, on its windscreen an official Hospital Car Park disc, emblem of liberty, proof of her place in a world beyond the four walls of her house.

'Still nostalgic are we?' James was smiling. After a glass of Scotch he was more perspicacious.

Kate turned from the window; she too smiled. 'Darling, do I sound sour? I don't mean to be. I love our babies.'

'If I remember right, this is just what you wanted. Lovely house, garden, babies. Every woman's dream.'

'It is, it is.'

'Spare a thought for your poor husband, toiling away in his office, slaving away to pay the mortgage . . .'

In a way he was right. Kate had met James when she was twenty, he twenty-six. She had been a secretary then, later promoted to personal assistant, a job into which she had slipped in her unthinking way. Never had she been bad enough at it to pull herself up and reassess what she

35

was doing, nor yet good enough to make of it a career and find within it a shape for herself. Instead she had muddled along and bided her time. Had a man and babies been hovering, her ready solution, her woman's goal? Once or twice she had made half-starts – collecting leaflets from the Canadian Embassy about opportunities abroad, enrolling for evening classes in one thing or another, hoping they would lead to more and abandoning them after three weeks because something more interesting was happening that night. Looking back she could see how directionless her days had been. The Tube had taken her to work, the Tube had taken her home; between the jammed journeys she had simply existed at her desk, fingers busy, body leaning attentively to listen to what Mr Bingham was dictating about revenue quotas. Only her fingers had heard. *Could try harder* teachers' writing on school reports. *Katherine must apply herself*. If she had applied herself, she could have made that job interesting and stopped it growing barren on her, as indeed it had. If she had tried she could have saved for a ticket to Toronto. Next year she had said she would, but next year she was married.

Kate said: 'Perhaps we should swap our roles for a day or two.' She sipped her Cinzano, supplied by the mortgage-earner. 'Perhaps that's what they're doing next door.'

From conversations over the garden wall she knew some basic facts. Samuel had been a civil engineer before he had discovered his vocation. Was it he who was now responsible for the hoovering noises through the wall while Jetta did the wage-earning, giving her therapy classes or whatever it was that took her off so briskly in her emblemed car? To the peerer through curtains she seemed the dominant one, even taking charge of the motoring while her husband sat in the passenger seat. At this James had frowned. 'Seems our literary friend is incapable of driving.' Far from making Kate despise Samuel it had rendered him endearing. Being married to a capable man, pinned firmly to his frame, her unpinned edges could wave at James's opposite blithely, at times wistfully.

'They're having a dinner party,' she said. 'I can hear it.'

They had been next door once, actually, for drinks. It had been a few months ago, shortly after they had moved in. Kate had gazed around the sitting-room, identical to her own in shape but the wrong way round – familiar yet altered, as in a dream. An arty room, the Greens', with a bohemian air reminiscent of the ˘ ˙0s – African masks on the walls, Red Indian rugs, Chianti bottle lampstands and in the bookshelves row after row of those orange and white Penguins, now orange and grey. 'Dates us, doesn't it?' Samuel had said, following her eyes. 'Archaeologists of the future will be able to do a pollen count in Penguins.' She had laughed. 'I wasn't thinking that. I was just admiring how many books you have. And what interesting things.' It made her own house seem tepid and unadventurous, with its flowery Sanderson wallpaper and bird prints given by her mother. Her Bromley upbringing had simply been transferred, unexamined. She had never been artistic or intellectual.

Kate had longed to explore upstairs, see the rooms whose sounds she knew so well. Until she had seen the bedrooms she never really felt she knew a household; the same syndrome, this, as the necessity of sleeping with James before she could relax. These Greens, she could not pin them down. Sam seemed quick and funny,

37

perhaps vulgar; could anyone be less like James? Jetta said 'frankly' too often; Kate distrusted people who did this. Also she found daunting Jetta's long body topped with glossy hair; her olive, expressive hands.

Noises from next door. 'They're going downstairs,' she told James. 'I can hear them through the wall.'

'Who?'

'The Greens, darling. They're going to have dinner.'

'I'm getting rather peckish myself.'

James and Kate also went downstairs. Parallel opening of ovens, parallel picking up of forks, parallel conversations of which the Greens', Kate suspected, must be the more thought-provoking. Less tricky to be sure, for the time had come for her to confess, not thank God that Joe had broken James's camera, just that he had unpopped its case and adjusted a certain number of dials, whose use was to Kate mysterious. She would not confess: if in a subtle way she could find out what they were for, then in a timely moment she could turn them back again.

'James,' she began. 'I've been thinking about photography. It must be having babies – you know, longing to catch them, all those fleeting moments.'

James brightened. 'Are you really? That'll be nice. I'll teach you.' He was a keen photographer and he was gratified that she shared his interest. He welcomed this sign of wider horizons.

Kate blushed. 'Could you start,' she asked, 'by telling me the basics? You know, how cameras work and so forth?' Saying this, she quite truly began to be interested.

'It must be fascinating,' Jetta was saying, leaning forward, 'working in a photographic studio.'

'Yeah,' said Ron.

'Photography's so marvellous – its immediacy, its power. I feel that it's the only truly democratic art form, don't you?'

A pause.

'Yeah,' said Ron.

They were at the chocolate mousse stage by now. Various topics had been raised. Some had died, lingeringly; some had been jolted into life by Sam, who switched into the conversation when he felt like it and switched off again. He had startled Ron by greeting him, for reasons best known to himself, in broad Yorkshire. 'Our Marion!' he had called up the stairs, 'our Marion, stir yourself.'

Now he was eating his mousse. 'Can't get the hang of cameras,' he said.

'Telling me.' Marion turned to Ron. 'He's hopeless at anything practical.'

'Used to have a box Brownie,' Sam said. 'Want to see my pics? Got a whole drawerful of fuzzy, decapitated aunts.'

Marion gripped her spoon. Would he jump up and show Ron that one of herself on Brighton beach, aged six and bare? She could not trust Dad.

He didn't. He went on: 'My whole past is out of focus, a nostalgic haze of wrong exposures.'

A pause. Was Ron going to join in? Marion concentrated on the twining ivy round the rim of her pudding bowl.

Her mother said: 'And you're an assistant there?'

'Deliver the stuff,' said Ron. 'You know.'

'Ah, I see.' A pause. 'How do you feel about that, Ron? Do you find that rather frustrating, if you're fond of photography?'

Marion looked at Ron. The last thing she could imagine him being about anything was frustrated. He looked too inert. How grey and pimply his face was. She felt ashamed of him; she inspected the ivy, stalk curling round stalk.

Her mother's voice: 'You must find, Ron, that you're longing to do the actual photography yourself, aren't you?'

Ron shook his head. 'Too much hassle,' he said.

Her mother picked up her spoon. Marion felt a tiny, surprising pang for her. Dad chuckled something about hassles with Hasselblads and poured out more wine. He drank, his eyes restless and amused; he had switched off from the conversation, he was sauntering away down his own paths and of course Marion could think of nothing to say, so they ate in silence. Thank goodness, thought Marion, that mousse doesn't crunch or crackle; just noiselessly slithers down.

The only bright spot was that this evening would eventually end. Eventually. What a relief, then, to tell her parents that she thought Ron was as awful as they must think him. She hadn't realized quite how dull he was until tonight, here with her parents. Before, seeing him amongst a crowd of his friends, she had gazed at him picking his nails and assumed he possessed enigmatic depths.

And how young he seemed. Despite the leather trousers and the nonchalant lighting of cigarettes she could see that his eyes, under the hair, were anxious and darting. Yes, she could not wait for him to go. Then they could gossip about him. She so seldom gossiped with her parents, being too inhibited nowadays, but it would be fun doing it about Ron – necessary, too, so they would not think she really had such dreadful taste.

'Heavenly mousse, darling,' said her mother, smiling at her. She turned back to Ron; her face went serious. 'Yes, I do see what you mean. Frankly, Ron, I think you're quite right. People don't realize that clambering up the career ladder is a pressure imposed on us from outside.'

A silence.

'I'm glad to see, Ron, how many of you young people are realizing this.' She gazed at him; on her chest, sincerely, her medallion shone. 'Realizing this and leading their lives according to their own priorities rather than society's.'

Ron stubbed out his cigarette in the remains of his chocolate mousse. Marion winced; she could have finished it upstairs. How could she have ever contemplated him! Worse, her mother seemed to be doing her sucking-up routine; but then she was inclined to do that. It was part of the reason Marion felt shy about bringing anyone home.

Coffee was served; the evening progressed. Sam and Jetta, as so often happened when they were bored, started bickering together. It was about an author, Illich someone or someone Illich, who was unknown to Marion. By and large it gratified her, the way her parents quarrelled about proper things like books and films and sterilization versus vasectomy (though her father could get embarrassing over this one). They were so different from other parents who never seemed to say anything much, TV flickering in the corner, deaf to each other in their small rooms. Her parents might be deaf to each other but that was because they were both so busy talking. They had met at London University and the way Dad jumped from his

41

chair still seemed student-like. He snatched a book to prove his point, rummaging through its pages, half his shirt untucked.

It could distress her though. She feared quarrels, she could never get used to her parents' lightning switches of mood. Halfway through an argument she would grow hot and loyal, stumbling in to placate, only to find that mysteriously the quarrel had dissolved away. They were too quick for her; she would be brooding over the angry words long after they were friendly again – indeed, over-friendly, snuggling together all refreshed and expectant as they did when they had had a fight. She was always out of step.

Tonight Marion was grateful for any diversion. Dumbly she sat on the sofa with Ron; they were spectators, their heads swinging from Jetta to Sam, Sam to Jetta, a verbal Wimbledon. Saved from the need for words the last hour fled by and soon it was late, Ron bestirring himself to leave.

Closing the door behind him Marion had a moment of pure, calm peace. Downstairs she could hear her parents chattering together, quarrel forgotten. Their moods came and went so swiftly. Probably they were giggling over Ron. Marion made her way downstairs.

Her parents, both in aprons, were at the sink. Practised hosts, they were also swift and efficient dishwashers. Marion breathed a sigh, loud enough to be heard through the clatter.

'Phew,' she said.

'What did you say?' asked her mother.

'Phew. I'm glad that's over. How *embarrassing*.' She waited anxiously.

'Knives please, Sam. Heavens, were we that bad?'

'Not you. Ron.'

'Ron?'

'You know, dull and everything.' She was glad their backs were turned. She mumbled: 'I didn't realize he was so awful, you see.'

Her mother replied: 'I thought he was most interesting. Plates please.'

'*Interesting?*'

'His views on squatters and things.'

'But he didn't have any views. Only the boring ones.'

Her parents had finished. They hung up their aprons and dried their hands. Her father looked twinkly and boozy. He said:

'Seemed dead keen on you, he did. I caught some languishing glances in your direction.'

'You didn't *like* him, did you?' Marion stopped.

'Seemed a nice enough bloke.'

Nice enough for me, your own daughter? Marion stared at him.

'Natty line in trousers,' he added, 'our leather lad. Bet it gets hot in there.'

'Don't be silly, Dad. You couldn't like him!'

Her mother turned to her. 'Darling, don't feel you have to apologize for your friends. It's sad to be uneasy about who you bring home.' She smiled. 'I hope no one can accuse us of being reactionary.'

'You aren't. But that's not the point.'

She looked despairingly from one to the other. Her mother was hanging up the dishcloths, tolerance and understanding even in the gentle way she was attaching them to their hooks. Catch me, declared the back view of her kaftan, calling them long-haired louts. Yearningly

Marion gazed at the embroidered cloth. Don't be tolerant about Ron. *Please*.

'Coming to bed?' her mother asked.

'Soon.' She lingered in the kitchen.

The stairs creaked as they went up; she heard the closing of the bathroom door, the gurgle of the water pipes. Then the closing of the bedroom door and silence. For a while she remained sitting at the kitchen table. She felt so empty.

Food. She got up and opened the fridge. Food at least could fill her up; food the comforter. Upon food she could always rely. She peered in; there was some lasagne left over from supper, still tepid under its foil. That would do.

Upstairs in her room she scraped out the congealing pasta and put it into her mouth. Stolidly she worked her way through it. It would make her even more hideous of course, but who cared? Actually it was rather a relief. Soon she would be so enveloped in folds of fat that she wouldn't have to bother any more at all. No more sweaty evenings shredding her napkin, clearing her throat.

She sat in front of the mirror licking the spoon, staring at her spots with a misery that was almost gleeful. She looked down, gloating on the fatness of her thighs, gloating on the stubbiness of her fingers, gloating on every spoonful of the cold and greasy pasta that was making her even more repulsive. She could sit outside her body, goading it on to eat more and more. Her parents were right, of course. She could see it now. For someone as hideous as she was only someone as hideous as Ron would do. They had said as much, hadn't they?

How right they were. Scrape, scrape, she scraped every morsel from the dish, the burnt bits at the edges, the soggy tatters that had stuck to the bottom, the little smears of solidified mince. On the bookshelves the teddies looked down on her calmly.

Next door the evening was devoted to cameras. The thoughtful discussion on photography, this new shared interest, had drawn Kate and James together. They had survived even the tricky moment when James had decided to fetch his camera and instruct Kate on a variety of points. He did not notice that the dials had been turned; in fact, he turned them a good deal himself. 'F.16,' he said, 'is the appropriate setting, at this distance, for sun.'

Impressive, this man who knew all about F.16 and F.32 and lenses, both fish-eye and zoom. Inside his skull was stored so much knowledge. Kate's feelings were helped by having shared with him a bottle of wine over supper. She felt warmed towards him, warmed and awed. 'So you turn this?' she asked. 'Have I got it right?'

Added to this, tomorrow he was going away again and already the poignancy of departure was settling upon him, making him elusive and hence desirable. It was Thursday. He had only been back five days this time; he had to be away a lot this summer. These three-day, five-day, sometimes ten-day absences created pockets of his life that were utterly mysterious to her. Upstairs in the bathroom lay James's tube of toothpaste, dented and squeezed in some Brussels hotel. Beside it her own looked humble. What did she know of this foreign James, who even spoke to taxi drivers in an unknown tongue? These evenings before his departure had an echo about them, a sense of the largeness of the world stretching out from the windows. When she saw his suitcase in the hall, minor squabbles were forgotten; pettiness dwindled away, dwarfed by the whine of planes in the night sky.

All this meant that, sitting in the living-room after supper watching *News At Ten*, they found themselves to their surprise caressing each other, turning from the television to kiss, putting their coffee cups carefully on the side table and finally easing themselves, still locked together, down on to the carpet. Wine and warm desire spread through Kate. Over James's shoulder she could see the TV screen; a man was standing at a microphone shaking his fist. Shake away, she thought; go on, get agitated.

They rolled on to their sides; she unbuttoned James's shirt and slid her hand inside, feeling his warm chest so hard and smooth, the familiar hairs. On the screen some tugs were towing an oil rig through the sea; a giant one with struts. Tow away you little tugs.

James was unzipping her skirt; with her hand she helped him, caressing his hand, unbuttoning his shirt cuff. She rolled up his sleeve and stroked his lovely known arm. She ran her hand down his trouser leg, bending down to slip off his shoes; it was a long time since she had undressed him like this. A long time, too, since this had taken place anywhere but in bed; this made her bolder, more desirous – only in novels, surely, did married people make love in their sitting-rooms. She bent down and eased off his trousers; she moved up and kissed him. She smiled into his eyes and, bolder now, she climbed upon him as he sank down on to his back.

She was just settling herself when he grunted; his face winced.

'What's the matter?' she whispered.

'Spine.'

'What?'

'Something's digging into it.' Very gently he moved her off. 'Rather painful, actually,' he said, grimacing.

He reached down and picked something up from the orange carpet.

Kate looked at it. 'Oh,' she said.

She sat up. Desire drained from her. James's best Parker.

'Goodness I'm sorry,' she said. 'I don't know how he could have got to your desk.'

James's face was not irritable. That abstract, intent look he wore in lovemaking had gone of course; it left his face resigned. 'Kate, it's the only place in the house, you know, that I'd rather Joe didn't go. I didn't like to make a fuss about the diary just when I'd come home, but . . .'

'Oh dear, it must have been when the doorbell rang and I wasn't looking. He must have rushed in here and got that drawer open . . .'

Her voice trailed off. Neither of them said anything. They sat there, gazing at the little pen.

'Never mind,' said James briskly. 'It's probably not harmed.' He stopped and glanced at her. Was he thinking that perhaps they ought to start again? Could he possibly want to?

Not really. They sat there on the carpet; their two bare bodies seemed large and goose-pimpled, all knees and elbows. Kate felt chilly.

They could not think of anything else to say. Who was to blame – Kate, James or Joe? Whoever's fault it was, the moment had passed. Kate picked up the pen. Separately they put on their clothes. Then they sat down

47

again in front of the television; *News At Ten* had not even finished.

Kate, though drooping with tiredness, went downstairs and did the washing-up with a thoroughness unusual to her, scouring out the pans and even scrubbing the greasy corners round the top of the oven. At least she could clean properly. On the draining board stood the empty bottle of Médoc. It was a shame really. Seldom was a child not awake, the phone not ringing, James or herself not distracted by something else, the hour just right with that friendly glow from a bottle of claret. Seldom, too, was she not too sleepy.

A problem, this sleepiness. So much of the night she was up, either feeding Ollie or else sitting in Joe's bedroom. Joe had developed the habit of waking up in the grey dawn and had to be rocked, a drowsy body in his damp pyjamas, while she sat in the chair, neither of them awake, neither of them asleep, their heads nodding, time, centuries of it, passing.

It was hardly surprising then that during the day she longed for sleep. Ten minutes of it, fifteen; she did not ask a lot. Her ploy was to nod off while Joe's attention was engaged elsewhere. This should be easy; often he got engrossed in something. While this happened she would arrange herself as though she were fondly watching – head in hand perhaps, or reclining on the sofa. A minute later, furtively, she would shut her eyes.

Joe knew. How did he? His fiendish radar. A clatter as he threw down whatever he was doing; the stomp of approaching feet. If in a moment of real desperation she covered her eyes with her hands, sticky fingers would prise them apart. Small ruthless hands would lift her head. So she did not sleep. Daily she suffered that most unrecognized of maladies – the dulling senses, blurred vision, sluggish responses and jerky awakenings, the narrowing of every desire down to the urgent need of ten minutes, five minutes, *one* minute in which to shut her eyes.

The strain of course was keeping it from James. Seven o'clock in the evening, when he returned home, was her lowest ebb. However, it would be small welcome for him to find her slumped over the kitchen table; he could hardly wish for his day's observations to be answered by snores. So often she felt herself slipping, slipping away from the wife he married; at no point must she slip away completely.

Kate, yawning, hung up the dishcloth. It dangled, damp and grey. Next door they must be livelier.

In fact, upstairs she could hear their front door closing; footsteps along their hall, descending to the kitchen, very close. Muffled voices – she pictured them lounging wittily round the table, swigging the brandy dregs and being rude about the departed guests. Upstairs in her own house Ollie was crying. She dried her hands on the dishcloth and went up to the bathroom to feed him. Unbuttoning her blouse she thought: an hour earlier James unbuttoned it – what did he see? A breast to be caressed. What did Ollie see? Milk to be drunk. Kate smiled at this, dozily. For its changing uses her body was needed day and night. Just for a moment, now Ollie was fed, she had it to herself, she could greet it at the end of its day. For five quiet minutes in the bathroom she could clean its teeth, inspect its face in the mirror, grimace at it. She lingered. Silence in the bathroom. She took off her clothes and was complete – naked, Kate.

Then she was in bed with James and the cat. Ginger only dared get in when she had arrived; he jumped on to her and sneaked into the convenient hollow made by the dent of her knee. James pressed one side, the cat pressed the other, shuffling round and round to make himself a nest. Still, she thought as James put his arms around her and Ginger shifted, his claws sinking in as he tried to regain his position – still, I should be pleased to be wanted. I am pleased, but I am *tired*.

The Coopers' cat was large, shabby and friendly. The Greens' cat on the other hand was a cool and neurotic Siamese; never did she deign to mount the stairs to Marion's room. Marion lay alone, under the bed the scraped-out dish.

Four

'No, it's not often that I complain,' said Alf. 'Not often that I don't have a smile, a pleasant word for anyone, but these hospitals, take my word for it young lady, these hospitals they treat you like a lump of meat. Honest. I said to them straight out, I said you just treat us like a row of blooming carcasses, if you'll pardon the language.'

'Oh dear,' said Marion. 'Was that when you went to Out-patients?'

'A row of carcasses, that's what I told them. I always speak my mind, I believe in it. Don't mind who it is I'm addressing. Those men in white, think they're blooming gods. That's what I told them. "Think you're blooming gods," I said. Think they can tell me when to come and go, think they can tell me to sit with me feet up all day like a blooming invalid. Gods, that's what they think they are.'

'Then they said you're worse?'

'Nurse? Nurse? No, I've nothing against nurses, don't get me wrong. Real little angels, they are, some of them anyway. You see some lovely girls, really lovely. Dunno where we'd be without them.' He shook his head slowly. 'My Pauline was once a nurse, you know, but does she ever come and see me? Not her. Not Miss high and mighty. Catch any of them coming to see their old Dad.'

'But they do live miles away, don't they? Doesn't Pauline live in Hull?'

'Catch them coming to see their old Dad. All gone off, none of them left now.' He gazed down at his plaid bedroom slippers; he always sat in the same chair and he always wore his slippers.

'Don't they write you letters?'

'Better? Not better, they said. Worse. Think they're gods; and one of them a darkie too. Pulmerry something, he said.'

'That's your lungs.'

'Pulmerry something; all long words, fancy names. And me an active man.'

'Can you still get to the corner shop?'

'What's that?'

'The *corner shop*.'

Marion felt theatrical talking to Alf, raising her voice and feeling her face stretch in all directions as she exaggerated her words. Once a social worker had arrived and with Alf between them they had shouted across him, their voices loud and mannered as if they were giving each other elocution lessons. Even their gestures had been overdone and stagey.

'Oh, I can still get the fags and things, least I could Tuesday, but yesterday I wasn't feeling so good. Me heart, you know.'

'It's your lungs.'

'Me heart, you see. Pain's terrible. Couldn't even get up them steps.'

Alf lived in a basement room on the other side of the High Street, in a road behind the Odeon. He had lived there for thirty years and when Marion first visited him she had hoped to be rewarded with colourful cockney anecdotes and sage insights into the past. She had not reckoned on Alf's deafness and his fondness for monologues, the majority about the way the Pakis at the corner shop had tried to short-change him but he had seen through their game. Her attempts to draw him back into the past had met with no success; remorselessly the conversation would be swung back to the present in general, and in particular those Asian fellows, and the wicked state of the pavements in his street what with all the dogs and nobody taking a blind bit of notice, and the way they'd put up all those barriers down the High Street so you had to walk half way to Littlewoods before you could cross the road. And the way nothing was printed clearly any more. Soon she realized that boring young people tend to become boring old people. Never mind; that her visits were not more rewarded only made her feel the more virtuous about coming at all.

A lot of the girls at school visited old people; it was part of a Task Force project. Marion stolidly kept on with Alf; it seemed too cruel to stop, no one else knocked on his door except the odd social worker and someone bringing a square foil-wrapped packet from Meals on Wheels; anyway it was nice to know that she was wanted.

So Alf came to occupy a larger part of her life than she had bargained for. As the weeks went by she realized with surprise that she was actually becoming rather fond of him. He was the only man in whose company she felt unembarrassed. He made no demands, in their two armchairs he accepted her, she accepted him, she need not worry about her spots because he was too short-sighted to see them. Besides, being with him salved her conscience, in some devious way, about her parents; the more she listened to him, alert and bright-eyed, the more thoughtful questions she asked, the less guilty she felt about becoming so uncommunicative at home. Added to this, her visits to Alf got her out of the house. Her mother knew about Alf, of course, but not about the frequency of Marion's visits; with any luck she might be thinking that Marion was doing something more exciting and suitable, more adolescent and sexy, than sitting about in this dank, musty room with its worn lino on the floor.

'That sounds a bit worrying,' Marion said. 'Your chest, I mean. Tell you what – ' she raised her voice and leant forward – 'I'll do your shopping today because it's Saturday and I'll come back on Monday after school and see how you are.'

Marion always saw the streets differently after leaving Alf's room. Usually she noticed nothing much; eyes on the pavement, she would be deep in her own thoughts. Sometimes she raised her eyes to look at the dresses in the shop windows and to think how much better she would look in them if she slimmed. After Alf's, though, she could not help noticing the shapeless old women with their pramfuls of washing, the shuffling tramps, the Irishmen with their puce faces and sleek sideburns loitering on the corners waiting for the pubs to open.

Marion walked slowly back along the High Street. Where the roads crossed at the Tube station there was an underground Gents. Steps led up to the outside world. Today she noticed the hand-rail that led up from the dark entrance; the attendant had polished it so beautifully, it shone in the sun. And when she opened the door of her house she felt half thankful to live there and half ashamed that she took it so blithely, so ridiculously, for granted.

Five

Several things were to happen that following Monday, the first day of June. It began ordinarily enough. In his attic study Samuel was uttering his daily prayer of thanks that he did not have to go to the office. The novelty still had not quite worn off. Monday morning. This was easily the best morning in the week, the pain of it for everyone else only increasing the pleasure of it for himself. The front door slammed; Jetta left. It slammed again; Marion left. Sam settled himself more comfortably.

From here he could see out of the window. He gazed down at the long narrow gardens. Deserted by the office-bound, they appeared tranquil and peculiarly his own. Silent, weekday flowerbeds – the yellow flowers seemed yellower, the blue bluer, the shady corners shadier and more mysterious. The knowledge that all over London people were jammed into the Underground made his own surroundings spring into life. His little room too – alert and confidential it seemed, his table with its row of pencils and pens, its big block of A4 typing paper, its constantly rearranged pile of notes. On Monday morning they clustered towards him as if all weekend they had been waiting.

Samuel sat back, his eyes roamed over the gardens noting the sunlight on the foliage, the branching trunks of the sycamores. He could do this for hours. Could have been an artist, couldn't he? He had novels in him but he also

55

had paintings. All this creativity and just imagine how he had suppressed it. Must have been insane to have stuck that office for so long.

'Must have been,' he had said to Jetta. 'After all, you earn pots of dough. You can keep me in the style to which I'm accustomed, can't you?'

'Sam, it's a sensible idea. Rather a brave one, really.'

'I'm rather a brave person. Can you keep me in gin?'

Jetta had smiled a swift smile. Her polished olive skin gave her a foreign look; over it Sam's humour rolled off harmlessly, leaving her face intact. In fact, there was an oddly impervious quality about Jetta as a whole. Being a psychiatrist, of course, she would have to be. Over her, people's problems might roll but she must emerge untouched. Was this why, with her smooth skin and clear confident gaze, as the years went by she looked younger?

'The world of civil engineering will be devastated. Motorways will halt, half-built. Bulldozers will flounder to a standstill in a sea of mud. "Which way did he say?" they'll cry. "Through this row of houses?" they'll shout, "or that one?" '

With distant eyes Jetta smiled. She would wait until Sam had got over his jokes as one would wait for a child to finish tying his shoelaces before one took it for a walk.

That was six months ago. Samuel slotted a sheet of paper into his typewriter. He straightened his pens. Poised, he sat there.

For a while he remained in the same position. He could see several things out of the corner of his eye. His pile of notes: should he sort them out again into usable and non-usable? His geranium: did it need some of that miracle spray stuff Jetta had bought? It looked a bit droopy. His packet of cigarettes: was he due for one yet? After all, the clock was creeping towards coffee time.

Sam got up and wandered back and forth across his room. By nature a messy man, he kept himself busy less by actual tidying than by moving things constantly from one place to another – rearranging his small space, as a hamster drags its bedding straw from one corner of its cage to the other.

Sam made himself some coffee. This little ritual, involving a complicated system of grinding and a rather fancy new percolator, difficult to assemble and to dismantle, took some time. He sat down again. Steam curled up from his cup, smoke curled up from his cigarette, propped against the ashtray. For a while he contemplated them in this otherwise motionless room. Tranquil, they drifted together, promising satisfaction.

He gazed at the paper slotted into the typewriter. It was going to be good; everything augured that. 'There are great things in you, Sam,' Jetta had said, gazing at him, nostrils flaring with belief. Her nostrils did that; her whole face was finely modelled, handsome and sensitive.

He believed it too, of course. Had he not already reached page forty? Not bad going, for six months. He hadn't exactly figured out all the details of the ending yet, but authors worked like that, didn't they. Some of them, anyway – the more inspired ones. Let it flow; let the characters gather up life into themselves and lead the plot on. It will unroll.

Sometimes it unrolled and sometimes, he had to admit, it didn't. Or it unrolled in the wrong direction and reading, in the clear light of morning, what he had tapped out so elatedly the night before left him with a mild sense of surprise. Especially the style, somehow, which had the habit of becoming – well, *freer* – as the night progressed. Odd how in full flush, rattling away on the old keys, it had seemed such peerless prose.

He had refrained, of course, from confessing any of these doubts to Jetta. If she was curious about the great work's progress she kept it well hidden. She wasn't the sort to sneak up and take a look; she would consider that dishonest, and for her dishonesty was perhaps the greatest sin. Sam leafed through the pages, gazing at the black rows of x's, all the testy little marginal notes he had written to himself: *Idiot! How could Norton have got to Hong Kong? Didn't this happen on Tuesday? Jesus! Arabella wouldn't talk like this*.

He gazed at page forty, as yet unblemished. Blankly it stared back. There was absolute silence. No – not quite; through the wall, from the direction of number twenty-three, he could hear the noise of a radio. 'You and Yours': Sam knew the radio programmes off by heart. He could hear the bouncy little signature tune that introduced it. What was Kate Cooper doing in there? In this street of emptied houses he felt that he and Kate shared their days. Like him she was alone – except, that is, for her two little brats who could hardly be the most scintillating company. Her husband, Sam knew, was abroad. What did she do all day?

Enough. Page forty. He had left Arabella at Singapore Airport. He must fly her back to London. '*Outside the sultry terminal*,' he wrote, '*the palm trees waved in the tropical breeze*.' Can it be sultry and breezy too?

Sam raised his eyes. Faint radio. Kate Cooper, mysterious beyond the wall, tantalized. Was she bending over the ironing? Making a bed? Dusting, her hair catching the sunlight? Housework, a wall away, appeared in his eyes idealized. He pictured her in a flowered apron. Did she really wear one?

Samuel frowned. Why the hell was Arabella flying back without waiting for Norton to arrive from Hong Kong? He had worked this out once, he was sure of it. Fuck me, he thought, what was it?

It was so much pleasanter thinking of Kate, her wide creamy English face and submissive body. Irresistibly his eyes strayed to the window. What looked like a stone on their lawn was in fact their tortoise. At night it retired to a box in their outside lavatory. That much he knew; yes, he knew some snippets about their life. He wanted to know more.

Jetta was not so keen. 'You know these housebound women, Sam. I'm not blaming them but they are inclined to latch on, aren't they.' It was one of the earlier surprises of his marriage that someone as detached from people as Jetta could yet be so very successful at a job whose main purpose was to relate to them.

He was not like that. Sitting here he felt cheered, imagining Kate standing on his doorstep. 'I wonder if you could lend me some sugar?' She would be holding out a teacup in a delightfully helpless way, her fair hair falling in wisps about her face. So pale her hair, spun in the sun; so downy her arms. Her cheeks would be flushed with embarrassment. Sam smiled at his sheet of paper. Unlike Jetta who was already tanned, Kate had just managed in an endearing way to burn the bridge of her nose pink. There was something altogether sunlit and vague and rumpled about Kate, as if she had just stepped from warm sheets. That startled and bemused look of the newly-awake.

Sam rested his elbows on each side of the typewriter. Did Kate Cooper, he wondered, ever think about him sitting so near her, day in, day out? Unlike Jetta she would be interested in her neighbours, he was sure of that. She seemed similar to himself in many ways – instinctive, emotional. Also, being nearer his own height she seemed friendly. They were rendered conspiratorial by their long, slender mates.

Desert Island Discs. Sam heard the murmured, reassuring voice of that man who introduced it. Twelve-twenty – he straightened his pens. Only ten minutes to go before his pre-lunch drink. Martini today or whisky? He frowned, considering it. Once he was up in his study these questions swelled in importance; the daily rituals rose up, peaklike, as they did when one lay in hospital. But that was because in hospital one was bored; here of course it was different, it was the strain of concentration and of solitude. This paper, this pen.

Five minutes to go. Martini, he thought, today.

Kate in fact was not in a flowered apron; she was still in her dressing-gown. A certain sluttishness descended upon her when James was away. To be more accurate – knowing he would not be home in the evening gave the day a different rhythm. No longer did she have to point her activities towards the expected tableau that should greet James – dinner and a wifely welcome. House cleared up, lamps lit. Instead she could wander through the minutes

60

and the hours, browsing where she cared to browse, responsible to nobody's needs but those of her own and her babies. No wonder she forgot to wind up the clocks; she no longer needed them.

Browsing, actually, was what she was doing at the moment up in the bathroom. Changing Ollie's nappy she reached for a newspaper in which to wrap it; as usual the page she opened caught her eye, its stories more readable now they were having another use than the one for which they were intended. She read: *Mammoth Order for Swan Hunter Shipyard*. It could jolt her, remembering there was a world out there. She dealt with Ollie and laid him aside; she heaved up Joe. This was her universe, this her production line – this succession of pink, spread legs.

She looked at the overseas report. What did she know of foreign affairs? That which she gleaned from the murmuring radio, most of which sank without trace into the thick layer of sponge that had come to line her brain, her cerebral insulation. The rest of the radio she could not hear over her rattling pots and pans. The odd snippet of news remained, to be inspected in the paper at nappy time. Once the babies were potty trained, no doubt she would subside finally into primordial, feminine darkness.

Kate sat dreaming. Joe got up, bored with this. She woke up, wrapped the nappy and consigned *Syrian Deadlock* to the pedal bin. Kate be brisk, she told herself. She was getting so soft and sluttish in mind and body, her and her spongey brain.

The more so when James was away. She could do what she wanted when she wanted, it was one of the bonuses of his absence. She could have a supper that consisted entirely of sultana cake – she could have it at five, have it at eleven, have no supper at all. Have two suppers. Who was there to know?

Or care. When she thought this, she missed him. All very well to slide into your own rhythms, but if you slid too far you became like poor Mrs Forsythe. It was in the evenings that she missed him most. Having a day full of children, the evenings needed to be re-charged by another adult otherwise they were inclined to just peter out in a solitary manner, her plate scattered with crumbs. The day's ending had a frayed feel, rather than being firmly stitched up. Anyway, when it got dark she needed company. Television was all very well but there was nothing so lonely as the hush when she turned it off: a solid hush, a peculiar post-TV angst, that filled the sitting-room and sent her scurrying to bed.

Kate lifted up the ironing and carried it out of the bathroom. The daytimes were not so bad, the missing of James being confined to a poignant tweak when, as now, she folded his shirts and put them away in the bedroom cupboard. She laid them one on top of the other; these possessions became filled with James once he was absent. His body was in Brussels but he remained with her in his shirts, his rows of shoes, his old St Bruno tin full of cuff links and collar studs. The surprising thing was that this did not happen gradually; the moment James stepped into his taxi, his cupboard belongings were transformed into relics. It was the same with Joe when he went to bed. Though relieved to deposit him at last in his cot, the moment Kate returned downstairs and found evidence of unnoticed events during his day – the letters on the hall mat, a little heap of onions inside the teapot – she would miss him, ridiculously, irrationally. And Joe was just a few steps upstairs, he was distanced only by slumber. Kate finished putting away the shirts. *Desert Island Discs*, a tinkling and a murmuring that had been floating round the room, was drawing to a close.

'. . . *and one luxury to take with you to the island?*'

Long past midday, and at the stroke of twelve her clothing like Cinderella's would be no longer appropriate. Dressing-gowns before twelve were all right; after twelve they could resemble Mrs Forsythe and should thus be avoided. Thinking about her absent husband, Kate climbed into her skirt. It was good, of course, his going away; it re-established them as individuals. How many couples had this chance of becoming again whole in themselves? But it was also unnatural: she resented the period of adjustment when he returned, the way they had only just started getting used to each other when he had to go away again. She resented the politeness – in other words the unnaturalness – with which they treated each other when they only had a few days together, neither of them wanting to spoil it by becoming normal. She missed them sharing the small things. When he left, flowers in the garden were buds; when he returned they were seeds. Were not small things the stuff of marriage? Many wives must suffer this, she thought. Days with their husbands come to resemble photo-albums – photos of weddings and christenings and events for which one has to dress up. Nothing everyday. The things that Joe had done seemed too trivial to tell someone who, when he returned home, had about him the largeness of Europe.

'. . . *and one book apart from the Bible, Shakespeare and big encyclopaedias.*'

Kate gathered up her companionable trio – Ollie, Joe and radio – and went downstairs to the kitchen to prepare lunch. Her children squirmed for food; without their insistent needs, how long would it take for her to become another Mrs Forsythe? She could imagine herself existing timelessly behind closed curtains, emerging to shop for eccentric items of food and to harangue the passing cars.

Kate stood at the sink chopping cabbage. The kitchen was in the basement; through the window she could see legs passing. Tramps shuffled past, she could see their tattered trousers. Women with prams passed, she could see up their skirts, sometimes their thighs were knobbly with varicose veins. In the afternoons school-children would dawdle, kicking the railings, their conversation, fuckin' this and fuckin' that, floating down to her and her two wordless infants. Occasionally a child would stop and squat down to inspect her as she stood at the sink. Otherwise it was from the waist downwards that she viewed the human species, an anonymous procession of legs.

Residents campaigned against the lorries but she liked them. She could see two of them now, large and travel-grimed, waiting at the lights; *Eurofreight* was written on one, on the other *Halifax Removals*. If she craned her neck she could see into the cabs and glimpse the profile of the drivers. Last night one profile might have been in France; tonight perhaps it would be at the top of England. Just for a moment though it was almost within touching distance of herself in her Marigold Double Durable Rubber Gloves. If she had the window open she could hear transistors playing; sometimes a driver would turn and wink at her, suddenly intimate – it gave her

64

a shock, that. But she did not mind; closed into her house all day, islanded as she was, the busy street kept her in touch with the outside world. With each change of the lights it presented her with a new and sometimes international arrangement. She would wither away in a suburban cul-de-sac.

'*And thank you,*' said the radio, '*for letting us hear your Desert Island Discs.*'

It finished; swooping violins. Kate stopped chopping. For some time she had been gazing at a pair of legs that had not moved. At the railings was standing, motionless, a pair of shabby trousers leading down to bedroom slippers. This was mildly surprising. She turned away to put the cabbage in the saucepan, she fetched the bread and butter. When she turned back the legs were still there.

Kate bent forward to look up at the man. He was old, with stubble on his chin. Underneath his jacket he was wearing a shirt that even from here she could see was stained. He was clutching the railings.

She had been seen. 'Miss.' She could hear him calling down, throatily. 'Miss.'

Kate hesitated, then she went upstairs and opened the front door. The man stood there; this close she could see that his eyes were bleary and his face oddly grey. He must be drunk.

'Miss,' he said. 'It's me chest.'

Oh yes? she thought.

He said: 'I'm looking for the little lady.'

He caught hold of the railings. She took pity.

'What little lady?' She looked at him again. On second thoughts he looked less drunk than ill. She paused. She said: 'Come in. Are you all right?'

She led him down the hall. How smelly he was! Into the sitting-room with its roses wallpaper he brought a waft of neglect. She glanced down at the faces of her two babies, so smooth and cherished. Joe was watching the man with calm blue eyes.

She asked again: 'What little lady?'

His gaze wandered past hers; either he did not hear or he was too far gone to understand.

'What lady?'

'Said she lived here. Brinsley Street, she said.'

'Do you know what number? Perhaps she – '

'Brinsley Street. Lived here all me life. Known Brinsley Street before she was born. Can't tell me nothing about this place . . .'

Kate gazed at him helplessly. There he was in his dirty tartan bedroom slippers, a piece of the outside world sitting here on her sofa. Had she been stupid, letting him in? For a moment she had thought he was ill; looking at him now as he clutched the arm of the sofa, his eyes vague, she realized he was probably only drunk. Swiftly she glanced at her handbag beside him on the cushion. Too late to move it now.

'Queer pains,' he said.

'What pains? What – '

'Queer. Got me inside. Right in the chest.'

Kate had picked Ollie out of his carry-cot and was holding him; she felt the need of putting her arms around something young. As she looked at the man a thought flashed through her mind: I'm glad James is not here. What would he say, an old tramp in his sitting-room? He was so angry when she let them in to do the windows. A second thought flashed through her mind: I wish he was.

66

James would know how to tackle this. Maybe this man would never go, he would just sit here on and on; maybe he would get nasty. At this apparent contradiction Kate smiled.

'Me throat,' said the man. 'Got a thirst, I have.'

I bet you have, thought Kate.

'Water,' he said.

'Oh. Water, yes, of course.'

Clutching Ollie, Kate ran downstairs and returned with a glass of water. She watched the man drinking it; he tipped his head back, on his neck she could see the folds of grey stubble moving. His hand was trembling, some water spilt. Then they both sat in silence watching Joe who was pulling all the blankets out of the empty carry-cot. Should she start the explanation? How Joe was pulling off the bedclothes so that he could get to the pictures of bug-eyed bunnies on the plastic mattress beneath? Joe had such vulgar taste.

Kate glanced at the old man. His eyes were gazing beyond the bent and busy figure. No, this was one person she did not have to explain it to, and anyway at that moment the man started getting to his feet. Once he was upright he staggered to the hall and, bumping against the wall, he reached the front door.

'Are you sure you can manage?' Kate hovered in the hall behind him.

'That young missy,' he mumbled. 'She said Brinsley Street.'

He stood outside in the sunshine for a moment. Then he clutched the railings as if telling them to stay where they were, and started off down the street, unsteadily. Kate watched him until he had turned the corner at the bottom. She was still not quite sure whether he was drunk or ill.

67

Something had been confusing him: had it been booze or pain – or sheer fuddled age? And what little lady? It could be any female down the street. How should she know?

Then a thought struck her and she hurried back to the sitting-room. She opened her handbag. After all, she had been out of the room for a minute, hadn't she, to get the water.

No, her money was still there. She rummaged about in the bottom. Ah, but her keys were gone.

Downstairs on the radio *Woman's Hour* began. Kate straightened up. Hmm, she thought. Still, perhaps she had left them somewhere.

She sat still for a moment, looking at Joe. He was gazing, tranced, at the bunnies with their toothy grins.

Kate carried the children and the lunch out into the garden. It was there that her second little Monday drama took place. She went to the outside lavatory, which was situated next to James's toolshed. When she pulled the plug, water gushed out of the cistern and flooded the floor.

Kate stood still for a moment, staring at the matting on the floor, now becoming submerged; she gazed at the tortoise's cardboard box; it was becoming soggier, dampness creeping up its sides. Up near the roof the cistern was grumbling on in an unpleasantly insistent way. Water continued to dribble down from some unknown aperture. Helpless, Kate watched it.

She knew that Samuel Green was eating lunch in his garden; she had glimpsed him as she emerged from her back door. As usual, though, she had said nothing, being English and shy; also being conscious of the preciousness of territory, of the fact that walls are more than just walls.

She ran out. 'Samuel!'

As if he had been waiting for this, Samuel vaulted over the wall. The lilac bush rustled. He made his way across the grass and now he was standing beside her. Together they looked at the swamped floor.

'What about the tortoise?' he asked. 'All right, is he?'

She looked at him. James would never have asked that. 'Oh, he's fine. He's out in the garden somewhere.' No. James would have worried about the state of the floor. But then, to be fair, Samuel Green didn't have to buy new matting, did he?

Sam climbed on to the lavatory seat and peered at the rusty cistern. He scratched his head, then he started poking in the cobwebs in a way that even she could see was ineffectual. James, of course, would have known what to do.

From his murky heights Sam turned and grimaced down at her; he shrugged and stepped down. At the same moment, mysteriously, the water ceased. There was a minute of suspense as they waited side by side, tense in the dark little room. Nothing happened. Of its own accord it had stopped.

Samuel said: 'My magic powers.' He smiled, his teeth white.

It was silent now the noise had stopped. After a moment Kate said: 'You've got a cobweb in your hair.'

She stretched out her hand; his hair felt wiry. She lifted the cobweb off, it clung to her fingers.

The lavatory seemed too small to accommodate them both. She stepped outside, they stood together in the little

69

back yard that connected the house to the garden. At the end of the garden Kate could hear Joe singing to himself but he seemed very far away. There was a silence. They both watched the tortoise who was crossing the lawn.

'What's his name?' Samuel asked.

'Well, we haven't actually got round to a name yet.' She did not add that she and James never seemed to have time to discuss things like that; somehow there was always something that was considered more important first. And that anyway, since James was a keen gardener and had discovered the tortoise munching his way through his choicest *nicotiana*, the tortoise had become one of those subjects which Kate avoided bringing up as it had been understood, since the *nicotiana* episode, that the tortoise must be got rid of. James surely had noticed that the tortoise in fact was still at large amongst his bedding plants, but neither of them had been inclined to reopen the topic.

None of this did Kate say as she stood there with Samuel. She glanced at him, taking in his bright eyes, his large nose, his mobile mouth.

She went over and picked up the tortoise. 'What shall we call him, then?'

'Tyne-Tees, I'd suggest.'

'Of course, it was on the tip of my tongue.' She paused. 'Why exactly Tyne-Tees?'

'He looks just like a town councillor from somewhere like that.'

She looked at the tortoise. He lifted his pedantic head and moved it from side to side. 'So he does.'

She put the tortoise down. She would not tell James, he would consider it affected. Anyway it would reopen the argument.

Samuel climbed back over his wall. How easily he had got into her garden. She had felt herself so inviolate, so islanded. Never had she gone to the neighbours to ask for anything, she dreaded being thought tiresome. And suddenly here was Samuel, nipping in and out of her day and leaving her thoughtful.

She went back into the house. Vaguely she started looking around for her keys, she peered under carpets, she opened drawers. She thought: I will not tell James about either of these things, the lavatory or the keys. There was no point, it would all be forgotten by the time he got back, wouldn't it. His life was so large and busy, her events ridiculously small. And they sounded so dull.

Still Monday, but it was four-thirty in the afternoon; Marion was returning from school. She was so excited that if she were three years younger she would be skipping, but now she was just walking rather slowly. Probably she was walking even slower than usual and looking even gloomier, but nobody knew, did they. It was all pent up inside.

Her parents were in the kitchen, drinking mugs of tea.

'I say, Dad!' she burst out – she always addressed him first. 'Dad, guess what. I've been made a prefect.'

She stood still. Hearing the words spoken by her mouth made them at last real. A prefect. Those two syllables reassembled her, re-shaped her, filled her full of good intentions. She knew she would be good – diligent, kind but firm. At last she felt important; it was a great honour. 'I start next term.' She added casually: 'There's only twelve prefects in the entire school, you know.'

'Marvellous,' said her father. 'Marvellous.' He was

71

rummaging through the biscuit tin, probably seeing if there were any chocolate ones left.

'I'm terribly pleased,' said her mother, 'though I must admit I thought your school would have done away with that sort of thing long ago.'

'What sort of thing?'

She said: 'We sent you to the comprehensive because we rather thought that one wouldn't find certain, well, hierarchies there. Still, I'm very glad for you, darling. It's obviously important to you, isn't it, sweetheart?'

Marion did not answer this.

'I'm sorry, darling.' Her mother looked at her kindly. 'I've obviously put that badly. You see, Sam and I aren't great believers in that sort of competition – not at your age. It's not the best of precedents, you see, for later.'

Never mind what you believe, Marion wanted to shout. Just be pleased.

Dad had found his chocolate biscuit. 'You must show us your little badge. Do you have a little badge?'

Marion was silent. She felt her excitement draining away. Had she got it wrong herself, thinking of the bonds of loyalty, the new camaraderie with the teachers, the sudden respect it had given herself, Marion, in her own mind? No doubt she had baser motives – power hunger, desire for a little badge.

They were always getting it wrong, school. They didn't understand the things that mattered, like wearing the same clothes as everyone else. Remember the funny shirts? When she was younger, before Brinsley Street, they had lived in a block of flats near Swiss Cottage. It had a hall porter and a clanking lift and endless carpeted corridors with central heating pipes along them. Every day

72

Mrs Rotherstein from the floor above used to come down and make Marion's tea before her parents got home from work. She had gone to a school then that had a uniform. The trouble was, everyone else wore the regulation nylon shirts and socks while she wore different, slightly yellowy cotton ones, because cotton was good for the pores.

'Mum, they're all looking at me. Their shirts don't crease and their socks stay up.'

'Darling, people always react to something that's a tiny bit unfamiliar, but it's seldom hostile. One's own interpretation makes it that, one's own insecurity. If one is strong enough to be different, to stand up for one's beliefs, one actually gains respect, you know.'

Marion had not wanted her to say this; she had just wanted her to get anxious, or cross, or, better still, throw the beastly things away and get her some proper ones. Now that she was older she could see there was some sense in what her mother said – cotton did let the skin breathe and in fact her mother was marvellously fair and reasonable. She saw both sides, she explained why a terrible girl called Cheryl was a bully because of her deprived background, she was sensible and humane. But at the time Marion did not feel this; she simply knew that her mother did not understand.

They did not understand; they made her feel silly. She had always liked, for instance, to be ready for school a good hour before it was time to leave in the morning; she felt safe, then. She liked to know where she stood; her parents were so casual; in bouts of enthusiasm her father might play with her but she could never predict when he might feel like it. It was lovely when he did, but she wanted to know when, in advance. They made her feel so plodding and dull. They had many friends; in the next room the squeak of the cocktail cabinet, murmurs, laughter. Sometimes they all clustered around her loomingly, but she never felt either pretty or original enough to be inspected and talked to, those adult faces poised to explode at the clever remark she might, if she were cleverer, say.

Tonight, when she told them about being made a prefect, her disappointment turned to anger. Why, why didn't they understand? Her father was a novelist, her mother a psychiatrist – fine on paper, fine behind the desk at the clinic, but what about her, Marion, fidgeting here beside the kitchen table?

It was then that the phone rang.

'Ah, Ron.' Her parents' tea mugs hesitated, half way to their lips. She put on a bright voice. 'Yes, yes, fine, of course. Yes, well . . .' She remembered that her parents were going out. She twisted the black flex round her hand. 'Yes, well I suppose you could come – yes, do come round here . . . right, about nine.' She pulled it tighter, binding her finger. 'And we can go to the pub or something . . .'

Marion put the phone down. She felt flushed and reckless, miserably so, also glad that her parents had heard. She would show them. Show them what? Just show them.

When they had left the house, however – it actually was *Battleship Potemkin* this time – her anger subsided and was replaced by fear. Now that they had gone, what exactly was she going to do? Ahead of her stretched a whole evening alone with Ron. She must get him out to

74

the pub. How could she do it? She was pondering this question when the doorbell rang.

Ron had a bottle under his arm. It turned out to be something called British Wine.

'So we're not going to the pub,' she said.

'It's cheaper, this.'

She inspected the bottle. 'Isn't this the stuff all those old men drink under the bridges?'

'Yeah, well they've got the right idea, haven't they. See, it gets you stoned quicker.'

Ron had washed his hair. This slight sign of interest alarmed Marion. But he looked better than usual, there was a little tinge of purposefulness about him that she had not seen before. He was looking round the room in really quite an alert way, with his shining hair. She glanced furtively at his pale, girlish face.

But that did not solve the problem of a whole evening's worth of conversation ahead of them. How do two people start, sitting side by side on the living-room sofa? He was blank to her, utterly blank. She only knew his name.

Well, there was a certain amount of bottle business – showing him where the corkscrew was, finding the glasses. And then twin gulps and comments on how it tasted. And then thank goodness Shiska came in, so there was a good deal of cat stuff: stroking her and admiring her, watching her in silence as she stalked around the room; comparing her slender duskiness with Ron's aunt's cat, comparing cats in general to dogs – cats being aloof, dogs friendly – a well-worn path this, but never mind. They patted their laps. 'Shiska,' they called. 'Here, Shiska.' The cat sidled against Ron's legs.

'You should feel honoured,' Marion said. 'She's usually so snooty.' She stroked her. 'Good girl, Shiska.'

Then Shiska turned away and walked across to the armchair; she climbed up and curled herself on a cushion. Marion and Ron fell silent.

Marion took another gulp of the British Wine. It tasted curious; she had drunk something like it for her tonsilitis. But who was she to care? She had another gulp and felt the warmth go down and spread out inside. She understood now why she disliked alcohol. The best way was to swallow it without thinking.

Marion got up and put on a record. It was *Sgt Pepper* – a bit passé of course but down here in the living-room it was all her parents' records and she had no intention of taking him up to her den, no chance. Already she felt a bit swimmy, already those silences seemed less leaden – they were softening, dissolving. And then music thumped out and that was better. She turned up the volume nice and loud and wandered around the room. She did not care to return to the sofa just yet.

Casually she straightened the curtains; she spoke some more to Shiska – never had Shiska benefited from so much attention; usually Marion avoided her, partly from simple dislike and partly because Shiska had the knack of making her feel fatter and clumsier than any human being had ever managed to do. Marion walked across to the glassed-in bookshelves and interested herself in the titles – *Arthur Koestler*: *Darkness at Noon*. *Lady Chatterley's Lover*. She tapped her foot to the music to show how much she was enjoying it – 'Fixing a Hole' was playing. She gazed at the row of books. In the glass she could see, reflected, Ron. At this particular angle he appeared to be perched, ghost-like, on the *Collected Works of George Orwell*. She moved away. She could not escape him – there he sat in the oval mirror. She could see he was pouring himself out some more drink. He looked up – hastily she shifted to the left, she did not want to catch his eye. She moved over to the corner cupboard which was crammed with objects. It was like a hall of mirrors – there he was again, a distorted midget on the bulging flank of her grandmother's silver teapot. He was everywhere, he was every shape and size.

She moved back to the bookshelves. In the glass she watched his reflection. It was getting to its feet. Marion continued tapping her foot; she hummed along with the tune, watching the reflection make its way towards her across the room. She took another gulp of her drink.

Behind her the floor creaked. She stopped tapping.

'Do a bit of reading then, do they?'

Ron's breath was hot on her neck.

She nodded, keeping her eyes on the books.

'Bertrand Russell,' he said. 'Wow.'

He was close behind her, she could feel his body against her back, his breath in her hair. She concentrated on the book titles – *In Quest of the Self*. Ron ran his finger down her back, she felt it. *The Problem of Pain*. His hand slid under her hair, it stroked her neck. *Edited by J. R. Guttenheimer*. His hand moved to the front of her neck and cupped her chin. He turned her face round and with quite a masterful gesture he drew her to him and kissed her.

In a way this was better. She knew this had been coming – now the tension was over she felt surprisingly grateful to him. She closed her eyes, she opened her lips, there was nothing she need say now, not with his body pressed against hers, his nose pressed into her cheek.

'She's Leaving Home' started. This was a sad song, too thoughtful for them. They remained glued together for its duration, suspended. The next started – 'For the Benefit of Mr Kite.' They heard the up-tempo'd beat, they up tempo'd their kisses. This was starting to be enjoyable. Once you had got over the awkward launching-in bit, you could forget everything but mouths and bodies and hands – Ron's were now roaming over her breasts but she did not want to stop this, to tell him not to. Ron was turning out to be a surprisingly expert kisser. She shifted to the side and took another swig from her glass; her embarrassment, she could feel it, was breaking up, melting. Head spinning, she ran her hands over his mauve tee-shirt, and when the record ended she knew they had worked up enough momentum to carry them over into the silence. In fact, momentum was mounting – in the sudden quiet Ron's hand was creeping up her leg and she heard the faint rasp as she adjusted them so that it should slide up the outside not the inside of her thighs – dizzy from British Wine, she was not yet that dizzy. Her head at moments was still clear, presenting her with little puffs of truth – that she felt cross and reckless, that Ron's warm hand wanted her, that she might be a virgin but Sharon and Jane and Lindsay weren't. And how hot her body was feeling – it was desiring the body that was pressed against it. Almost it could forget itself, and the over-bright lights, and the panting silence now the record player was stilled.

Ron pressed closer; fascinated, she compared the Ron of half an hour ago with the hands, expert and un-Ronnish, that were moving over her body, knowing it, tingling the skin wherever they touched. And why not? His hand finally slid up, her thighs welcomed it. Events were moving fast but who was she to care? Didn't they presume it, her friends, her parents? And her magazines – sex, sex they were saying, those girls with their casual bronzed limbs and parted lips. Sex, sex her body was saying, fattish and not at all bronzed but eager all the same. And Ron wanted it; wasn't he now fumbling with her zip?

'Wait,' she whispered, jammed against the bookcase. Over his shoulder she could see the clock. 'They'll be back from their film.'

'Let's go somewhere,' Ron muttered, still busy.

Her den? No, it would be wrong with her books and pictures watching. She would feel odd there afterwards.

'Come with me.' She struggled from his arms. Clutching her skirt around her waist she led him out to the back door. She unbolted it, stepped outside and took a breath of fresh night air. With the air came rapid thought – was Ron good enough, could she make him seem good enough? She must – before they did it she must, she owed it to her body. She could see it was ridiculous but she made a hasty list: He wasn't too short – in fact he was quite tall; he was amiable and easy to please; he didn't embarrass her by ever asking her about herself; he wore trendy clothes which was good, and he lived in a squat which was even better. She could not think of anything else.

She opened the door to the outhouse, which was carpeted and really quite comfortable, with its washing machine and piles of clothes. No one would think of looking in here. In fact she often came in during the day, it was a secret place in which to dream and brood.

There was a lull while she quite boldly got to work on the heap of clothes lying ready for the washing machine, arranging them so that they would be comfortable. She hurried; she did not want to have second thoughts. Neither did she put on the light; enough filtered through the window from the house. Ron was outlined fumbling with his trousers. Now that she had arranged the mound she did not know what to do – should she wait or take off her clothes?

'Sodding trousers,' she heard Ron mutter. 'Zip's stuck.'

'They're lovely though,' she said, trying to sound conversational. 'I've never known anyone with leather ones before. Where did you get them?' It would be nice to talk during some of this; she had the suspicion that it could all be a little friendlier.

Ron was struggling and did not hear. Please hurry, she thought; her embarrassment was waiting, a wave ready to engulf her.

The trousers were dealt with now; Ron got down beside her on the washing. She could bury herself against him while he got to work on her clothing. That he had obviously done this on a good many previous occasions reassured her; it also confirmed that she would refrain from telling him about her own lack of them. She kept her eyes closed; briskly he pulled off her tights. No, it was better that they did not speak; especially now that he was turning aside and fiddling with his wallet. No, especially at this particular moment, when he was – well, dealing with that side of things. A faint noise of tearing paper; he was hunched over himself.

80

Thank God he was silent; all she could hear was his breath, heavy with concentration. He climbed on her properly now, into the washing she sank.

Marion stifled a yelp; she dug her fingernails into his backbone. She opened her eyes and stared over his shoulder; faintly glimmering, she could see the round glass hole of the washing machine. Rhythmic, it appeared and disappeared over his shoulder. It was watching them like an enormous Cyclops eye. She looked back, she concentrated on its glazed stare. Slowly her panic began to ebb away and for some extraordinary reason she began to feel quite calm. This was it, then. The Cyclops stared back. Yes, it said. Uncomfortable, isn't it.

Uncomfortable it certainly was. She would prefer to be back against the bookcase. Pressed against the glass she had actually felt rather warm and amorous; all that had of course now stopped, here in the struggling darkness. Already she felt sore. Ron though seemed to be all right, with his quickening grunts.

Shouldn't she be doing something? She felt she should but it seemed impossible, pressed down here amongst the sheets and pyjamas; if Ron went on much longer she would suffocate. She had already sunk down – the Cyclops eye was now out of sight. What was it thinking, staring at these bare legs and bottoms? People actually wrote poems about this, she realized with surprise. On the window ledge she could see the black silhouette of the detergent packet. *Persil Washes Whiter, And It Shows*.

She closed her eyes. Pictures flashed through her mind – the metal lift-doors at Mount Court, the way they caught her fingers when they folded – creak of the cocktail cabinet – brass doorknobs too high to grasp – the thin, sallow legs

81

of Mrs Rotherstein when she was opening the fridge to get Marion's milk.

With a shudder and a grunt, Ron finished. That's it? She was drenched in sweat; Ron's sweaty skin stuck to her chest. Outside in the garden a tom cat cried, furtive and male. With small moist noises Ron was unpeeling his body from hers. He climbed off and began struggling into his clothes. Bent over in the faint light he looked furtive too, he was hurrying to get on his awful leather trousers. They made a slithery noise as he pulled them up his legs. She wished he could slink away like one of those cats; the thought that they would actually have to speak at some point in all this made her want to bury her head in the washing. If she covered up her face, perhaps when she uncovered it he would be gone.

He was still there. All too close, he cleared his throat. She opened her eyes; his black shape was sitting on the washing machine. Was he about to say something? She lay still; now she was cooler she was conscious of the wetness between her legs, under her arms, under the hair on her scalp. Her body felt clotted and sour. If only he would just slink out.

Ron cleared his throat again. She froze.

'Getting dressed, then?' he asked.

She struggled to her feet. Ron actually passed her skirt to her, which could have been nice of him. Wordlessly she snatched it. She thought: I am being as dreadful as he is. Perhaps worse.

What was that black shape thinking? It was lighting a cigarette – nervously, indifferently? How could she tell?

She fumbled amongst the washing for her bra. Everything seemed to have got tangled up. She found her

82

father's underpants and an awful old girdle she sometimes secretly wore; in the faint light she held them up to see what they were. But no bra. She felt flustered; her hands were clumsy. Bare bottoms, she thought, pushing in and out; bodies rubbing together. Men rolling off with a grunt. The bra – she found it. She put her arms through the straps and with awkward fingers she tried to hook it together. The cigarette glowed, watching her. Compared to what they had just done, so very quick and simple, it seemed so complicated to get dressed. The hooks sprung apart; with surprise she realized that her hands were trembling. She tried again; into each other the hooks clicked.

Marion felt around for her knickers. She picked up something light and cottony and held it up. Her mother's. She rummaged around, her hand burrowed under towels and shirts, at last she found her own. The cigarette glowed; if only she could be quicker, if only her hands would stop shaking. She had to stand up, unsteady on the lumpy clothes, to get them on. How ashamed she felt, struggling into them, lifting her legs; how large and bald her body felt, how dreadfully unloved.

Men – fat men with bellies heaving themselves into women, thin ones like Ron pressed on top of her, his face buried in the washing, pushing. She scrabbled amongst the clothes for her blouse; she managed to button it up, probably to all the wrong buttonholes. She wriggled herself into her tights: the indignity of it. It took so long and her hands didn't help, at least it was too dark for Ron to see they were shaking. If only he had looked at her once, if only he had said something, anything; if only *she* had said something. She pulled up her skirt.

They went into the house. Nothing more was expected,

Ron seemed perfectly content to leave. She closed the front door behind him; for a moment she stood there, holding the cool knob.

Temples throbbing from the VP Wine, she thought: Well, I've done it now. In the midst of the thickening headache she felt a small glow of pride. Upstairs, as she took off her clothes she remembered that today she had been made a prefect. Only today? Echoingly distant it seemed, very far and flimsy. Her parents had been right, of course. Silly to have got so excited.

She pulled up the sheets. She would make her mind a blank, she would think about something absolutely ordinary and reassuring. Something mundane like Alf.

Suddenly she realized: I said I would see Alf today. I promised him; I said I would do his shopping. Monday, I told him.

Never before had she broken her word. She would just have to see him tomorrow, wouldn't she?

Marion pressed the sheet against her face.

Six

That Thursday was turning out to be one of the bad days. Ollie never stopped crying, Joe never stopped whining, the four walls closed Kate in and she was so sleepy she could scream. She hesitated at the sitting-room door. Joe was pulling all the books off the shelves and throwing them on the floor; the baby's nappies were sopping wet. She must carry Ollie up to the bathroom, but was it worth returning to pick up a kicking Joe, carry him away from his beloved shelves and shut him up with her while she did the baby? Was the distant thud of books in the sitting-room preferable to the nearer shrieks in the bathroom, the rattling of the doorknob as he tried to get out? Round and round her weary head the question swam, sluggishly. And it was not as if his interest in books was the remotest bit intelligent; ostensibly examining them, he was in fact trying to prise up their endpapers. Those whose endpapers remained firm he threw to the floor.

All this had its positive side – it made her yearn for James. She was bored with her children. Tomorrow, Friday, he would be arriving; she would fling herself into his arms. She had the suspicion that they had not done enough of this lately – well, they would now. Suddenly she needed him simply for his adulthood, she could talk to him and get a proper answer, he would not cry. Sometimes she doubted that she could still actually use the correct words. She had a vision of herself leaning across the supper table. 'Jamey want a glass of winey-piney?'

No, she would pull herself together and become a better wife than she had been lately: affectionate, efficient, asking thoughtful questions and listening to the answers rather than wondering whether she had turned the oven down or left it at Mark 6. She might blame him for listening with half an eye on his newspaper but wasn't she as bad? She must remember this. When James was away her good intentions mounted up; the longer his absence the more of them joined the queue, like people gathering for a delayed bus. This was because the longer he was away, the more she forgot those things about them both which in practice made the intentions so very difficult to keep. There were no crosscurrents and petty irritations to muddy something which in his absence grew more idealized, more crystal clear. A worrying thought: did she admire and cherish him better when he was three hundred miles away in Brussels?

She would go shopping. She collected Joe from the sitting-room. In her absence he had lost interest in the books and transferred his attention to James's desk. Kate threw up a prayer of thanks that James was coming home tomorrow and not today. The floor was scattered with a snowstorm, a million paper circles shaken from James's hole-puncher. Into the crevices of the hole-puncher Joe was now inserting a pencil. Kate stopped and gazed at the intent figure. Joe seldom played with his actual toys – unless they were broken, in which case he could be happy for hours, pushing an amputated tractor wheel round the floor or gazing with fascination at a crippled teddy – but it never failed to amaze her how much he could find to do with anything else. To her, a hole-puncher punched holes. To Joe it could be propelled along the carpet like a bulldozer, it could disgorge a blizzard of fragments, it could have pencils thrust into its bowels and be shaken to produce a rattle, it could be banged up and down in an aimless but gratifying manner . . . if Kate were not in such a bad mood she might have smiled. When one grew up one learnt the use for a thing but one also unlearnt all its other possibilities. It seemed a waste.

'Come on, Joe. Lovely shops. Walkies.'

Joe, whining, refused to come. Kate grabbed his wrist and dragged him across the carpet. No, it would be good to see James. Tonight she would prepare for him both in mind and body, shake off the rhythm of these clockless days, clean up the house, submerge herself in a scented bath and work out how she was going to tell him about losing the front door keys. If the old man had taken them, perhaps she should have changed the locks? She also liked to roam through the rooms, clearing up and finding, as she did so, that she was instinctively editing her James-less days. In other words, discarding those things of which she was ashamed – old chocolate wrappers, well-thumbed women's magazines – and leaving *in situ* those things with which she was pleased to have occupied her time – deep novels, wifely sewing. Once she had even checked that the radio was tuned to Three rather than One; when he next switched it on she would like to reassure him that the woman he married had not turned into the zombie-like female who could only cope with the idle tinklings of Radio One (as was, by and large, the case), but was still the comparatively *compos mentis* former assistant to the South Eastern Divisional Manager, a woman who tuned in to classical quartets and discussions on Goethe. Not only might this reassure James; it also reassured herself, Kate.

She heaved Joe upstairs to change his nappy. Then she took him downstairs, slowly this time because he insisted on touching each one of the banisters. In the hall she lifted him into the pram and lodged him next to Ollie's feet.

'Blanket,' he said.

Joe was lost without his blanket. Upstairs she went to fetch it; downstairs she came and gave it to him. Grabbing it with one hand he put his thumb into his mouth, his eyes far away, his pupils shrinking to pinpoints, on his face that unreachable, inward look every baby has when it starts sucking.

'Book,' he said, withdrawing his thumb.

Upstairs she trudged to fetch his book. Just lately he had formed a violent attachment, not to one of his carefully-chosen picture books but to a small maroon volume entitled *A Portuguese Primer*. It must have been its interesting pliable feel.

Book blanket rattle, she thought. (Joe insisted on a rattle now, to copy the baby.) Keys (the spare set) shoes shopping bag. Sometimes it took so long to get ready that by the time they went out it was just about time to come home again. Now that she had two babies, each small square of pleasure had found itself fenced in by a growing number of chores; one had to clamber over so many obstacles to reach the sunlit patch for which one was aiming.

Kate slammed the front door and sallied forth with her jammed pramful, the baby stirring as Joe, who was sitting across his legs, adjusted himself more comfortably and opened his book. Down Brinsley Street she pushed the pram and turned off along a similar terrace. All around her stretched identical streets – rows of houses leading to more houses, stretching as far as she could walk. She knew all these roads.

It was early June now, heavy and warm; fumes from passing lorries filled the air. Not a blade of grass could be seen – down the High Street the only sign of summer was *Seasonal Reductions – Get Your Gas Central Heating Fitted Now*. Admittedly, in the window of *Eileen's Café Hot Meals All Day* the geranium had flowered; a large woman, no doubt Eileen, had brought her chair out on to the pavement and was watching the passing mothers, most of them fat, wearing sleeveless summer dresses that showed the red blotchy skin at the back of their arms. Otherwise it was the same as ever – a London shopping street, seasonless, busy.

Down the High Street Kate pushed the pram, feeling sluggish. She did some shopping, gradually the pram became weighed down with bulging plastic carrier bags. She could shop in her sleep, so well did she know the interiors of Sainsbury and Tesco, their arrangement of counters, the empty space by the crate of Schweppes where she could wedge the pram. (Ollie's sleeping face, waxen amongst the labelled boxes.) When she had finished her shopping she wandered on, unwilling to go home. Despite the thundering traffic her pramload was peaceful. As yet Joe was too young to ask endless thoughtful questions about death and electricity and when the Muppets were coming on – worse still, to make loud and embarrassing remarks about the passers-by. Guiltily she would like him to remain the age he was, in this particular aspect so undemanding. She could slip into a dream, a peaceful,

89

dullish dream as she walked along, the silence in her pram broken only by the little popping noises Joe was making with his mouth. He thumbed through his book, on his face the sombre, withdrawn look James wore when he was reading the financial page. Kate read over his shoulder: '*Quero fazer uma pintura/uma permanente. I want my hair tinted/permed.*'

Kate turned the corner and pushed the pram towards the canal. Here it was quieter; children played in the street and from the open windows of the little rag-trade workshops came the rattle of sewing machines. This area was full of small industries run by Cypriots and Pakistanis; their cassettes filled the air with warbling songs.

Kate felt the sun warm on her arms. She would like to tell James about her mornings and her afternoons, but they sounded so humdrum. Indeed they were, weren't they, compared to Brussels meetings and Eurodeals? So she did not tell him much; walks like this, sunlit ones, were closed away into her day, just as his incomprehensible office was closed away into his.

She arrived at the canal, she pushed the pram down the ramp and walked along the towpath bordering the water. Here lay a narrow strip of summer, tall cow-parsley spreading its sweetish scent around her, bees buzzing. Far away she heard the traffic humming and the rumbles from the factories that loomed up on either side. She loved the secret water here. Few people ever came; today there was nothing except a bundle of rags. On second inspection it turned out to be a man peacefully slumbering, his empty bottle nestling amongst the daisies.

Joe raised his eyes from his book. 'Bye-byes.'

'Man's gone bye-byes,' she whispered. On a day like this, even a wino looked romantic.

What had happened to that old man on Monday? The thought crossed her mind as she walked on down the towpath, past the grimy walls of the ABC Bakery. Its ventilation grills breathed hot air on her as she passed. Ducks idled on the water, fed too fat to bother with the white bread thrown out to them from the bakery windows; on the dark water the pallid slices floated. It would be nice to walk along here with James, but when he was home he was either too busy or else he liked to go on a proper outing to a proper place like Hampstead Heath. Her weekday wanderings along back streets and along this canal with its oily water and flowering banks were through territory unknown to him. He would consider the canal sordid. It was, of course.

'Listen to them.'

Kate jumped. She had turned a bend and there, on a bench, sat Samuel Green.

'Listen to what?' She collected herself.

'To those poor buggers.' He pointed to the factory. 'Slapping down row after row of indigestible buns.'

'So hot. So boring.'

'Lucky, aren't we.'

'Not working? Shouldn't *you* be?'

'Ah, but I am.' He tapped his head. 'It's all in here, see.'

'And water gets the old inspiration flowing.' She felt quite familiar, as if she had been talking to him for hours.

'Of course.' He stood up. 'That's a delicious dress. It shows your freckles.'

Kate bent down and busied herself with the babies.

She straightened up. 'Actually I miss work,' she said. They walked back along the towpath together. 'Sometimes anyway. When the house closes in and the children nag.'

'I don't believe it.'

'No, really. I miss working with men, being treated as an equal.'

'Now it's just randy husbands at parties.'

'Who don't like to talk about what they do because they feel it wouldn't interest me, a silly little housewife. I see them getting polite when I ask. But I'd like to know, else I *do* become a silly little housewife. I've been thinking about it a lot this morning.'

She also thought about the dress showing the freckles on her shoulders. No one had ever noticed them before.

He asked: 'What's the solution, you frustrated one?'

They talked about solutions; none of them workable, but still it was nice to discuss them. They talked about Samuel's book.

'Have no qualms, I can talk about *my* work for hours.' He plucked a stalk of grass and twirled it in his fingers like a dandy. 'Till you pass out, crushed by the sheer weight of my egocentricity.'

'Go on then.'

And he told her how it was a high-class spy thriller, lots of pace, lots of sex, three deaths so far, two of them violent, all the right ingredients. 'Bound to be a block-buster,' he said. 'Once I've figured out the end.'

The sun glinted on the water. Up the towpath they sauntered, beside them the cow-parsley, masses of it, white and filigree-fine. It was quiet here, a tranced place with its motionless, floating slices of bread. Up above in the streets the world rumbled on and in Brussels James was sitting at his desk on the tenth floor – or was it the eleventh? She had never known.

Joe leant out of his pram. 'Bye-byes.'

Here there was no one but the floral slumberer. He had turned on to his back and kicked aside his bottle.

Sam said: 'A presumptuous little wine.'

They heard the snores. Kate read the label. 'VP British.'

'Found one of those in my outhouse the other day.'

James would have had a fit. 'Did he climb over the wall?'

'Guess so.' Sam was humming. He tilted his head to read the leaflets Joe had grabbed from the bank. '*Access Takes the Waiting out of Wanting,*' he said. '*Soon you'll wonder however you managed without one.*'

Kate smiled up at the blinding sun. Along the concrete towpath they walked and up the ramp into the street. They wandered along the pavement and stopped outside a baker's shop. They went in, Samuel asked for three buns with icing on the top.

The man put them into a paper bag. 'One for Mummy,' he said, 'one for Daddy, and one for the little lad.'

They munched their buns; they made their way back towards the High Street, as Samuel said he had to go to Marks and Spencer.

'So do I.' Kate surprised herself; there was no reason for her to go there, no vests that needed buying, no socks. No reason but a disinclination to leave Samuel and go back to her pile of washing-up.

To distract herself she said: 'Look at those.' She pointed to the shops they were passing, the Pakistani greengrocers' with its cardboard box full of knobbly roots, the Gents Tailor. *West End Misfits*, his sign read; she had needed someone with whom to chuckle over this – look, here he was, Samuel.

It was nice, chattering as she walked down the street, her usual pleasantish pram-pushing silence broken; broken, too, her usual boring calculations – how soon would Joe tire of his Portuguese Primer and demand a lolly? If so, would she give in?

They passed the Gas Central Heating showrooms. Kate said: 'What sort of person gets it fitted in June?'

'The sort who lays out his clothes the night before.'

'Someone sensible.'

'The sort who buys his swimming trunks in the January sales. The sort who reads *Which?* before he buys anything.'

Kate blushed for James, who read it. She resented Samuel saying this; she also resented James for perusing *Which?* and missing the secret water.

They wove their way through the shoppers and reached the doorway of Marks and Spencer. Samuel said: 'Jetta's too busy to choose my shirts with me. Guess where she's going this afternoon.'

Kate asked feebly: 'Where?'

'Wait for it. To a seminar in Tooting. "The Touch Taboo." '

Kate burst into giggles. They pushed the doors; ahead of them stretched long rows of garments. Shoppers moved about, fingering the clothes.

Kate confided: 'I always feel so embarrassed in places like this. My pram bumping into people's legs and Joe grabbing things with his sticky fingers.'

'Be proud, fecund woman. Hold up your head. They're envying you.'

'Who are? They couldn't.'

'The women are envying and the men are lusting. Look at that ratty little floor manager in the toupee. He's slavering.'

'He's not!' she laughed.

'Kate, look at yourself. Blonde, voluptuous . . .'

'James says I'm fat.'

'He says what?'

Kate fell silent. Quickly she transferred her attention to the shirts. She held up an emerald one, crackly with cellophane. 'What about green, to match your name?'

'I was fancying some executive stripes.'

She smiled. 'I've never seen anyone look less like an executive.'

'I was, once.'

'Oh yes, I forgot. Were you bored and restless, your creativity struggling to get out?'

'That's me.'

'Did you scribble furtive scenarios on the back of memoranda?'

'One day they'll be priceless. Librarians from Bryn Mawr University will rummage through the filing cabinets.'

'Plans for chapter one, embedded in plans for Hounslow By-Pass.' She was feeling quite witty – for her, anyway. For a Thursday morning. For a mum. Shoppers paused to glance at this talkative pair.

'Would you go for me in this?' Against his chest Samuel held a flowery package.

'Oh dear. You look like somebody terribly creative in advertising.'

'I like flowers.' He looked at her, head tilted. He raised

his thick black eyebrows. 'I imagine you hoovering in a flowery apron. Say you do.'

'I do, I do.' She paused. 'I don't.'

'Another fantasy withers.'

'Fantasy?'

'What you do all day. I like to picture it.'

'Samuel, do you?' *50% Cotton/50% Polyester*. She inspected the labels. *Non-Iron £5.65*. Did he really?

'I shall buy the green one,' he was saying.

She said: 'When I hoover, actually, I'm usually in a filthy temper. James bought me an enormous thing, far too elaborate.' After consulting *Which?*, she forbore to say. 'Its insides are always going wrong.'

'Like Charles Atlas with a weak digestion.'

Kate's shoulders shook with laughter, she leant against the handle of the pram, causing Joe to shift his position. 'Sorry, darling. Sweetest.' She felt a wave of fondness for him; she kissed his fair head, bent over its book.

She looked up and said: 'I hope and presume that it's you that hoovers at number twenty-one. After all, you're the houseperson.'

'Of course not. Jetta's so much more efficient than me.'

'That's not right. *You* should, sometimes.' She smiled. It might not be right, but she still smiled. 'Yes, get the green one.' She picked up the shirt.

'And some socks. I'm always wandering about the house in my socks. They're full of holes; want to see?'

'Mine are too. What sluts we are.' They moved over to the sock counter. 'It's all those stairs. Much quicker in socks. What about these sandy ones?'

'Nice. Won't show the holes. And some brown ones for when my tan's improved.'

They rummaged for his size. She concentrated on the socks, deciding whether he should have beige or brown, discarding the patterned ones as too nylony. Odd to share his buying of these things.

While he paid, Kate waited. She gazed at the counters: socks, shirts, waiting to be bought, to be claimed and pulled on to feet, buttoned round chests. Today they gladdened her. Samuel, writing the cheque, said something to the girl at the till; she smiled, it swept like sunlight across her sallow face. Kate felt pleased to hang his carrier amongst her shopping, to share these purchases at once so ordinary and so intimate. For whom else had she chosen socks? As far as she could remember, only James; and then, alone.

They pushed out through the swing doors. The brilliance of the day startled her: dazzling, the multicoloured summer dresses. What was the time? She had no idea; this expedition had gathered its own momentum. Judging by the loud and smoky interiors of betting shops, it must be lunch-time. In fact Ollie was stirring, starting to utter irritable creaks, his prelude to crying. He had kicked off the blanket; he jerked his froggy legs.

They walked towards Brinsley Street. So alert, Kate felt, to the sheen of the fishmonger's mackerels, to the luminous plastic weave of the now vacated chair outside Eileen's. They passed a Cypriot workshop; there was a poster on its wall – the Mediterranean, of the brightest homesick blue. Had she never noticed these things before? Perhaps she had simply never put a name to them.

Ollie's creaks, like a car shifting into fourth gear, shifted into wails. Joe, for a moment taken aback, paused and joined in.

'Copy cat,' said Kate.

Sam leant towards Joe. 'I know you, little bruiser, lead your mum a dance don't you, make her run up and down those stairs wearing out her socks, make her all hot and bothered. See, can't keep nothing from me.' He leant further forward. 'Don't fool me, those goody-goody curls. So you be nice to your mum, eh? Else I'll come round and pinch your blanket.'

They stopped at the top of Brinsley Street. Kate was about to reply, but Sam said he had to nip along to the paper shop for *The Times*.

'For the telly. My miserly Jewish soul stops me buying the *Radio Times*, so I go out and spend fifteen pence a day on a newspaper instead.'

Kate, smiling, watched him as he walked around the corner. A smallish but compact man, one would notice him in any street, there was an alertness about him. His fuzzy black head turned to look at the houses he was passing. What was he thinking – scurrilous thoughts about the neighbours? She longed to gossip.

But the babies were restless. She turned and pushed the pram down the street. For once she hardly heard their crying; her gingham dress shifted itself against her body as she walked. Cars drove past. Watch me – do I mind? Watch me as I walk.

She reached her doorway. Searching for her keys she heard the lower purring of a taxi; it slowed down, a confidential mutter behind her. Bending down over her handbag she heard a door slam; so oblivious was she, it took a moment for the man's voice to become recognizable.

Kate swung round.

'Goodness. James.' She gaped at him. 'James! What a lovely surprise.'

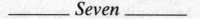

Seven

'This is marvellous!'

Kate fumbled for her door keys. Fluster crowded in: how had she left the house? What was she looking like? If only the babies would stop crying!

She got the front door open. 'Darling,' she said, 'this is so nice. Why are you back today?'

James and his suitcases followed her into the hall. 'Tomorrow's meeting was cancelled, so I thought I'd come home today instead.'

He looked tired and drawn. 'Come into the living-room and sit down,' she said. Then she remembered. 'Oh. Wait a minute.'

They stood squashed together. The hall was so narrow. Both babies continued yelling. 'Er, one moment,' she said. 'Let me just nip in there first.'

'What's up?'

'Nothing, nothing.' She flashed him a smile. 'Could you pick up Joe? That might stop him screaming. I've just got to sort something out.'

'What on earth is it?'

'Well, you see – well, Joe got your stapler – '

'Can't hear!' James had to shout over the screams.

'Sorry, I mean your hole-puncher thing and there are a few holes on the floor.'

'Holes?'

'No, you know – solid holes. Non-holes. Shut *up*, Joe!'

She pushed her hand through her hair. 'You know, the bits the holes are made from.'

'Ah.'

'Sorry! Just let me get in there first.'

'Kate, it doesn't matter. Look here, darling, let's do something about the children first. I can't hear myself think.'

James bent down and picked Joe out of the pram. As he lifted him, something scattered over the floor. James put him back in the pram; there were crumbs all over the legs of his pin-stripe suit. He dusted them off.

'Heavens! Sorry.' Hurriedly Kate fetched the clothes brush.

'What's he been eating?' asked James. 'Seems to be sticky.'

She dusted his lapels. 'Just a bun. An iced one.'

'Aha.'

'What a mess. Naughty boy!' She bent over Joe. 'So bad for his teeth too,' she muttered.

James was edging past. 'Never mind, darling. Let's just get into the sitting-room, shall we?'

'Yes, yes! You see, I wasn't quite ready for you.'

'I'll make us a drink.'

'Yes, but what shall I do about Ollie? And I ought to feed Joe and . . .' She trailed off. She looked at James and smiled. 'Wouldn't it be nice just to switch the babies off? Unplug them. Just long enough for a drink.' She put her arms around him. 'Some homecoming!'

He smiled back. 'Kate, you think I mind more than I do. I don't like to see you getting so harassed.'

'So petty, you mean.'

100

'Anyway, you're all looking very well. Quite sunburnt, in fact.'

'We've just been on a marvellously sunny walk.' She stopped. 'Look, why don't you go in and have a drink. I'll deal with these awful babies and join you in a minute.'

And she disappeared down to the kitchen.

James poured himself a whisky. Quiet descended.

He tipped his head; he drank the amber liquid. It warmed him, it soothed him, it was his welcomer – today, more of a welcomer than his wife. Was it the children that were bogging her down?

In front of the television lay a plate containing the remains of what must have been Kate's supper. Sluttish of course, but also rather touching. Solitary plate, solitary glass. No, he wouldn't sit up here waiting for her; he would go downstairs right now and tell her about the events of his week.

Kate was spooning food into Joe's mouth. James leant against the fridge and told her of his double-booked hotel, the complicated situation with the French, the series of meetings . . . 'and then there was a legal hitch and I had to rush down to Strasbourg.'

'Really?' she said. 'Come *on*, darling!' She pressed the spoon against Joe's closed mouth, hurrying him.

'But then it turned out that one needn't have gone. All a great waste of time but it meant that I had a spare hour and had a good look round the cathedral. You'd have liked it. I've meant to go there for years, but you know how I hardly ever get time to do things like that . . .'

Kate looked up. 'Do you like this dress?'

James was taken aback. He thought she would have

101

liked a conversation of this sort. 'What a funny question. I mean, you've had it for ages, haven't you?'

'Yes, yes.'

'Well . . .' He looked at it. 'It's not bad, I suppose. Your bra strap's showing, though.'

There was a moment's silence, then Kate turned back to Joe.

James wondered: What's the matter with the woman?

Somehow James and Kate could not quite get into step. Not that evening; nor, surprisingly, through the night and into the next day. Was it that Kate had been caught off her stride? James's sudden arrival, cutting short her fond and leisurely preparation-time, cheated her of hours of herself, Kate-hours, which she now had no chance to regain. Loose ends in the house, in herself. She was not ready. James had had to drink his whisky alone. To return to wifehood Kate needed advance notice – silly, but she did.

It had happened before. Arriving unexpectedly one evening, he had surprised her sitting in front of the television in her childhood dressing-gown, watching *Nationwide* and eating a mound of Heinz Spaghetti Hoops. He had stood in the doorway; bashful, she had felt. Also a feeling, well hidden from her darling husband, that she was being intruded upon. Separate souls, all of us; this she had felt, in her shabby brown flannel.

This time it took them a while to find their voice, their shared tone. James was preoccupied, busy with some work crisis that was too complicated for him to explain; she would not have understood it anyway. Kindly he asked her about her days, but in the hurried telling they flattened and shrank until they seemed hardly worth mentioning. Her life had no headlines; it was all small print and he had no time to read it.

No time. The harder he works the less he sees of us. He is too busy maintaining a household to enjoy it. He comes home exhausted, he trips over toys. Once it was different – before the children, when I earned a wage and wore silky knitted suits unblemished by egg, we would have a drink together, we were equals, I would lean forward with a tinkle of ice, listen and talk. I worked for Shell International, whose very name created vistas. I was in the mainstream of life.

But what is the mainstream? This, surely this. Kate gazed down at her baby. She was bathing him, soaping his bendy mottled limbs, soaping his head, its pulse beating beneath the skull. Ollie with his needing mouth: his mouth was funnelled, searching; his small hand gripped her finger. What is Strasbourg to this? What is Brussels and In-Trays?

Kate put the children to bed. It was Friday, the day after James's return, and they were going out to a cocktail party. She liked parties, even the despised cocktail variety, though her pleasure was mostly in the preparation – the shared dressing in the bedroom, the companionable, slightly shaming drink together before they left, the rekindling sight of each other in rarely-worn clothes.

She lingered over her row of dresses, willing James to remember about the party and come home in time. Downstairs Marion was already ensconced on the sitting-room sofa.

Of course James was late.

'Who on earth *are* these Forsters?' he asked, flinging his briefcase down on the bed.

'Darling, I've told you a million times.'

'You didn't tell me we had to go out. To a *party*. I was going to finish repairing those back windows tonight. You would have liked that, wouldn't you?'

'James, I did tell you. You just didn't listen. Just because you don't want to go . . .'

James rummaged through his ties. 'You know how I feel about do's like that. A thimbleful of sherry and I'm always collared by some tedious old buffer everyone else has steered clear of.'

Kate smiled. James, the first to rush into the blazing house, the first to lead his men over the top, but ask him to go to a cocktail party . . . 'Please,' she said, 'for my sake. Elaine Forster's got a boy Joe's age, you see. I do want to get to know her better.'

'Why don't you go and have tea with her then? A Tupperware party. Whatever you women do.'

But he was dressed now, and briskly tying his shoes.

In the car he said: 'You'd better fill me in.'

Kate smiled again, an expert in the one-minute potted biography; usually it was left until they had arrived, a gabbled whisper during the few strides between car and unknown front door.

'Elaine's a social worker. Jack's something to do with the *Financial Times*.' She added brightly: 'He's always going to Europe; you'll have lots in common.' She was also an expert in selling her husband their own friends – another wifely skill, little recognized by those without husbands. Without husbands, anyway, like James.

The first person she saw was Samuel. This gave her a shock. In a roomful of strangers there was the back of his head. No mistaking that fuzzy black hair, that enquiring tilt. He was talking to a tall girl with red curls; something he said made her laugh.

'Shame there's no one you know,' said Elaine Forster, giving James and Kate a drink. She was a stringy, worthy, talkative woman, for Kate the representative of a whole new classification: a fellow mother who must be cultivated for the sake of her child.

'Actually,' said Kate, 'I've just seen someone.'

'Marvellous. And how's Joe? Thought about playgroups yet?' Before Kate could move Elaine had launched into some fellow-mother chat, of the sort liable to make James beside them shift from one foot to the other. Playgroups came into it, so did inter-sibling rivalry and, shame upon them, the different types of dungarees to be found at Mothercare in the Holloway Road. Shame upon them because, despite her evening elegance, her grey slithery dress dating from childless Shell days, Kate found the dungaree question absorbing. My mind has gone, she thought, remarking that yes, the denim ones were remarkably long-wearing.

Elaine said: 'I do like butch clothes for little boys, don't you?'

'Joe's got some dungies with "Firestone Tyres" written on them. When he wears them I feel quite in awe of him, as if he knows all about the inside of our car.' Beside her Kate heard James clear his throat.

There was no knowing where the conversation would have gone from there; it was interrupted by the arrival of Jetta. Brisk by daylight, in the evening she appeared softened, indeed alluring, wearing a thin blouse that revealed a certain amount of tanned cleavage. Without looking at James, Kate could feel him brightening.

105

'Funny,' he said, 'to come all the way to Hampstead to meet one's next door neighbour.'

Beside her, Jetta and James started talking. Shamed by the proximity of Jetta, Kate steered the conversation from dungies to Elaine's work.

'Such a sad case on Tuesday,' Elaine said. 'Old man who lived alone, quite near you, actually. Children didn't want to know, lived miles away, and on Tuesday morning you'll never guess.'

Kate tilted her head. 'There the poor old boy lay, slumped in his chair.' She sighed, concern switching to brightness as she spied a new guest. 'Died where he sat.'

'Goodness! What from?' The fuzzy black head was leaning closer to the red curls.

'Lung-clot. That's what they said when we took him in. He was quite a nice old thing really. My department used to visit him every week.'

Kate remembered her old man. What had happened to him? In the Shell days this might have led to reflections on life and death; certainly to further interested questioning of Elaine. Tonight she just wondered: When shall I tell James about the key? Shall I have the lock changed, quietly?

What a little housewife I am! Fretting, my chores still clinging to me. Even here, am I unable to shake off my daytime self? She looked down at her hands: her fingernails, she noticed, were jammed with Plasticine.

James and Jetta were talking about Brussels, she could hear them.

'. . . conferences,' Jetta was saying. 'Once a year. And then of course I studied there for six months when I was training.'

'How very interesting,' said James. 'Where did you live?'

106

'The rue Dauphine. Near the Bourse.'

'Of course I know it well. In fact, there's a restaurant, Chez Noel it's called . . .'

'I ate there nearly every night.'

Kate looked down at her nails. *Plasticine*.

'You don't say! James, what an extraordinary co-incidence.'

Elaine had got back to babies. 'It's council-run, this playgroup, so it fits in with my working hours.'

'Reading my textbook over an artichoke.'

'In fact, Tom sometimes won't come home at all. Simply refuses to get into his pushchair. So hurtful!'

'In its heavy grey way,' Jetta was saying, 'the city has charm, doesn't it.'

'Sometimes I have to bribe him with his teddy.'

'You're right. Bourgeois and self-respecting. Solid values, solid buildings . . .'

'Sometimes, shamefully, with food. But only crisps. Never sweets. He's mad on Smoky Bacon.'

'I'm glad you like it,' said James. 'People say it's dull but I'm fond of the place myself.'

Kate looked up sharply. James always complained about Brussels to *her*, his wife. Why not to Jetta? Why, for heaven's sake, did he start going on about its bourgeois charm?

Kate turned back to Elaine, but Elaine had launched herself towards the newcomers. Kate, never having set foot in Brussels, let alone inside the chic, artichoke-laden atmosphere of Chez Noel, drained her glass and edged towards Samuel.

'. . . I'm funny that way,' the redhead was saying. 'Silly, I know, but I *always* have to have a book with me. You know that, Sam; I simply adore reading.'

She was smiling at Samuel, showing a row of even white teeth. As Kate came up behind, Sam said something which she couldn't hear.

'Sammy, you're priceless!' The girl laughed, red lips parted. 'Be a sweetie and give me a signed copy when it comes out.'

He said: 'Only if you buy it first.' Then he did a nice thing: without turning to Kate he took her empty glass and filled it from the bottle he was holding.

Kate said: 'I see you're an expert on cornering the booze.'

He turned to her. 'At Elaine's you have to be.' He was wearing the green shirt they had bought; also an enormous floppy red bow tie. 'Found any husbands yet?'

'Only you. I'm too frightened about saying I'm a housewife.'

'Kate!' He smiled, looking her up and down. 'Not quite a housewife.'

Kate gazed at her hands. 'I've got Plasticine under my fingernails.'

He took her hand and inspected it. 'Blue. What were you making?'

'Blue sausages. Joe only likes me making sausages.'

'Do you really want to be pushing bits of paper round a desk?'

'Not really.'

'Or sweating away in your bakery overalls, shoving buns in the oven?'

She smiled, back beside the canal. 'No.'

The redheaded girl asked: 'What's this about buns in the oven? Sounds saucy.'

Suddenly reckless, Kate said: 'A few years ago I would have been so embarrassed, that man saying "one bun for Daddy". There are some advantages, being twenty-six.'

His answer was drowned in a burst of laughter from the people behind them. Kate drank some more, feeling absurdly flattered that Sam was listening to her rather than the girl whose hair curled around her face in meant red tendrils. Over the other side of the room she could see James thoughtfully speaking to Jetta, then at her reply smiling. Kate thought: I bet he's not noticing her bra straps. No doubt James was noticing – well, Jetta's equivalent of freckles. On second thoughts: noticing but not realizing he was noticing. There were some compensations in being married to an unobservant man.

'Kate.' Elaine's hand was gripping her arm. 'You just must meet Gloria. Her Abigail is nearly three – just right for Joe.'

Funny how just when Kate had struggled out, she was pushed back in. She was led away and planted firmly back into the world of toilet training and educational toys. Over Gloria's shoulder she could see James and Jetta, now joined by a group of serious-looking men.

'Ashamed,' Gloria was saying. 'They mustn't feel that, must they. I just let her *see* the potty . . .'

James was saying something; the others were listening. Warmed with wine, Kate felt for a moment rekindled, seeing her husband speak, wondering what he was saying – watching the man, usually so familiar, distanced and glamorized by the party. He rubbed the side of his nose; a sign, this, that he was gaining momentum, becoming more interested in what he was saying. She remembered him as she had first met him, a tall calm stranger, in his hand a glass of cloudy punch. Across a crowded room he had once intrigued her. Still did, of course.

Alert, Kate caught two of his words. 'Council's responsibility.' At once she knew the whole conversation. He was talking about the dustmen's go-slow. By heart she knew the argument that had preceded and would follow that audible pair of words. He had been going on about the go-slow for days.

Deflated by this, her eyes sought Samuel's. He was working his way towards her. Several people waylaid him; he obviously knew half the room.

'I can recommend the trainer pants,' Gloria was saying. 'They've got a plastic lining.'

Sam, nearing her, caught her eye. Kate smiled over Gloria's shoulder.

Gloria said: 'It catches the pee.'

'We must escape Elaine.' Samuel arrived beside them. 'That remorseless, bony hand.'

They retreated to the dining-room, where they had a view of the crowd. Samuel started gossiping about the people they could see.

'That brawny woman,' he said, 'with the small and servile husband; she's muscled her way into everybody's beds.'

Boldly Kate asked: 'Yours?'

'No, I don't go for gym mistresses.' He paused. 'Well, I might, but not that one.'

'And her husband?'

'He languishes after that pallid Pre-Raphaelite in the corner, who's pretending to thumb through the books.'

'And the gorgeous redhead?'

'Oh, some media groupie.'

By the way he said this, over-casually, Kate knew that he had slept with her. Out of the boozy haze this slid into sight, then slid out again.

'And him?' she asked. Their eyes skimmed the room, alighting on faces, pausing at James and then tactfully bypassing him. Elaine, arm outstretched, approached to separate them but was deflected by someone else. Kate felt reckless and amused. There seemed nothing more pleasant than leaning against the polished table, their wine glasses side by side, and being tipsily bitchy. So unlike her normal style.

Just then James appeared at the door. 'Kate, do you fancy pushing off? I think I've had enough.'

'But I'm just warming up.' She heard the glug as Samuel refilled her glass.

'The thing is, I'm a bit whacked,' he said. 'Also peckish. There's only peanuts here.'

'Oh, James, don't be a spoilsport.' Then she turned to Sam and said: 'James hates parties. They upset his evening's routine.'

Now as she said this she could stand aside and see that it was not nice – see, in fact, that it was the cheapest of all marital ploys, that of the barbed remark to one's spouse in the presence of a third person. But she was fuddled with wine; also, Sam's bright eyes and loose scarlet tie made James look pale and constricted.

Then she felt ashamed, for James said: 'Listen, darling, why don't I take a taxi? You can come home when you feel like it.'

He humbled her – he was too nice for her, too nice for Sam. She said: 'Do let's go.'

*

111

One bowl of dripping and half a tin of Kit-e-Kat. *Kit-e-Kat*.

Marion, peering into the fridge, felt her heart sink. No food? Well, some butter and what on closer inspection turned out to be a paper bag containing three rashers of bacon. All stiff and curled, the bacon was.

Ridiculous to be disappointed. But she had not realized, when she had agreed to baby-sit, how she had relied on finding food. It was not official of course – after all, they were only at some cocktail parry – but the official food was invariably disappointing anyway: usually a bit of cold chicken and some limp lettuce. It was the family leftovers under the inverted plates – half-eaten trifles, bits of tasty, picked-at pie that mothers were too ashamed to offer to baby-sitters – that she craved.

And tonight – especially tonight she craved. It was only a day or so since she had heard the news; her loss, her awful guilt, why wasn't it getting better?

She closed the fridge door. Her disappointment was replaced by indignation. What a hopeless housekeeper Mrs Cooper must be. Hopeless wife. She did nothing all day and still she couldn't cook anything decent. What, pray, was she going to give James for his supper? There he was, slaving away in his office, and what did he come home to? Half a tin of Kit-e-Kat.

Now if she were married to him – to James (to herself she called him James, such a lovely manly name) – if she were married to James couldn't she imagine the spread! Candlelight, a dainty starter, then something nourishing and meaty – big piece for him, small piece for her. Just watch his face light up! Then on with the starched apron, open the oven door, bring out, with a flourish, the steaming lemon soufflé all moist and yellow. Watch his face then.

She watched it. But to concentrate on any face meant that it changed to Alf's. His was the head that filled her brain, blocking out everything else. His stubbly face was lodged inside her; his moist eyes saw everything she did. Alf – he had needed her, in his way, sitting there, hands clamped round his tea mug, droning on about the Pakis, he had needed her.

Marion sat down at the kitchen table and stared at the large cold fridge. Oh, if only she had known. Stupid, stupid not to have seen how ill he was. Stupid to have let herself get so tangled up and hurt about her parents and then say to Ron: yes, do come round.

Some time that night Alf had died. No one would ever know exactly when; no one had been there to see. Just him in that silent room. And her in that other room with Ron. Perhaps it had happened at the same time. Who could tell, now? Had he been waiting for her, expecting her to knock? He must have been. Had he put out a teabag for her beside his solitary one; washed, painstakingly, a mug?

She had gone round after school on Tuesday. The door opening – too quickly, Alf never got to his feet so fast. A strange woman's face. 'You'd better not come in here, dear.' Marion had just stood there; for a moment she did not understand what had happened. Had she come to the wrong door? Alf lived alone, yet there were murmurs behind the woman, the sound of something – a chair perhaps – being moved; there were several people in there. Then the woman had said: 'There's nothing we can do now, you know,' and Marion had realized.

No doubt Pauline in Hull had been informed, but to Pauline it would have been a burden lightened, a merciful release. And the social workers: they no doubt would be brisk and businesslike. But nobody really cared – nobody except, strangely enough, herself, Marion, sitting here at the kitchen table working her way through a bowl of Sugar Puffs – yes, she had found something to eat – feeling so painfully and alarmingly bereft. Spoonful after spoonful, she filled herself with Sugar Puffs. She would tell no one: Sharon and Lindsay would not be that interested, and her parents . . . something stopped her from telling them. She knew, sinkingly, what their reactions would be – her father would be too flippant; her mother, in some mysterious way, too sincere.

Marion washed the bowl and put it back on the dresser so that nobody would know it had been used. Slowly she made her way upstairs. No, funnily enough the only person she could imagine understanding would be Mr Cooper – James. She stopped in the hall to gaze at the coat rack, at his large unmuddy raincoat and, on the shelf above it his row of clothes brushes with leather backs. She was getting to know this house quite well by now; when baby-sitting she spent a long time lingering over his things. James would neither be too flippant nor too sincere – he would just be tall and comforting and calm. Neither too many questions nor too few. There was something reassuring about him – unlike her father he could be relied upon. She loved her father but in some terribly important ways he was disappointing.

She compared James to her friends' boy-friends, so weedy and silent and unfinished, sitting about limply on sofas. She did not want to think about Ron yet – she could only rather cautiously think *around* him, avoiding his face – but in every respect these specimens, so shuffling and pimply, just did not start to count when it came to something that really mattered like the fact that three days ago Alf had

114

died. The only person she was absolutely sure had needed her and she had not even said goodbye.

No, every male had let her down. James was the only one, she knew it in her bones, who wouldn't. He wouldn't let her down, would he?

'I've just remembered,' said Kate. 'I haven't got anything for supper.'

'Oh.'

'Sorry. I could open a tin.'

They were driving down Haverstock Hill. As they descended the road Kate could feel her party spirits sliding down into the everyday.

James said: 'Keep a look out, can you?'

'What for?'

'Panda cars.' He inspected the rear-view mirror. 'Don't want to get done.'

That James knew he had too many milliwhatsits in his bloodstream, that he therefore drove with caution, was eminently sensible. Of course it was.

Up above them spread a June sunset. The warm evening had brought people out from their houses; they filled the pavement, strolling, looking in shop windows. Above them the sky was a blushing pink. Even through the car windows Kate could feel something electric in the air – the ending of a summer's day with voices echoing and the coloured lights switched on above the pubs, the beginning of a Friday night.

She said suddenly: 'Let's stop and get some fish and chips.'

'Fish and chips? You mean, now?' James paused. 'What about that girl?'

'Oh, Marion'll be all right. We won't be long.' She

added brightly: 'It'll be fun. We can eat them out of newspaper.'

James halted outside a café labelled *Fish Dinners: Hot Pies a Speciality*.

'Look,' said Kate, 'we can even have pies with that lurid green sauce.'

'We could,' said James, accustomed nowadays to expense-account eating and starched napkins.

It was a summer's night, an evening like this, that Kate had first met James. She remembered the scrolled and mottled marble of the mantelpiece against which he had leant; the party took place in one of those Edwardian mansion blocks belonging to someone in the Ministry of Agriculture and Fisheries, or someone whose father was in it, or whose cousin. She had never known. Sally, her flatmate at that time, had known this someone's sister. It had been a grander gathering than either of them had bargained for, its participants murmuring and mature. Sally and she had both been twenty years old, two giggling girls from Bromley feeling amateurish and awestruck in their swopped dresses – she in Sally's, Sally in hers. Merely a secretary then and humble within her role, Kate had felt, looking at the men in their suits, that one of them might suddenly swing round and tell her to take dictation. It was only the fact that she wore Sally's dress and was therefore in disguise – more pert and Sally-like – that emboldened her to approach this calm and isolated man, leaning against the marble mantelpiece like a well-tailored Muse.

A night like this it had been, and James and she had eaten fish and chips afterwards in some unknown London street – in her memory as unreal and misty as the setting

116

for a musical: a lamp-lit square of pavement, a backdrop of brick wall, the rest hazy and unglimpsed.

Tonight, six years on, they stood at the counter. 'Haddock, we could have,' suggested Kate, 'or even, if we're bold, rock salmon. That's dogfish, you know, only they don't like to say so.' James was silent. She urged it to be fun, for the evening not to die on them. It was so seldom that they went out.

They took their hot parcels and carried them outside.

'Where do you suggest we eat them, then?' asked James.

'Here on the pavement.'

'But we'll get in everybody's way. We can't just stand here.'

'Against that wall then.'

'What, over there?'

'Why not?'

'There seems so much paper to manage. It's all going to fall out.'

'Well, where do you suggest?' Kate's anxiety to make this fun was putting her on edge.

'We should have sat at one of those tables inside,' said James.

'Why on earth didn't you say so?'

'It was you who seemed to be doing all the organizing.'

'Don't be silly. I only *suggested* it. You could have said no.'

'You know how you suggest things, Kate.'

'What do you mean?'

'Nothing, nothing. Just a certain emphasis. Bloody hell, this thing's hot.'

'Where shall we eat it then?'

'Anywhere, but let's make the decision quickly, darling, shall we?'

117

They eased themselves back into the car and sat side by side, opening the paper.

'Messy, isn't it,' said James. 'I'd forgotten just how messy.'

'*Fun, isn't it*,' he had said then, after the party. He had fed her a chip; at his hand, feeding her, she had gazed.

There was a silence as they explored their steaming packages.

'Take care, can you, darling, of the floor.'

Prickling, Kate asked: 'Why me more than you?'

'Kate, you know that you're, well, you're inclined to let things get into a bit of a mess.'

'You mean the house? You mean it's a mess?' Oh dear, if he had altered, so had she. She said: 'Anyway, I'm eating them perfectly neatly. Neater than you.'

'Don't be childish, Kate. Perhaps we should have taken them home and eaten them in the kitchen.'

Suddenly Kate felt depressed. When had they stopped finding this fun? Beside her, James was making a certain business about separating the fish from the bones; he did it with a finicky concentration that had always annoyed her. Also it made her feel guilty, as if she had put in all the little bones one by one just to goad him. Over it all hung the irritable guilt, growing clearer now that she was more sober, that she had misbehaved at the party.

Fussed, James asked: 'Don't we have any tissues in this car?'

'*Here, take my handkerchief*,' he had said that night. '*Don't spoil that beautiful dress*.'

'Yes, here.' She passed him a Kleenex.

They ate in silence for a while, then James said: 'I just wonder if we should phone that girl. Tell her we're late.'

'*I'd like to just be here for ever*.'

118

'But it's only half past nine,' she said. 'Anyway, we'll be going home in a minute.'

They sat there, a married couple wiping their hands with Kleenex while outside the street was humming, car doors slamming.

'Finished?' asked Kate.

She took James's greasy paper, scrumpled it up and got out of the car to find a litter bin.

People pushed past her; she smelt cigarette smoke, perfume, expectancy. Two girls in white summer cardis, linking arms, pushed open the door of a pub; music briefly blared; they went in. Opposite the chip shop was a place called Tariq Late Nite Foods. Inside it was neon-lit and bustling, young men inspecting the freezers, girls queueing to pay; outside cars stopping, engines running, winkers winking, people nipping in for a loaf of French bread, a packet of fags . . . single people, flat-dwellers, addresses scribbled on matchboxes . . .

Suddenly Kate was seized with an urge to run. Where? Anywhere. Run, run, high heels clattering, run down the road, be jostled, submerged, be swallowed into a pub, into a cinema, be swallowed into Belsize Park Underground, be a woman alone in her slithery silvery desirable dress. Cheque book she had, handbag, money (James's money, *James's money*); take a bus, take a train. Why not? Sit boldly on a bar stool, stare at strangers, be gazed upon. Gaze at my breasts, my freckly shoulders. Never mind the babies waiting, Marion waiting, James waiting, the washing-up waiting; that they were all waiting made her want to run the faster. London was full of other evenings, the unknown Kates she could, if she clattered down Haverstock Hill, become. Lights all through the city; seats waited for her, didn't they? Seats, spaces, as yet unknown, they were there for her to occupy if only she wished to find them. So many choices there suddenly seemed, so many seats other than that one in the car, next to James who would by now be looking at his watch.

Kate was not running, of course. With her bundles of paper she was standing at the litter bin. Her breasts ached; all of a sudden the milk spread, warm and damp, across the front of her dress.

She smiled; she pushed the paper into the bin. Slowly she went back to the car.

As they drove home James remarked: 'He certainly knows how to hog a bottle, doesn't he.'

'Who, darling?'

'What's-his-name next door. Our immortal bard.'

'James! You know his name perfectly well.'

'Terrible manners.' James changed gear. 'And trying to monopolize – well – people like you.'

Kate raised her eyebrows and found that she was smiling. So it had been Samuel who had irked James. There had been a concrete reason, an understandable one, for the vague disappointment of this evening. All James's irritability could slot, with a pleasing click, into the slot for jealousy.

What a relief; because there was nothing to be jealous about, was there. Kate picked the Plasticine out of her fingernails.

Some day he'll come along, the man I love
   And he'll be big and strong, the man I love . . .

Big and strong. Brown hair, brown voice, deep brown eyes with such a sadness in them. Yearning, yearning,

Marion sank into the cushions, she sank into his arms, into the whole warm manliness of him. Outside the window, beyond the spikey TV aerials, the sunset spread across the sky.

He'll look at me and smile, I'll understand . . .

The music filled her up, it was warm syrup spreading through her body, down her limbs, filling her to her toes and the very ends of her fingertips. It meant James, this song, she knew this. He would understand about Alf, and what it was like at school, and how she so often had to keep things in because nobody quite understood what she meant. How, in the last week, she had glimpsed two voids. He would understand all that.

And in a little while, he'll take my hand

And though it seems absurd, I know we both won't say a word . . .

Where would be the need? No stupid voices spoiling things, no worry about what she should be saying next. Just the deepest of silences, his arms around her shutting out those mournful spaces. Above them the sunset and the technicolour clouds, the limitless future.

Somehow, too, the past. The woman who sang understood that as well. Alf was understood in those words, his dying, the light cast back upon his years and cast forward too upon the time ahead. And herself, Marion, everything echoing around her – herself, yearning.

The song finished. Before the next one started she wanted to put back the needle and hear it all over again. She inspected the record cover. Peggy Lee, with her bleached hair, looked rather ordinary. How could she know so well? She was singing for Marion.

Soon James himself would walk through that door.

Marion rather dreaded this – surely he would see what was written all over her face? Her feelings had been growing for days, even weeks – by now could she keep them hidden? She had always been keen on him, of course; it was only lately, though, that she needed him.

The Coopers did not possess as many books as her parents. They did have some Wordsworth, however. She pulled the volume from the shelf and arranged herself on the sofa. She was wearing her long blue skirt, which in itself looked soulful and also hid her thighs. She must not have James thinking of her as the silly teenager who only read *Honey*. Poetry was appropriate. Just holding the book made her feel deeper; a magic tablet in her hand, it solemnized the surrounding air.

This was how she would be found. At least, this was what she planned, but by some unwelcome coincidence just as the car stopped outside, Joe woke up. Marion scrambled to her feet; with a thump, Wordsworth fell to the floor. Into the hall she rushed, her plans scattered. Wails floated downstairs; a loud insistent yelling. Should she be discovered, the diligent baby-sitter, running upstairs to Joe, or should she greet them all casually, the relaxed one?

She hovered, undecided. The key turned in the lock; Mrs Cooper appeared.

'He's just woken,' Marion told her. 'Only just.'

Mrs Cooper smiled. 'Don't worry.' She looked at her. 'Marion, are you all right?'

Marion blushed. Mr Cooper, grave and beautiful in his dark suit, closed the door. He said: 'Sorry if we've kept you. We just stopped for some fish and chips.'

Fish and chips. She must picture this later, in detail.

He went upstairs and returned, Joe a pyjama-clad bundle

in his arms. It was then, truly, that Marion fell in love with him. He was just standing there, tall and protective, holding Joe all curled up. So reassuring and large, he looked down at the tiny child. Then this lovely, grave man smiled; with his hand he smoothed back the hair from Joe's forehead and said gently: 'Sleepy boy.' Marion's heart turned. So gentle, that hand was: its large size made it painfully gentle. It cradled Joe in his Pooh Bear pyjamas.

Marion moved a step closer, ostensibly to say goodnight to Joe. As she said it, though, she was scarcely conscious of Joe's sleepy, flushed face – it was that charcoal flannel that she saw, inches from her nose. If she moved closer she would touch it. She did not feel weak: her weakness was stored up for when she went outside.

The front door closed and she stood on the pavement. It was dark by now and she was alone feeling, indeed, shaky. Now would begin the luxury, delicious beyond description, of going over everything that had happened in the hallway – his grave goodbye full of regret, his placing, with meaning, of that pound note in her hand. For a moment the pound note was precious beyond money. Fish and chips, he had said – a chink into his life. She would do anything in the world to have eaten fish and chips with James. Mrs Cooper, a harassed, peripheral figure at the best of times, dissolved away; it was Marion sitting there on a park bench beside James . . . sunset above . . . murmured words . . . the loving sharing of the crispest, darkest chips. 'Here, darling. I've saved this one for you.'

Marion's head swam with confusion and yearning. It seemed too mundane to just open her front door and go home. Her parents were out but only at some drinks party;

any minute they would come back and then she would feel crowded.

There was no way she could go to the outhouse. She used to creep in there and think, but now of course it was spoilt. She did not want to go near that place. By now the flattened sheets and dirty shirts would have been bundled into the washing machine, its Cyclops eye opening; they would have been taken out, dried, ironed and folded into crisp piles to be put away. Painlessly laundered.

It was then that she remembered Alf's room. More to the point, Alf's front door keys.

'Mind you, can't have everyone knowing about this,' he had said. 'Don't want any young hooligans breaking in, do I?' With his stick he had pointed to a row of bricks edging the flowerbed; they had been standing in his little patch of front garden. 'Keep my keys under there, don't I.' He shook his head. 'No, used to be all open doors down this street, everyone knowing everyone else, didn't have to lock your doors then, young lady.' He had straightened with a grunt. 'Blooming thugs everywhere, those squatters steal the coat off your back.'

What can they steal from you? Marion thought. Sadly, so little.

He went on: 'No harm in you knowing, mind – don't want me being taken poorly and them banging the door down, do we?' He had shuffled back indoors, muttering. 'So I keeps me spares there, and you can keep it to yourself.'

Marion walked swiftly down Brinsley Street. Which brick?

Kate was watching Joe's eyelashes. Sitting on the sofa with him in her arms, gazing down at the top of his head, the only way she could tell whether he had gone to sleep or not was whether they blinked. They blinked. Kate sat very still, willing him to close his eyes, willing the letters James was opening (this morning's; he had not had time earlier) not to *all* be bills. Poor James: from the way he inspected them swiftly, woodenly, and put them aside, she knew they were. Deflating to come home from a party to find awaiting you a pile of envelopes, beige and windowed.

No, now was definitely not the time to ask his advice about the keys. Not the right moment. Surprising, really, how nearly every moment was the wrong one for telling him news like that. One would imagine those long evenings together and long weekends and presume that the opportunities were endless. Unmarried people would presume that. Married ones would know better: how can one spoil the nice moments – the walks in the park, the lazy Sunday mornings? How can one interrupt the preoccupied ones – the reading of the newspaper, the measuring of the downstairs window? And if it is a bad, quarrelsome moment, who likes to worsen it even further by telling the unwelcome news that an old man got himself into the house under false pretences and made off with the keys?

Kate glanced down at the lashes. The tender, twin fringes were stilled. Joe slept, thumb in mouth, wrist lacquered from nose-wiping, on his stomach Pooh Bear rising and falling. The question was: should she, when she took him upstairs, change out of her dress? Now she was back home she could hardly remember the party, and her silky dress seemed inappropriate. Damp, too. But would it be unromantic to change out of it? James looked so preoccupied he probably would not even notice, and what is the point of wearing something cripplingly tight under the arms and draughty down the back if one's mate is busy with bills?

Keys, dress, Ollie's feed . . . the usual little questions came crowding in, it was as if she had not been out this evening at all; life was back to normal, the moment beside the litter bin was like the brief flare of a match in the dark.

'Just taking Joe upstairs,' she said, 'and changing out of this dress.'

James glanced up; Kate left the room. Back he turned to *Fuel cost per tonne 2385p, Units Consumed 3057*. He was not reading it. The writing was in front of his eyes but it was Kate's face that he was seeing – Kate's face at the party, and how the animation had drained from it when he had approached. It had: he had noticed.

She had looked so pretty too, in that dress. Flushed, alive. Why didn't she keep it on?

Amount Due: £86.07. Kate returned, wearing the same boring old jeans, the ones with the coffee stain on the knee, that she had been wearing all day.

Eight

Which brick? Alf's front flowerbed, less a flowerbed than a sooty square of soil, was edged with a row of them: the terracotta edging slabs with wary tops common to the older sort of city garden, along with cinder paths and neatly-staked chrysanths.

Marion crouched, furtively, and lifted the edging slabs one by one. Beyond the railings the street was deserted; in the sodium light the terraced houses stretched away into the distance. Many of the façades were boarded up with corrugated iron, their upstairs windows gaping holes, their front gardens submerged under speckled laurel bushes and soggy mattresses. Those still occupied wore the secretive look of houses in a condemned area; only old people were left behind twitching lace curtains, and sometimes squatters, patterned bedspreads pinned up against bureaucracy. The desolation, the sense of the years having passed, filled Marion with delicious melancholy.

She found the key. It was tied up in a paper bag saying *It's Clean It's Fresh At Sainsbury's*. She pulled off the rubber band; her fingers were grubby with earth. Never again would Alf shuffle testily to Sainsbury's – worse than that, would anyone notice that he didn't?

After only four days, rubbish had drifted against his front door. Was he buried now, deep in the earth? How quickly he had been forgotten. Marion fumbled with the lock. No doubt she could have climbed in through the

127

window; the Social Services people must have got in that way but it would be tricky and might attract attention. Besides, even after Alf's death she felt obliged to use his scheme and to respect his careful ways. No one else would.

The door creaked open; she hesitated. She did not know what to expect – perhaps the room would be left as it was, cold tea in the pot.

She was wrong; the room was bare. The floor had been swept, Alf's meagre belongings had been taken away. The room seemed larger and curiously altered in shape, its ceiling loftier, its corners more apparent now that there was no furniture to hide them. The curtains remained at the window and the lino remained on the floor; otherwise there was nothing left. Thirty years he had lived here; as she crossed the room her footsteps echoed.

She stood at the mantelpiece. She gazed at its painted surface; Alf remained in the row of parallel brown stains where he had laid his Woodbines and forgotten about them. Never would he lay them here again. Never, ever, she repeated to herself, the words rolling round her head. Never again would the lino creak as he made his way to the scullery. What had died with Alf – last week's virginal, listening Marion?

She had never known anyone die before – only a distant aunt she had never met. She had not realized how remorselessly the room would exist after Alf's death; how life would continue, outside the cars hooting heartlessly. Through the letter box a card had been posted; it lay on the floor: *Blocked Drains? Leaking Pipes? Contact Our Fast Plumbing Service*. Didn't they know?

Nothing left, nothing. Rubbish against the door. From

digging about in the soil Marion's fingernails were black; she picked the dirt from them and let it scatter on to the lino. In this room she felt moved and holy; things she had once thought familiar had been altered, they cast long shadows now. She felt expanded; all over her body her skin was tingling; the folds of the curtains and the jutting mantelpiece seemed pressingly *there*. Loss made them real. She walked round the room, her footsteps echoing. She felt so strange: it was not frightening; it was a release being here, feeling these things. And there was nobody to watch her or to spoil it. No Ron to damage her, no parents to disappoint her, no silly little worries crowding in to confuse her. Here she felt large and knowing. The orange glow from the street lamp lay mystically over the room. Soon this room would be destroyed, the house first a mound of rubble then flattened and concreted over, new houses rising. She stood picturing this. The long past, the long future – painfully, deliciously she was glimpsing them.

This will be my special place, thought Marion, moving from the mantelpiece and putting the key back into the Sainsbury's bag.

Aloud she said to the room: 'I'll be back soon.'

Her voice, loud and portentous, alarmed her. Clutching her paper bag she escaped.

She did go back soon, on the following Monday, when she got out early from school. She was doing her A levels and at school a dispersal had taken place. Several of her friends had already left and taken jobs. The remaining ones had been claimed by boys, as a consequence becoming moony and dull, presenting to the plate-glass windows their soulful

Garbo profiles. Or else huddled and clannish, murmuring together about late periods and their boy-friends' stealthy exits at dawn. Despite her technical admittance to this club, this gathering of the experienced, Marion still felt unable to contribute to this particular topic. Subjects, too, had claimed them, taking Sharon to the Biology Lab and Lindsay to the Art Room. Being sixth-formers now they were considered adult, able to leave the building when their class had finished and not remain until the bell at four.

It was half past three. Again the street was empty but this time Marion had a large canvas bag with her. Feeling bolder, as if she owned the room – in some sense she felt she did – she rummaged for the key and walked straight in. Wasn't it she who knew Alf best; who had, in her soaring way, mourned him?

Still, she closed the curtains. No sense in people knowing. In the sombre room she stood for a moment, pushing out of her mind the intervening weekend and the busy day at school, urging back the feelings of Friday night. She stood still, getting herself into the mood.

It worked. The hurtful way Sharon had gone to lunch with Jane instead of her; the excruciating way Mr Hilbert had said '*Really* Marion' in front of the whole English class when she'd thought a bawd was a sort of medieval platter; the meeting with James in the street and the discovery, when she got home, that all the time she had had an enormous white blob of toothpaste on her lip; the way her father had said in front of all those people that she was going to a skin specialist; the fact that, though she couldn't have borne it if he *had*, Ron had not phoned . . . in this quiet room they fell from her. Standing in the silence, she need not even blush.

Out of the bag she took four candles. She had not tested whether the electricity had been turned off; it was candles she needed for the right atmosphere. She put them in a row on the mantelpiece and lit them one, two, three, four . . . in their flickering light she could see Alf's cigarette burns, amber streaks. She thought of the Paki newsagents', on its shelf the packets of Woodbines Alf would no longer buy. Again that queer, expanded feeling.

She bent over her bag and drew from it the red woolly rug from her den. No longer situated in front of her gas fire, she now laid it in the place where Alf's had been. Then she drew out a packet of Ginger Nuts. Here in this candlelit room she could really eat.

She sat on the rug and opened the packet; in the silence the crackling wrapper startled then reassured her – a friendly food-noise. She felt the room settle around her comfortably, become *her* place. She put a Ginger Nut into her mouth; she held it there a moment against her tongue, feeling it soften, releasing its sweetness; she gazed at the candles, she put her palms together and after a moment's concentration she did what she would never in a thousand years admit to her parents that she did – she said a prayer.

'Ashes to ashes,' she said slowly, sonorously; the marvellous words rolled around the empty corners of the room. 'Ashes to ashes,' she repeated, filling herself with the terrifying and weighty sentences; Alf crumbling into the earth; Alf scattered. 'Oh Alf, rest in peace . . .' She was chanting now, making up the words, their momentum

131

quickening, carrying her along: 'Sprout up flowers, sprout up trees, into the roots of the soil, into the deepest black, sink, bones of Alf . . .'

She swept on, away from Alf. It did not matter how long she went on; they were lovely, the words, sweeping her along ever more hypnotically – she wished that at school they would sing, in assembly they didn't any more – 'Watch over us Oh Lord, watch over the flowers and the trees, watch over James and protect him . . .' It was lovely that there was no one to hear. Sometimes if she went on long enough she could make the tears come into her eyes.

One dreadful time she had been praying in her bedroom and she had forgotten to lock the door. Years ago it had been, when she was eleven and she had been praying for a sister – not a brother, a sister whom she could look after and whose hair she could brush – and suddenly who should walk in but her mother. She had pretended that she was on her knees because she was looking in her chest of drawers – 'Just finding a vest,' she had said, airily. But it must have looked daft; she was miles away from her chest of drawers, she was right in the middle of the carpet. Still, her mother had not guessed. She would not guess something like that; she simply would not believe it was possible – her own daughter, who had been brought up so sensibly, with all those balanced discussions on Buddhism and atheism and Christianity.

Marion sat back on her haunches and ate another Ginger Nut. No, here she was safe. She would bring along more things next time – magazines, perhaps a cushion if she could smuggle one out of the house without anyone noticing.

At this point Marion glanced down at her bag. There were still two more things left, of course. She remained in the same position because she did not want to admit, not quite yet, that they were in there. She sat motionless on the rug, her bag in front of her. Dare she get them out? She was starting to feel a bit peculiar about them – not guilty of course, just a bit, well, tentative. It was such a bold thing to have done.

Even here, alone, Marion could feel the blush spreading. But she leant forward and opened the bag.

Blocked Drains? Leaking Pipes? Contact Our Fast Plumbing Service.

Joe laid the card on the ground and smoothed it flat, lovingly. Breath hoarse with concentration, he dug his spade into the sand and heaped it on to the card. He heaped on more until it was a little mound; he thwacked it with his spade. Then he pulled the card out, scattering sand in all directions, and put it in the pocket of his dungarees.

He had been inseparable from this plumbing card all day. It was one of those sudden fierce bonds that, in the manner of the Portuguese Primer, sprang up mysteriously. Ever since it had dropped through the letter box it had been clasped in his hand, all the way to the playground.

'Want spade.'

A small boy was standing in front of Joe. He watched Joe banging it about in an aimless manner. 'Silly likkol boy,' he said.

'He's two years old actually,' Kate said. 'On Friday.'

'Gimme spade.' He grabbed for it.

'You can't have it,' Kate said. 'It's his.' She glanced

around, shiftily, for his mother. Playground lore, in fact mothering lore in general, dictated that one might jump up to rebuke one's own child but never on any account a child belonging to someone else – in fact, one must be exaggeratedly, unctuously polite to it. The boy's mother, however, appeared to be over by the swings; Kate grabbed back the precious spade. This most basic of lores made for strain in large gatherings, each mother poised to rebuke ostentatiously her own child, while tensely ignoring the fact that it was being half beaten to death by someone else's.

'Did you got a sweetie?' the boy asked.

'No.'

'Did the likkol boy got a sweetie?'

At this Joe stiffened, alert, and came stumbling over. 'Sweet?' he asked. 'Sweet?'

Kate gathered him up. 'Let's go on the swings.'

'Sweet!' Joe yelled.

Kate picked up his plumbing card and his spade and carried him across the asphalt to the boxed-in infants' swings; crated bundles swung to and fro, pushed by vacant mums. She eased Joe, wriggling, into a seat. 'Sweet!' he yelled, struggling, but to Kate's relief his voice was stilled, as always, by the novel sight of his fellow bundles and the interesting sensation of the playground swooping away under him, then swooping up again.

A busy place, this. Situated in a triangle of grass behind the High Street, it drew its inmates from a variety of homes. They could be identified by outfit: the smart children in white socks and hair ribbons, whose small brothers and sisters reposed in gleaming new prams like bishops lying in state – these came from the council flats. The shabby children grubbing about in jumble-sale jerseys, needless to say, belonged to the posh houses in the smartened-up streets; their mothers, striding aware women in nipply tee-shirts, shouted to their children in the fruity, confident tones of the middle-classes.

Kate knew a few of these women, less by name than by gynaecological history. As a bank manager identifies his client by his credit rating, so Kate, in the peculiarly intimate way that mothers of babies exchange information, identified these women by their methods of birth control and number of stitches. Occasionally a husband would appear to fetch his spouse; breezily polite to the other ladies, little did he know how his wife's post-natal dryness during intercourse was as familiar to them as the bench upon which they sat.

'More, Joe?'

Kate continued pushing; Joe's face swooped up close, then away, on it the fixed concentrated look it always wore in the company of other children. The transformation of the Joe she knew, so swaggeringly self-confident within the walls of his own home, to the playground Joe, the awestruck onlooker, never failed to surprise her. In fact, tears had pricked her eyes when on the edge of some busy sandpit group she watched him hovering, blanket trailing, thumb in mouth, while someone else played with his spade. So placid and innocent, playgrounds seemed, until one looked closer.

'Sweet!' Joe yelled suddenly. Kate, stopping the swing, had to admire his sharp eye, even if it was in fact only a wrapper. Joe stumbled off in its direction. He shamed her by his loud and unwholesome lust for sweets; rejecting the wrapper, he now set off on a search for more, picking up bits of paper and inspecting them.

'Joe, how about that roundabout thing? Shall I go on it with you?'

Joe ignored her and made off in the direction of the sandpit, the other boy trailing behind in a way that looked faithful. There was another tedious exchange about the spade. Kate watched the confrontation, the boy wiping his nose with the cardboarded sleeve of his jumper. Sitting on the concrete edge of the sandpit she disclaimed responsibility; that was what made playgrounds so relaxing. Instead she looked at the other children patting the sand, banging it, scooping it up and trickling it through their fingers, burying their feet in it. She pondered the inescapable difference between girls and boys – an unfashionable concept but demonstrated simply enough by the patient row of sandcastles along the edge of the sandpit. There were already eight of them; she did not have to look at the bent figure just producing a ninth to know that it would be a girl.

It was nice coming to the playground. She could direct her footsteps here. In the vague days of routines and petty errands the playground stood out as something solid, its sturdy iron structures reassuring her that for an hour, at least, Joe's directionless energy would be employed upon something *meant*. Out of the ether of infinite naughtiness had been constructed this playable sand, these slides and swings bolted firmly in place; they were created neither to make coffee nor to powder one's nose (two objects she had snatched from Joe that morning); they were created simply to be enjoyed.

Except, actually, Joe wasn't. He had climbed from the

sandpit and was bending, fascinated, over a grey, spat-out bit of very chewed chewing-gum.

Kate clambered to her feet.

The candles flickered. They were a little shorter now and at their base wax had spread, anchoring them more firmly to the mantelpiece. Spreading over the painted wood they looked settled; they belonged there.

He belonged there too.

Marion gazed at James. How long had she stood there, gazing? Never in real life could she raise her eyes to his; she did not dare. Now she could. Every bit she had inspected in turn – his straight, firm eyebrows, neither too thick nor too thin; his thinnish but resolute and lovely mouth (she had leant between the candles and touched those lips with hers). Best of all, his eyes – beautiful dark understanding eyes, kind but sort of smouldering too . . . they were looking directly at her. Wherever she went in the room those attentive eyes followed.

She would have preferred colour, but black and white was better than nothing. It must be a studio photo because there was no background, just a radiant glow, and James was just a little bit younger. Some sweet little tendrils of hair clung closer round his temples than they did now – not that he was getting bald of course, just more distinguished. The candles flickered. James, enshrined.

It was all Mrs Cooper's fault. Leaving her back door open, setting off with her pram – anyone could get in, couldn't they. There was no doubt that she could look after neither her house nor James – garden door open, house a fearful mess. Marion had actually worked herself up into feeling quite self-righteous over the dirty dishes in the kitchen, the matchbox on the stairs with all its scattered matches and in their bedroom Mrs Cooper's face powder all over the floor. Wandering around the house Marion had felt her indignation growing; in fact she had actually lingered over these things to help it grow some more – the more it grew the less she felt guilty about being there at all. By the time she had got to the top of the house she had actually managed, by nurturing this sense of moral outrage, to feel that it was herself, Marion, creeping uninvited around the rooms who was perfectly within her rights and that it was Mrs Cooper who was the culprit.

Whether these rights extended to pinching a photo Marion did not like to ask. Anyway she had only borrowed it, hadn't she? She would give it back soon; nobody would even notice that it had for a short while been out on loan. Besides, Mrs Cooper had James in the flesh; she possessed him all the time. It only seemed fair for Marion to have just a tiny bit of him. Mrs Cooper could not grudge her that, surely? She should be pleased, come to think of it, that somebody was keen enough on him to take it.

By this time, standing in the bedroom, Marion had felt almost honour-bound to put it in her pocket. In fact, wasn't it her duty to rescue it from its obscurity behind all those other photos and oozing, half-used pots of make-up?

'Can't trust them nowadays,' Alf had said. 'Steal the coat off your back, they would.'

Very, very slowly Marion took out the last object. She wished she did not remember Alf's words.

She gazed at the shirt. Somehow the photo was not quite the same thing – it seemed more a symbol.

Still, she had only borrowed it. Slowly she drew the shirt to her; she pressed it against her face, she buried

138

her nose in it, breathing in James's scent, the faintest, miraculous trace of him. It was not exactly sweat, she decided, just warm man. With the cotton pressed against her eyes she could blot out her unease. Blot out the way she had actually picked it up off the bathroom floor where it had been lying amongst all the other washing. She honestly truly had not meant to take it; she had just felt the need to wander round the house for a bit while Mrs Cooper was out – commune with James.

Well, here it was. Saved Mrs Cooper washing it, hadn't she? And anyway she would never notice it was gone, it was just one amongst many others lying in that great untidy heap.

Still uneasy, Marion kept her face buried in it. It was a striped shirt, one of her favourites. She had often seen James wearing it when she sat behind the curtains and watched him come home from work. She could hardly believe that she actually possessed it. She inspected it. On one of the cuffs a button was missing; gazing at the small tuft of thread she felt touchingly bonded to James, sharing his tiny moment of exasperation, commiserating with him about his wife. Catch her, Marion, letting him go to work with a button missing!

She took the shirt away from her face. Now she had got it here, what exactly was she going to do with it? In this empty room there was nowhere to put it.

Down at the Town Hall the clock chimed five. The echoes closed the room in, made it safer; still, it was time to go. She took the shirt and hung it on the handle of the scullery door. Yes, she would take it back in a day or two; it looked eerie, as if James had come home from work and just casually slung it there. It hung limp and

139

pale, pastel-striped. James, are you behind my shoulder? Shall I turn round?

He would be standing there, chest bronzed in the candlelight. Beautiful sinewy chest, she had seen it when he was gardening; not an ounce of fat, enough hairs to be masculine and not enough to be alarming – at the swimming baths some men looked shocking as gorillas. Dad too was all matted. In her daydream James still had his trousers on, of course; she did not want to think of any part lower down.

No, just his chest; his torso, perfect as a Greek god's.

'Yes, I had a terrible time with this one here. Sasha's head, you see, was enormous. I had the works – fourteen stitches, forceps, you name it . . . and then they got infected of course; idiot midwife didn't know what she was doing, I couldn't sit down for weeks. *Ben!*'

The woman lunged after the boy, picked him up and returned to Kate. 'Sorry, he seems bent on molesting your little one.' She went on: 'No, after Sasha was born I told myself – never again.'

Around her face she had a fuzzy triangle of hair that during this sort of conversation could only suggest its sister triangle below. 'Ben sweetie, your *nose*.' She turned back. 'No, I blame it all on the epidural.'

Kate wished she found these conversations less absorbing. Three years ago, her womb small and unused within her, she neither knew what an epidural was nor cared. Playgrounds such as this she had passed, briskly. A swift, incurious glance, perhaps, at the mothers; a vague wonder at how they passed their days – depending on her current circumstances this wonder could be pitying or envious.

Their rhythm of life was that of another race; they kept different hours, emerging with their pushchairs long after she had disappeared into the Underground and vanishing off the streets to nursery tea and 'Blue Peter' long before she returned at night. Those long slack mornings, long slack afternoons: what did they *do* with them? The shopping that she concentrated into a busy wedge of Saturday morning – was it that, spread out and watered down, which kept them occupied? Their physical skills – the manoeuvring of prams over kerbs, the juggling together of carrier bags, babies and pushchairs – were to her mysterious and unlearnt.

Well I've learnt them now, thought Kate, swooping up Joe, settling him on one hip, extracting from his mouth a wizened apple core, swooping down for his spade and his plumbing card, carrying him to the pram, readjusting Ollie's blanket, shifting her shopping bag, dumping Joe in – look! All with one hand.

It must be five o'clock. She needed no Town Hall chimes to tell her; Ollie's seeking mouth was her human clock, her tender timepiece. Between the houses she could see the home-bound cars jammed at the traffic lights; office girls, bored with their work, would be fidgeting; James, absorbed with his, would not.

They made their exit, a laborious and shuffling one, through the gates. Emerging into the road they passed a husband who had arrived to fetch his family. Fresh from the outside world, a rolled-up newspaper under his arm, he glanced with a smile at the childish apparatus and appraised the women. Kate prickled, femininely. What did he think of this daytime, mother's world? Of her, just another mum?

On the pavement Joe got out of the pram and squatted down. He pointed. 'Ladybird,' he said. He knew the name from the motif on his Ladybird books. Kate bent down to inspect it with him; the ladybird was clambering over an empty Woodbines packet. 'Ladybird.' Joe's fat finger pointed at it, informing Kate. Companionably they squatted together, watching it walk across and ease itself down the other side.

She lifted it up and put it safely on the grass verge. They meandered on along the peaceful pavement. Beyond the houses cars were blaring their horns; on other pavements people pushed past each other, hurrying blindly to their destinations. On this pavement Kate and Joe were humming tunelessly. What did James, what did that other husband know of this – the slow procession along the street, the sticky hand in hers, the frustration, the joy?

It was at this point that she saw a familiar figure.

'Look, Joe. Marion. Look, over there.'

She pointed Marion out. Marion was walking in the same direction but on the other side of the road. She had not seen them. Kate watched her – a large, pale girl with black hair like her father. It was a heavy profile but there was beauty there – there would be beauty soon, if Marion could see it. In her surgical-looking platforms she walked with tight, self-conscious steps. She held a large bag and she wore a cardigan carefully buttoned over the breasts that she carried like a burden, her woman's punishment. Would someone, some day, delight over them? Would some day even Marion?

She looked so stiff and inward as she walked along, her eyes on the pavement, enclosed within her own thoughts. Herself at sixteen, Kate remembered it. The day her grandmother died. She was sitting undressed in her bedroom, inspecting her stomach because she had just read that the perfect body when in a seated position showed two creases in the belly. It was painful of course about Gran, but marginally more painful was the discovery that upon her stomach she could see plain as plain not two creases but three.

Marion must be thinking about stomach creases, Kate decided, or clothes or boy-friends. Whatever it was it had her full attention – there was no child to tug at her sleeve, to distract her and lift her eyes from her ruminations upon herself. An adolescent, she seemed a different species from the playground mothers with their casual bodies, bending down, wiping noses, pulling on socks, lifting and carrying – bodies that were by their owners scarcely noticed, merely dressed and undressed, fed and attended to in the snatched moments during the day when this was possible.

Kate called: 'Marion!'

Marion swung round, alarmed.

'It's only me,' Kate said cheerfully, crossing the road to join her. 'Just out from school?'

A slow blush – Kate turned away so Marion would not see she had noticed – spread over Marion's pale face. Her spots reddened but so did her cheeks, making her pretty.

'No,' said Marion. 'I mean, yes.'

They walked to the crossroads and turned left into Brinsley Street.

'Put that great bag into the pram if you like,' suggested Kate. 'I can load up the pram till it groans.

We bulldoze our way along the pavements, scattering pedestrians.'

But Marion seemed disinclined to part with her bag, a stiff canvas affair. She clutched it and mumbled something Kate could not hear. *Am I that terrifying?* Kate wondered.

To spare Marion having to talk, Kate changed the subject. What an awkward girl she was – worse than usual. Anyway Kate felt like talking, having spoken to no adult except Frizzy Hair all day.

'I was thinking, Marion, what a different breed we are. Mothers, I mean. I still have a surprise sometimes when I wake up and realize I don't have to go to work – to that sort of work anyway. That I'm one of *them*, pushing my pram along the street.'

Marion said nothing. Kate, trying to be confiding, to relax Marion (us two girls together), said: 'I remember so well being your age and creeping upstairs at night so my parents wouldn't wake up.' She laughed. 'Now I creep upstairs so my *babies* won't wake up. Not nearly so exciting.' A pause. 'And policemen look so young now, which means I must be getting on.'

Still Marion did not reply. Kate thought: how egocentric one is made by shy people! Battling on about oneself. 'I only realized the other day,' she said, 'how I must be getting older. It was just up the road here, you know that street where half the houses are empty? Some boys were climbing through a basement window and they fled when they saw me coming. I felt quite flattered.' She paused. ' – you know, that I was old enough to be awe-inspiring. It seems only yesterday that I was doing that myself. Do you feel that?'

A pause.

Kate laughed: 'You know, that it could be *you* climbing into some empty basement, all wickedly?'

'What?' Marion looked startled.

It must be dreadful, Kate thought, to blush so much, at every single innocuous remark. Poor girl.

Nine

Again a Monday. Again Samuel up in his attic, but it was stuffier now up here under the roof, midsummer drawing near.

4th girl wanted, super mews flat, S. Ken. £18 p.w.

Are you cheerful, sociable, aged 25–30? Girl wanted, own room, Fulham Rd.

A fly settled on the newspaper. Sam swatted it.

Sixth girl for sunny garden flat . . .

Sixth girl! Six of them. Imagine - in the bathroom six pairs of tights dangling, six little notes pinned up to take their Pill. These Knightsbridge girls, he could fantasize about them for hours: these English roses with their headscarves and their Daddies, straddling their ponies no longer, straddling him, Samuel, so unsuitably Jewish – he, whose parents had fought the long battle from the Mile End Road to Golders Green. What would their Mummies think?

He should be working of course. He had only bought *The Times* for the telly. As usual he had become engrossed in it right through the overseas news, criticisms of unknown Welsh operas, the Court Circular (yes the Court Circular), and now the Personal Column. Soon there would remain just the advertisements for compost accelerators and rubber knickers for the incontinent and then he would have to work. But then it would be lunch-time.

And hadn't he known these girls, these Sophies and

146

Fionas, these wearers of Gucci shoes with those classy little chains? For him, hadn't their narrow South Ken beds creaked; hadn't they, un-Englishly, moaned? For him, so hilariously unlike the firm-jawed young merchant bankers with whom their pedigrees should lead them to couple.

Jetta had understood. He might not have told her in so many words, but it was to her lap that he returned to lay his penitent head. Encircling him she had taken him back into her, smiling at his delight. Such poignant, shuddering reunions, his passion singed and curled at the edges by his remorse. Impulsive he had been but not truly unfaithful, she would know that. They had talked about this for hours in the early years of their marriage; long discussions they had had about the inadequacies of the English language, the way that one word 'love', providing the adults involved were sensible, could in fact range over a large number of interpretations, that different kinds of love could co-exist peaceably, enhancing a marriage and returning the original partners to each other enriched. Jetta had been wholehearted about this during those midnight talks, the level in the whisky bottle falling and the ash in the ashtray rising.

Yes, but what about Kate?

Samuel removed *The Times* and looked at his typescript. No longer did he cross out with x's; latterly the pages had become scored with the passionate slashes of his blue Biro. No doubt about it, Kate was playing havoc with his plot.

For a start how could he concentrate? What with her radio and her hoovering; her voice, raised to praise her babies or shout at them, raised, on occasion, in song.

Then there was the creak of the stairs and the nearer murmurs when she was in the room adjacent to his – on his calculations this must be the babies' room. She seemed very close then. And what about the thud of her front door shattering his train of thought? Awful the struggle not to jump up, dash into Marion's bedroom and catch a glimpse of her as she walked down the street. Today he had lost the struggle and been rewarded – no, tortured – by the sight of her in a halterneck dress that revealed a whole new stretch of sweetly pinking skin.

Worse of course was the garden. These hot days she appeared there constantly, but summer had played a trick on him; while prompting Kate to shed a delightfully large number of her clothes it also covered the bushes in a blanket of foliage. Between the leaves Kate could just be glimpsed, tantalizingly. This meant that a constant watch had to be kept at the attic window. In fact, it was almost a relief when he made his way to the front room and discovered that she was going out.

It was getting out of control. Ridiculous trying to prolong that meeting at Marks and Spencer, buying all those woollen socks in the middle of bloody summer; ridiculous that enormous amount he had drunk at Elaine's party after Kate had left, that inane flirting with Chlöe who had never meant a jot, all those things he had whispered to her simply because he was upset and wanted her to be Kate; the despising of her for believing him.

Other women he had managed all right. But then none of the others had been like Kate. There had been an element of using and of being used which had made his own justification easy. Upon a part of him they had

148

not impinged; concurrent with them he had remained in love with his wife.

Sam, hot and uneasy, ran his hands through his hair; in its fuzz his fingers tangled. Why could he not get Kate out of his mind? Was it that she was the first woman who was altering him?

'*I imagine you hoovering.*'

'*Sam, do you really?*'

He was getting obsessed, no doubt about it. But why Kate? Why choose one's next door neighbour for heaven's sake, a faithful wife, anyone could see that, a woman whose nearness was lunacy because if anything went wrong there she was literally on one's doorstep? His others, now he thought of it, had always lived a good distance away, several stops on the Tube. If he nipped out for a packet of Gauloises he was highly unlikely to bump into them on the pavement.

Kate, you have crept under my skin. You have become a dear and familiar part of me; I know your hours and I feel their rhythm, their pulse is the pulse of my day, a wall away; you are sweetly spreading into my life as you are spreading into my book.

He glanced down.

'*The moon filtered through the leaves and shone on the lawn*' – no, '*touched the lawn with silver.*' That sounded better. '*Behind Arabella rose the spotlit pillars of the Embassy, with its lit windows whence issued the merry tinkling of glasses and the murmur of civilized voices.*' Clichés there? Re-read tomorrow. '*Arabella leant languorously against the balustrade, her young, tall, slender body draped in silk, glimmering white as a swan in the moon.*' Good, he had thought that. Was it? ' "*Come here*"

149

she murmured. Baxter hesitated. Could she be trusted? Had Norton told her about the documents in the pocket of his tuxedo?' Do tuxedos have pockets? Check this. '*Ah but she was bewitching! Her hair, a glossy chestnut bell, her lips, full and inviting, her breasts, small, high, their nipples straining against the silk . . .*'

Samuel stopped there. He sat hunched over his manuscript; he read it again. Any better? No, worse. Why had it lately become so unconvincing?

Kate had done this. Unwittingly of course, but she had done it. His book had seemed perfectly all right – in fact, extraordinarily good. Then along had come Kate; all at once he had felt impelled to pull open the curtains and let in the fresh air. Why? Her honesty; the knowledge that she existed next door, so candid. And what had he seen? Flimsy painted furniture, shoddy artifice, worn patches on the carpet, the cynicism showing through, clichés. Take Arabella for a start. He had considered her lovely, all his South Ken girls rolled into a delectable whole. With relish he had created her and now she seemed nothing – false and second-hand, her chestnut hair a wig. Kate, you living, breathing Kate with your imperfect, charming face . . . He looked down at Arabella. She was lifeless as a dummy.

Samuel paused. He picked up his Biro and started crossing out.

Again the flickering candles; again the canvas bag. Outside in the warm summer night the Town Hall clock struck eleven: one, two, three . . .

Before it had finished Marion was unwrapping the newspaper; as eleven struck she took out the cut glass

150

bottle in which, miraculously, James was distilled. It was his aftershave, a scent redolent of those trembling moments in his hall and their sudden closeness as he passed her the pound note.

She must be mad. Obsessed. Wasn't this proof?

'Off again?' Dad had remarked, eyebrows raised, when she had crept downstairs.

'Oh, just out.' Her voice calm. She had not expected him to walk out of the sitting-room like that.

'Lock up, sweetie pie, when you get in.'

Half past ten and he had not even asked where she was going! Nor why she was taking a bag. She might be running away for all he knew. Nor had he shown any interest in the fact that lately she was so often out at night. A relief, of course, but a hurtful one. She used to think it was absentmindedness but lately it had got worse, he always had his mind on something else when she was talking to him. Gradually she was realizing that he simply did not care. She was losing any illusions she had pathetically held about Dad.

Her mother was as bad, sitting at her desk, poring over files from the clinic. 'Crisis time for Karen Phipps,' she had said. 'You know, Sam, that girl with the problem father. Mother's just gone into hospital.' She wrote something in the file and closed it with a snap. 'I'm seeing her three times a week now. You see, she needs it.'

And what about me? Marion had thought, staring harder at her homework. What about Alf dying (she had not told them the news but surely they could sense it)? What about Ron? What about crisis time for me, your daughter? Do I have to come along to your precious clinic before you'll manage to understand?

151

By contrast, her love for James seemed so simple and pure. Marion lowered the bottle from her nose and replaced the stopper. She put it on the mantelpiece next to the photo; she bent down and took out the three leather-backed clothes brushes.

It was funny really. That first time it had been an impulse. Afterwards, though guilty she was also proud of it, like she felt after that thing with Ron. It was so dramatic, so unlike her – dogged, law-abiding old Marion, so dependable they were giving her a little green badge at school to prove it. She seemed so interesting – just the psychological stuff her mother would have loved if she had known. This time, purloining the brushes and the aftershave was more like a dare she had set herself, an adventure – noting that both houses were empty, that the Coopers' back door was ajar (not so surprising, these hot days), selecting the two things and taking them back to her own house until dark. It proved to herself that she could do it.

Of course she wanted these four bits of James; it was lovely touching them – curiously, it made James himself seem less important. But she would take them back soon; certainly she would take no more. She did not like the thought of James – even of Mrs Cooper – being alarmed. No, it was just that doing it a second time stopped the first time from seeming so creepy.

For the same reason she had stopped praying and talking to James out loud. Even alone, this had made her too self-conscious; the sounds made her nervous for herself. She crossed the room and sat down on her cushion – last week she had brought it along, also some books and a couple of posters. The place looked more homely now.

152

She gazed at the photo and the dangling shirt. At school they were doing the Crusaders in history. She had derived a twitch of comfort from the list in her textbook of the mementoes hidden in the knightly armour; it gave her bizarre little collection a precedent. Not that she needed it, she reassured herself. After all, most of her friends had sentimental locks of hair secreted about their persons, to be smugly produced during a cloakroom huddle. Alison even had her boy-friend's football socks, which she refused to wash. Everyone carried photos in their wallets; nobody thought that strange. They would pull it out and say: 'This is Donald.'

She took out the little cardboard box. In this tranced and stealthy room, its walls dancing with shadows, the label reassured: *Lyons Blackcurrant Pie*. Midnight feasts, giggles – she was quite normal really, wasn't she? She had quite a stock of food here, of course, but the amazing thing was that she had not yet worked her way through it. At home nothing lasted more than a night, but now she had this secret room she was finding (she did not dare put this into words, it just lay, a glimmer at the back of her brain), she was finding that she actually was not eating quite so much. She did not feel the need.

Still, a pie was a pie. Munching, she remembered yesterday's incident; she had forgotten it until now. It was six-thirty and she had been sitting at her window waiting for a glimpse of James coming home from work – would he be wearing his beautiful light-weight suit today? It was then that she had noticed the cigarette. It was stubbed out in the saucer underneath her rubber plant. A French cigarette, so it must be Dad's. Do you know, she had felt absurdly flattered? Silly, but when she was younger he had often come into her room and chatted. He used to browse through her books and notice that she had rearranged her china horses, that sort of thing. She had not shown she was pleased but she had been, for what is the point of rearranging your china horses if there is no one to notice? He would sit on the window ledge with her and make rude remarks about the passers-by; they had laughed together. But since she had got older both he and her mother had stopped coming in casually; they had respected, elaborately, her privacy. Or perhaps she had put them off.

When she saw him coming out of his study across the landing she had pointed to the stub and called: 'Been snooping on the neighbours then?' in a cheerful sort of way, and you should have seen his face! She had never seen Dad look uncomfortable like that.

She could not understand it. Had he found something? But there was nothing to find; she had stopped smuggling food into her room now she could take it to Alf's – in fact, she had almost stopped smuggling food at all.

Then James's front door slammed. She had missed him, just at that moment when her stupid head was turned.

She could have strangled Dad.

Ten

'Bics! Bics!'

'That's right, Joe. Lovely biscuits.'

Behind the barrage of Daz and Persil Jetta recognized the voice of Kate Cooper.

'No, Joe. *No*. Well, all right then. All right then. All right, Mummy put them back and *Joe* put them in the basket.' A silence. 'No, Joe, in the *basket*. Joe! Give them here.'

Jetta had to smile. Poor woman. She need not hear the words; she could tell by the timbre of the voice, its brightness hushed into irritation, exactly what was happening. Countless times she had heard it over the garden fence, through the walls, today in Sainsbury's.

'Darling, in the *basket*. Look, lovely basket. You can have one later. *Joe!*'

In Sainsbury's they might be but a yard or two apart but what worlds separated them. Kate emerged, pushing her laden trolley towards the cheese section. She had not seen Jetta, so embroiled was she with her son. One had to admit that she looked a mess – half her hair down and wearing some garment with a halter neck that showed where she had failed to tan. The little boy was half out of his trolley seat, leaning forward and trying to grab one of the packages from amongst the shopping.

'*Bic.*' His voice, loud and firm; one could hear it over the noise of all the other shoppers. Kate, glancing

155

round furtively, gave him a quick slap. A slap. Jetta saw it.

Fancy that. Jetta with a sigh reached for some Fairy Liquid. An ostensibly easy-going woman like Katherine too. However trying Marion had been at that age – and God knows had any child been so annoying? That clumsiness, those adenoidal sniffs, that slow, maddening stare – never had Jetta allowed herself to lose control. She had remained calm, and explained, gently. One wouldn't slap an adult, would one?

Jetta gave a swift glance at her shopping list; she set off towards the cat food. Into the trolley went the tins, four, five, six. She swept up a packet of coffee, a packet of tea, some packets of Corn Flakes and Sugar Puffs (one of life's smaller mysteries was where five packets went each week). Briskly she tapped across to the meat counter; into the trolley she threw a chicken, a leg of lamb, half a dozen pork chops. 'Jetta, you're amazing,' Sam would say. 'My bionic woman.' These weekly blitzes never took longer than twenty minutes. Sam would take two hours and come home with half the stuff forgotten. So she dealt with it herself despite her full-time job. 'Upon you,' he said, 'I rely.'

Kate, she could see, was still dithering over the cheese. The occupant of her trolley now looked calm; he had lifted up his shirt and was pointing out his stomach to her. Kate leant over and gave him a kiss. How impulsive! With a mother like that any child would be confused. She watched Kate turn back to the cheeses. Irish Cheddar, or Mild English at five pence more expensive? Her day must be so narrow, her preoccupations so petty. Jetta, standing now at the checkout, felt a wave of pity for the woman.

156

She watched Kate push her trolley to a checkout further down and struggle with Joe over the rack, adjacent to the till, of craftily-placed sweets. Kate, flushed, swept the hair back from her face. Jetta had to admit, actually, that there might be some men who could find her attractive, the sort of men who liked their women helpless – probably men who in themselves were rather inadequate. Kate wore unremarkable clothes and looked as if she had never quite had time to finish dressing; Jetta herself, being tall and striking, could carry off her own bolder and more bohemian designs with verve.

She watched Kate reaching over her trolley. Men who preferred large breasts, Jetta suspected, were a dying breed. She herself had never met any. Over her own firm, small breasts Sam delighted. He would nuzzle them. 'My athlete,' he would say. 'My lithe one.'

Swiftly Jetta packed her shopping into a large cardboard box; swiftly she carried it out to her waiting car. The old man in overalls as usual tried to help her; as usual she waved him aside, smilingly. 'I can manage, thank you.' She looked at her watch: 9.30. Her first patient, Mrs Good, was due at ten. She felt strong and capable running the house, running the clinic, synchronizing her times and fitting it all in. That she was supporting the household pleased her; also, more obscurely, it pleased her that Sam could not drive. *Upon you I rely*. Mrs Good relied on her, and Karen Phipps, and the four other patients who this morning would be preparing themselves to walk through her door – herself, the centre of a radiating web of need. She revved up the engine and let out the clutch.

The sun swept across the buildings as she turned to the left. This morning she felt particularly strong and confident, to tell the truth, being bolstered up by Samuel's book.

She had not meant to look at it. She respected his privacy and his need to finish it before he asked her opinion. It was just that at that dinner party last night, when Chlóe Sims had asked him how it was going, he had said that he was stuck. Rather abruptly he had said it, surprising them all. Jetta's first thought had been: Funny how one learns things at dinner parties. Her second thought had been: I see – it's a cry for help. Ashamed to ask her directly he had communicated his need in the presence of a crowd. She had understood; they knew each other so well.

When he had nipped out this morning she went up to his room and gave it a glance. The page on the typewriter was much crossed out. It was the description of some woman. '*Her hair, a glossy chestnut bell,*' Sam had written. This was slashed through with Biro. Above it he had written: '*Her pale hair, fastened to the top of her head, escaped in charming wisps that caressed her sweet, wide face.*'

One hand held the steering wheel; with the other Jetta touched her hair – yes, her chestnut bell. Today she wore it down. It surprised her, how moved she felt. It was rather marvellous, after eighteen years of marriage, that Sam should describe his heroine in those particular words. That his ideal heroine, his central woman, should still be his wife.

Jetta changed into third gear and drove up the hill. Right and proper of course to cross it out. She knew as well as Sam did that art meant a certain detachment; one had to distance oneself in order to create. Anyway, though she could hardly imagine Sam being embarrassed by something like that, he might think it would embarrass

158

her to find her body so lovingly intact upon the pages. Of course she was not embarrassed – she was flattered, deeply. And with what emotion had he crossed it out! The Biro lines through the chestnut bell – and through the '*small firm breasts*' that he had changed to '*full and inviting*' – well, they were not so much lines as slashes.

All this was doubly welcome because, now that she was reassured, Jetta could admit to a small corner of herself that recently, just recently, Sam had been – well, just slightly less demonstrative. She was sensitive to this, she had noticed it. Sam was a passionate lover; that he had lately been a shade less ardent presented itself to her, now she had glanced at his novel, as intensely moving.

Jetta's smile lingered as she drove through the gates and parked her car into its allotted space. *J. A. Green* said the sign; her compact Renault fitted exactly. She got out and straightened up, her chestnut bell swinging round her face. Up the path she walked, past the main entrance to the hospital, towards the modern extension where the clinic was housed. Markham Centre, it was called discreetly, so that no one should be ashamed of entering its doors. She walked past the dental surgery – she heard a high whine – past the crêche – a chorus of yells. The crêche had been one of Jetta's innovations, due mainly to the difficulty she had experienced with child-minders when Marion was small – they had been so unreliable, she had nearly lost her job the amount of days she had had to miss work. Consequently she felt a keen and practical sympathy with working mothers.

She pushed open the swing doors. The Markham Centre was bright with pot plants, cushions and Van Gogh prints on the walls; after ten years' work here, she headed the team. Annie the receptionist called: 'You look cheerful. Gorgeous day, isn't it!' Jim Morris approached with a file: 'Ah, there you are. About Mrs Dean . . .' 'Jetta!' called Barbara, 'could you spare a moment?'

Jetta felt herself swept up into the world she loved and that demanded so much. She dealt with Jim, she dealt with Barbara and now she was settled in her room, her first patient, Mrs Good, seated opposite: a slight, bowed woman, fiddling with her handbag.

'I don't like to waste your time . . .' Mrs Good always began like this. With an unfaithful husband and two suicide attempts behind her, Mrs Good possessed a highly-developed sense of inferiority and guilt; possibly a referral case for Jetta's special Wednesday group sessions.

'. . . it's when I found these letters, you see,' she went on, 'all coming from *her*. Found them in the place he keeps his fishing gear. Never look there usually.' She looked down at her anxious hands. 'Six or seven of them, tucked away inside his wellington boots; you know, nice and safe.'

Answering her Jetta thought: how alien to Sam and myself is deceit! At will I can roam through *our* house.

'. . . so I said that, and now he treats me like dirt. Honest, I wouldn't tell this to anyone else, but you know how I told you he flaunts her? Well, it's getting worse. He says she makes him feel like a man again, really he does, he lays it on, he says – ' she cast down her eyes and fiddled with the shiny clasp of her handbag – 'I don't know how to put this, but he says how good she is – you know – at what he calls her performance. Compared with me, that is.' Her eyes darted to Jetta's. 'It's disgusting.'

160

'And how do you respond, Mrs Good? You say it's disgusting; why do you choose that particular word?' Jetta leant forward, alert, professional; as she moved a cushion of warmth shifted itself comfortably inside her – the warmth of Sam's faithfulness, that central heat from which she could look out on the world and, secure in herself, reach out to the Mrs Goods and the Karen Phippses. And he, Sam, such an emotional, highly-charged man too. Always women found him attractive.

At her core Jetta smiled while her outer self nodded seriously, listened, ushered out Mrs Good, wrote down some notes, ushered in Karen Phipps – Karen Phipps, pinched and pale, three months' pregnant, her mother in hospital and her father periodically in prison. Today Jetta was concentrating on the mother relationship; Karen, she had judged, though still hostile, was ready for this.

'Try and explain, Karen, just what you mean by "cramped". Take your time.'

'Well, she just cramps me, like, hems me in. Least, before she went away she did.' Mrs Good had fiddled with her handbag; Karen fiddled with a frayed hole in her jeans. Three months' pregnant, she would soon be bursting out of them. 'Got real heavy, you know, all the questions – where I'd been, who I'd been with, all that.'

'What did you tell her, Karen?'

'Didn't tell her nothing, did I? What did she expect, fucking step by step account? Unexpurgated? Me Dad hit me once when I wouldn't say.'

'And what did you do, Karen?'

Jetta thought: when will these parents learn? From their children, always the same cry: they crowd me, they interfere. Frankly Marion should consider herself fortunate

161

– fortunate that this last week or so, when she had been starting to stay out every night, she had a mother who understood and who did not pump her with questions. On the contrary, who was pleased for her. It was so unlike Marion, this series of unexplained absences, this creeping back at midnight – unlike Marion but absolutely in order for a first sexual experience. To tell the truth Jetta was rather relieved; Marion had appeared to have so little confidence in this respect. No doubt it was Ronald; Jetta had lightly mentioned him once and been rewarded with a blush. She had told Marion, obliquely of course, how Marion must not feel in the slightest way ashamed or worried, she need not tell them anything if she did not feel the need to, but that if she had any queries – birth control, anything like that – then she must not hesitate. After all, they had had thorough discussions throughout her adolescence, Jetta had made a point of this, they had covered most topics – masturbation and so on. Marion had looked, she thought, relieved at this. She had said nothing, but Jetta could tell by her ducking head that she had been grateful to have parents who simply acknowledged their daughter's sexuality. Who did not find it a threat.

Small surprise that Jetta had been asked to Stockholm. When Karen had gone Jetta picked up the collected papers from last year's conference; this year her own name would join the ranks of distinguished specialists. 'Youth, Sex and Society' was the topic. It was rather an honour to be asked, as Stockholm was recognized as the most relevant of the international get-togethers, and this year's theme more urgently relevant than most. But then she herself was bound to think this, wasn't she? It was her speciality.

162

Going downstairs for coffee Jetta glanced at the date: 14th June. In ten days' time she would be standing up in front of them, row upon row of balding, thoughtful heads. Into the microphone she would be speaking, her voice booming round the hall. Yes, quite an honour. As she walked round the corner she was smiling.

'James. James Cooper.' Jetta stopped in her tracks. 'Fancy seeing you here,' she said.

James, too, stopped in his tracks.

Jetta pointed to the sign above his head: Dental Clinic. She raised her eyebrows in enquiry.

He nodded, smiling lopsidedly. He mumbled: 'Mouth numb.'

They had given him a whopping injection, that was why.

'Some tooth!' the dentist had said. 'Riddled with holes. Riddled with 'em. What's the name of that cheese?'

Emmenthal, James would have told him if his mouth were not full of instruments. Why did dentists do this?

'That holey stuff. Aw, never mind.' The dentist was an Australian; with his twangy voice he called James Mr Coper. He had straightened up. 'Well Mr Coper, that's one helluva tooth you've got there. Fix up a date with nurse here for an extraction, could you?'

So here James lay, a strong man brought low. The dentist's chair was one of the alarming kind that flung a person on his back, facing the ceiling. Rather than just one's head, it made one's whole body an offering. James found this disturbing.

'By the way, Mr Coper, no one ever told you about your plaque?'

James, mouth propped open, shook his head. The

163

dentist, too, shook his head, regret mixed, in a way peculiar to dentists, with jauntiness. 'Well, after your extraction you just ask nurse to fix you up with the oral hygienist, okay?'

Humbly, James nodded. What else could he do? Inside he felt annoyed at this bossing about, this reference to his plaque, the looming ascendancy of this puny man who in his office would be the merest filing clerk. Who was this oral hygienist anyway? Creeping Americanisms. Mr Johnson had never had an oral hygienist. Sentimentally James remembered the pleasant, old-fashioned surgery with its yellowing copies of *Country Life*. That was when Kate and he had lived in the flat in Holland Park. Here it was copies of *Newsweek* and a surgery like a spaceship; this man wore one of those side-buttoning jackets which James upon instinct distrusted.

'Nasty stuff, plaque.' The dentist shook his head again. 'Wouldn't like it if I showed you the mirror, Mr Coper. At your age, you know, it can get a grip on the old gums.'

Stung, James stared at the ceiling. How preferable was Mr Johnson to this dwarfish and over-familiar Ozzie. Mr Johnson never mentioned plaque; nor did he refer to James's age. The man returned with a needle. James kept his eyes averted.

'Now just a little prick.'

James clenched his hands. Ridiculous to clench them. He concentrated on the man's chin, inadequately shaven.

'Right. Now let's just wait a minute shall we? For it to work.'

James, horizontal, nodded. His throat was too dry to speak. The dentist moved out of sight. Unnerving little clatters; with the nurse he must be assembling the instruments. James had not had an extraction since he was a boy; under his armpits he felt the dampness spreading. To distract himself he stared at the white ceiling. Chatty, callously unconcerned, their voices reached him.

'Warm enough for you, Janice?'

'Lovely isn't it, Mr Musgrove.'

'You're getting a nice little tan on you.'

'I sunbathed all weekend.'

'Lucky neighbours, eh?'

James's gums prickled, the numbness spreading.

'I'll guess,' the dentist said. 'Your bikini's yellow. Right?'

'Turquoise.'

'Mmm. My fave shade.'

Approaching footsteps. James stiffened. The dentist put something into James's mouth.

'Feel this, Mr Coper?'

James asked: 'Feel what?'

'You're numb then. Right, let's tackle this big fella, shall we?'

The nurse loomed into view. Things began to be done inside James's mouth. Leaning close, a sweet cachou on his breath, the dentist said: 'Go topless do they, in Wembley?'

The nurse giggled. 'Honestly, Mr Musgrove!' She passed him something sharp and shiny. 'What do you take me for?'

'I'll take you any day, sweetie.'

James, irritated, lay stiff, this gay banter passing back and forth over his offered mouth. A tug: cracklings, creakings – surprisingly distinct, a noise of tearing. Oak, tugged by its roots. His head jerked forward; painlessly the roots snapped. Could this be happening inside his

165

mouth? He stared at the unprepossessing chin, at the nostrils choked with hair.

The dentist lifted something out. 'Janice, take a look at this.'

'Ooh,' she said.

They whisked it away. James lay there; he felt left out. *His* tooth, wasn't it?

'Okay Mr Coper, rinse out now.'

Up came his chair; their faces swung close. James felt included; he bent to sip. Janice, who was indeed tanned, became for a moment his. Ministering to him, she wiped his chin; she wiped at the long red strings of saliva that kept sliding down from his mouth.

'Hold the cotton wool there,' she murmured, pressing it against his lips. Then she deserted him, joining the dentist somewhere over the other side of the room. Already they were getting the files ready for the next patient. The dentist asked for some coffee: 'And two sugars, sweetie. Remember this time, eh?'

James kept the cotton wool against his mouth. It was getting wet and no doubt crimson. Janice went out and the dentist returned. He leant over James, smiling.

'Feeling all right, old cobber?'

Suddenly James was overwhelmed with fondness for the man. He had liked that irritability over the coffee; they were two males together.

'All over now,' the dentist said.

James felt sweaty with relief. With thankfulness too. Now he had finished, the way the dentist removed the cotton wool and gazed into his mouth seemed suddenly tender. Goodness, he could really like the fellow.

It was over. James closed the surgery door behind

166

him. With elastic steps he strode down the corridor, braced, alert, every pore in his body breathing thanks. This corridor, along which he had slunk but half an hour ago, appeared on his return journey illogically pleasing: the white walls sparkled, the posters showing apples and toothbrushes looked shiny and appropriate, even the idea of an oral hygienist seemed a concept at which one could be amused.

So it was in an uncharacteristic state of mind, chatty with relief, that he bumped into Jetta.

'Mouth numb,' he said, and then: 'Do you know, I'm a dreadful coward about these things. Never dared tell Kate, but I am.'

'Stiff upper lip. You must come from a public school.'

'How can you tell?'

'It's written all over you, James.'

She told him that this was her coffee break. Still chatty, he asked if he could join her.

'Should you drink coffee?' she asked. 'With your mouth in the state it's in, James?'

'Do me a power of good.' He paused. 'But can you spare the time?' She had shiny neat hair; under her arm she carried papers. A working woman – he was impressed.

'Just for twenty minutes. I know a nice café.' She left her papers at the reception desk; she glanced at the clock. Here was a woman who would not ink in her tights.

He opened the door for her and they went through the gates and down the road to the High Street. It had a busy weekday air, rarely glimpsed by him. Delivery vans were unloading, cars sounding their horns, people passing in and out of Marks and Spencer. Everyone either pushed a pram or seemed terribly old. Eleven o'clock and he should not be feeling this forbidden Friday sun warming his face.

'One feels a truant,' he confessed. 'Should be at work.'

He had not felt like this for years, not since school – the wary tightness of the skin, the alertness one felt in a street, however ordinary, once it was out of bounds. Altogether rather pleasant.

'I used to sneak out of school and take the bus into Exeter,' he told her. 'Wander round the streets.'

'What did you do, James?'

'Oh, one browsed through records, got the man in the shop to play them until he realized one was never going to buy any, eyed the grammar school girls. Didn't dare speak to them of course; just yearned for them over the Lonnie Donegan LPs.' He laughed ruefully. 'Actually I could never think of much to do really. After a bit I'd take the bus back to school again.'

'James, that's so touching.' She showed him into a café. In the window were counters of buns and cakes. They went through to the back where there were tables.

'To tell the truth I felt rather guilty,' he said. 'I was an only child, you see. My parents were quite old; it meant a lot to them, getting me into public school. There was never much money around.' Coffee arrived; he stirred in the cream. 'I was never that brilliant. I had to work hard – for them, really.' Why was he so chatty? Must be his tooth; in his mouth the numbness was lifting, he felt the throbbing beginnings of pain. He resisted the temptation to explore with his tongue. If he kept talking he could almost forget it.

'They bought me books they could ill afford,' he went

168

on. 'Dictionaries, atlases. My father made a bookcase out of an old dressing-table and put it in my room; one term when I got home there it was.'

Jetta sipped her coffee. 'I see.' She really did; he could tell.

'So very kind, they were. They believed me capable of anything; the sky was the limit. One felt so damned responsible not to disappoint.' Why didn't his conversations with Kate resemble this one? Household things blocked the way: children, arrangements.

James's tongue poked the hole; he winced. It was shockingly deep – deeper than he had expected.

'Would you say you were ambitious, James?'

James thought for a moment. 'Lately, more so. Since Kate had the children. Responsibilities, you know.' He steeled himself to take a sip of coffee. It stung. 'Yes, I suppose one's been working a good deal harder since then.'

'I saw Kate in the supermarket today,' said Jetta. She paused. 'Do you think she suffers, you working so hard? Being so busy?'

'But it's for her I do it. Do you know, I remember the exact moment – how strange. We were going to what was the Old Vic; she was very pregnant with Joe and I could only afford gallery seats – you know, the cheapest ones.' He took another cautious sip of coffee. 'Anyway, watching her huffing and puffing up the stairs . . . well, one felt so inadequate. I decided to change my job, even though it meant more travelling abroad and longer hours. Next time, I told myself, we would afford the stalls.'

'Did you tell *her* all this?'

'It must be obvious. She can see.'

169

'You should tell her, James. Discuss it. I believe one should discuss everything.'

By now his whole jaw was throbbing. Dare he probe again? It held a morbid magnetism, the great crater. He said: 'And what's happened is that now we can afford the stalls but we somehow never get to go. Ironic, isn't it.' His tongue poked it; he flinched. 'What with the children and my travelling abroad so much of the time.' He stopped. 'This is ridiculously egocentric. *You* talk. Tell me about yourself.'

'No, it's fascinating. Go on.'

'You are such a very good listener.' It was true; he seldom talked like this. The ease of it. She looked so sympathetic, leaning forward like that, yet something distant about her too – a sheen of professionalism over her like cellophane. He was thankful for this.

'Yes,' he said, 'one sometimes does wonder about, well, priorities.' He took a breath; he said: 'Do you know, sometimes, when Kate and the children are playing and I come in – do you know, I see them stiffen. Distinctly.'

His jaw throbbed.

'She gets so fussed and flustered nowadays,' he said. 'Anxious about little things, thinking I mind much more than I do. Somehow she seems to be shielding me from my own family. She says to Joe: *don't bother Daddy*.' He gazed up at Jetta. 'But really, you know, I want to be bothered.'

His hole was sore; his whole mouth felt swollen. What a confession, and in this most ordinary of places, so loud and clattering, so unconfessional. 'Two custard slices!' called a waitress, 'two iced buns and four cups of tea!'

At exactly the same moment, Jetta and James looked at their watches.

'Look what you've done,' said James.

'Good grief,' said Jetta. 'James, you shouldn't have been so interesting.' She looked at him. 'Just one thing, James. Tell her. Tell her your feelings. Talk to each other.'

Outside on the pavement they hesitated. James frowned, remembering. In this disjointed day something had been overlooked. 'It's Joe's birthday.' Helpless, his tooth paining, he asked: 'What on earth shall I buy?'

Next to the café was a stationer's. Their eyes rested on its small offerings of toys, placed between a display of pens and special offer typewriters.

'Why don't you get him that post-box?' suggested Jetta. 'Perfect for a two-year-old. You post those different plastic shapes in. Teaches them to select and differentiate.'

She sounded authoritative. 'I shall get it,' he said.

Jetta added: 'And don't for heaven's sake tell your wife I chose it. Say you thought of it yourself.'

'Why?'

'James!' She looked at him and smiled; the cellophane fell from her.

He smiled too. 'I see what you mean.'

She bid farewell. James said: 'Thank you for helping with the post-box,' too inhibited to say thank you for everything else. Had he been disloyal to Kate and said too much? He watched Jetta make her way through the shoppers; in her black and white striped dress she made them look listless.

He watched her until she had disappeared into the crowd. A fine-looking woman, nice and tall too. To be honest, though, she was not really his type. Curiously

171

cool, she was, and sexless. But such a clear brain; he had to admire her. She must be a marvellous mother for Marion.

James bought the post-box and set off for the Underground. He tried to bundle the parcel into his briefcase but, the briefcase being a slim business model, it would not fit.

_____ *Eleven* _____

Despite the cool gaze and the striped dress, Jetta was wrong more often than James had imagined. She was certainly wrong about Kate and the cheese. Far from tossing up between the Irish Cheddar at 69p and the Mild English at 74p, Kate was not even focusing on the massed yellow blocks. Her eyes were seeing James – James, and their marriage and the aftershave.

Things were not going well. This had been creeping up on her; when she was away from the house, in a bright impersonal place like this, she could see it all too clearly. Sinkingly so. Ups and downs: of course all marriages had them, but once in a down who can remember, or hope again for an up? Not her, anyway. Why had they degenerated into this loveless irritability?

This morning James had been particularly edgy. First there had been the fuss about the shirt. James, searching in the cupboard, had turned round.

'Kate, where the dickens is it – you know, the one with the thin blue line in it? I haven't seen it for weeks.'

'I don't know. Is it missing?'

'You should know. You ironed it.'

A sudden sadness. In the early days had it been so briskly taken for granted that she ironed? 'Kate you *are* sweet,' James had said when, the young wife, she had bundled his shirts under her arm. Both of them had found this piquant. 'Don't bother with much,' he had smiled, the indulgent

173

husband. 'Just whizz over the collar and cuffs. Honestly, nothing more.' Since when, she wondered, had it become so much more? The wordless mounds deposited in her laundry box, the assumption that by now she would be doing far more than whizzing gaily over collar and cuffs, that she would be pressing, sharply, a crease down the centre of each sleeve otherwise when he was dressing he would look – well not annoyed, James was not as bad as that – just faintly surprised. When, wondered Kate, did the one reaction slide into the other? Why has neither of us noticed?

This depressing thought was replaced ten minutes later that morning by a more urgent, indeed sinister one. James in the bathroom: 'You haven't seen my aftershave, have you?'

Kate, struggling with Ollie's nappy, froze. A casual voice: 'Oh, Joe must have taken it off somewhere.' He had not. She had searched the house from top to bottom.

'Darling.' A weary look and the day just starting too. 'Darling, you know how I feel about it.' Whenever he bought aftershave he would decant it into the special bottle. 'Couldn't you possibly keep a slightly better eye on things? It belonged to my grandmother; really rather valuable.'

Kate, busying herself with Ollie's kicking legs, had breathed a sigh that at least he had not noticed the absence of his photo in its priceless art deco frame – solid silver. Nor had he noticed that instead of his row of clothes brushes in the hall there remained but a row of hooks. Was she becoming soft and confused, the addled housewife, or had they really been stolen?

Kate woke to Sainsbury's. She looked around. No

longer did the other shoppers look bland and harmless – any of them might be guilty. Which one had been stealing through her house, causing its stairs to creak? Which one had snooped shadowy in her bedroom, lifting lids? The old man perhaps, but he hardly looked capable of such a careful, though puzzling selection. Perhaps he had passed the key on to someone else or had it copied. Had ten copies made. The mere fact that her key was in other hands than her own made Kate feel draughty with unease; it transformed the most harmless of strangers into a suspect. What was the good of James doggedly reinforcing the back of the house when they were creeping in through the front?

Before she had come out today she had made sure, of course, that the back door was locked and the windows shut. Henceforth she would make a habit of this. But what about the front: shouldn't she change the lock? At breakfast she had decided that the time had come to confess to James. Quite apart from the keys, her over-familiarity with the old men who cleaned her windows was a touchy topic; she had started in a roundabout way to tell him about seeing the legs at her railings. But across the teapot she had seen James's glazed radio face. When could she find the right moment? Always at breakfast there was the BBC News and the rustling *Times*. Between them how could she compete? He had looked attentive, but she could tell he was trying to catch the details of some damned work-to-rule at Heathrow. Irritated, she had thought: what's more important, work-to-rules or us? He lifts his *Times* like a barrier.

She had turned, over-chirpily, to Joe. 'Tomato sauce, darling?' She shook the bottle.

'Whoops.' With a glug it flooded Joe's bowl, it engulfed his chopped-up segments of sausage.

'Kate!' James looked up. He disapproved of tomato ketchup, its plebeian ruining of good food.

How over-controlled, therefore tense, James was this morning. If it were anyone else she would have put it down to the impending dentist, but James always said that he did not mind things like that: even an extraction.

To divert James from the blood-red bowlful Kate said: 'Oh by the way, about Joe's birthday . . .'

James shifted in his seat. Poor James; he must be working out exactly when, in his crowded day, he could fit in a visit to a toyshop. And once he got there, what on earth one was expected to buy a two-year-old. Kate refused to feel guilty that she had not offered to buy Joe's present for him. James was his father.

'Yes, yes,' said James. 'I'll be back nice and early.' He paused. 'What would you suggest? You know, something that won't get, well, spoiled or broken.'

Oh dear, another touchy topic. 'He doesn't spoil everything.'

Kate watched Joe spooning ketchup into his milk mug and stirring it. The milk turned pink. These touchy topics: week by week more added themselves to the list. Topics around which one must steer, topics prickly with irritation – don't touch or they will sting. The tortoise eating the plants, the state of the kitchen, Kate's carelessness in stopping Joe from ruining his toys, the rubbish bags . . .

With Joe's spoon Kate dredged up a piece of egg. She lifted the spoon to his face; at the last moment he turned and she fed his ear.

No, she must postpone this conversation about keys

until a more suitable time when it could be approached by the correct, tactful route via whisky and small talk subtly orchestrated up to the words: 'By the way, darling, you know you were wondering about your aftershave . . .?' Breakfast was not one of those moments – but then lately what was?

All this was passing through Kate's mind as she ambled home from Sainsbury's. This was the heatwave summer of 1976; every day dawned with a bright blue sky. Ollie lay in his pram, piglet-pink in his sun bonnet; Joe as a birthday treat was working his way through the packet of Garibaldis which in the supermarket he had so loudly demanded.

Joe leant forward, generously he offered her a sucked one, its edges limp. Knowing the fuss he would make if she refused, Kate took a bite. She pictured James's shocked face. A man inclined to be prim when unhappy, James's pained presence at Joe's mealtimes imposed a strain upon Kate, causing her to become by turns anxious and defiantly over-hearty with her son. What, she wondered, would he say to the greedy lunches she shared with Joe when James, the patriarch, was absent – the abandon with which the two of them ate, Joe rummaging about in his bowl, Kate hunched over some progressively stickier women's magazine? What oh Lord would he say to their food exchanges – Joe kindly passing her a piece of his liver to which she was partial and he was not, she fishing out from her yogurt a reciprocal redcurrant? Their swopping sessions, tender and smeary.

Smiling at this, Kate pushed the pram along the pavement. She turned to Joe. 'Well, birthday boy, what would you like to do today?'

177

She expected no answer of course. Kate talked to her children for the same reason that people talk to their pets, to keep herself company. Hours would go by, days when James was away, without her hearing another grown-up voice.

'Big kiss,' said Joe. At least that was what she thought he said.

'Darling!' Ridiculously flattered, she swooped forward to embrace him. He pushed her aside.

'Biscuit,' he said, reaching for her uneaten half of Garibaldi. She was always hearing him wrong. Rebuffed, Kate gave it to him; he put it into his mouth.

Kate felt more solitary than ever; the sun failed to warm her melancholy. As they passed over the canal bridge she glanced down – how nice it would be to see Sam sitting there on the bench. The seat of course was empty. Silly to long to talk to him when he only lived next door anyway, but she could not just knock on his door and say: Talk to me. Make me laugh. Don't even bother to make me laugh, just *be* there. I'm bored and I'm lonely.

And he was not in his garden either so she could not talk to him there. This fact she ascertained through the back window as soon as she got in. Her shopping bags, as she lifted them from the pram, were heavy.

Joe made his way across the sitting-room. Whining, he fumbled with the television knobs.

'Joe, not today. Not in the morning – not when it's lovely and sunny.'

Joe got into position. The sun outside made the sitting-room appear stuffy and degenerate. Kate looked at him sitting expectantly in front of the dead TV; she did not know whether to laugh or cry. Limp, she had not the strength to argue; she switched it on. What did he want – Open University programme on Vector Analysis, something in Hindi or the Colour Card?

Vector Analysis, she decided. She left the small, tranced figure and took the shopping downstairs. As she dumped it on the draining board she remembered the sturdy row of theories she had set up before she had actually produced any children; upon the arrival of Joe and Ollie how flimsily they had fallen, one by one. Fathers, so seldom seeing their offspring, could keep their cherished ideals intact, they could despise the mother for cajoling with sweets and for switching on the television because she was too hot to argue, because Ollie was crying and because otherwise Joe would insist on unloading the shopping and would see the chocolate mousse she had sneaked into the bag for his birthday tea and would whine for it until she either lost her temper or shamefully gave in. Oh the shaky edifice of bribes and substitutions – fathers had not the first idea of it.

Kate unwrapped a herring; it stared up at her with its glazed eye. From the sitting-room she heard a flat Midlands voice: '*If we now take the calculated ratio of space versus the already demonstrated ratio of volume, multiplying the result by four . . .*'

Kate carried to the fridge her wet and wordless fish.

As the day drew into the afternoon Joe grew whinier. As James's tongue had against all common sense sought out the throbbing hole, so Joe was drawn perversely towards all the objects that any fool could see were bound to trip him up, sting him, bump him or otherwise cause him pain. And of course once one is irritable everything is vexatious

– the fact that there is too little milk in one's mug or too much; the way the Marmite lid won't come off; the way, when you put it back, it won't go on. By the end of the day Kate was a jangle of nerves, made worse by her inability to shout at Joe because it was his birthday. Joe carried his birthday around his head unknowingly, like a halo. It deflected Kate's angry darts – shamed by his being two today they bounded off sideways, redirected towards the cat, who after a certain amount of bullying slunk upstairs and escaped into the garden.

Outside, with maddening golden serenity the day was drawing to its close. Oh to have a moment to stand silently and breathe in the balmy air. But Joe was tugging at her skirt. Fretful at the end of his long day, he was ready for bed. She had already put him in his pyjamas; his face wore the transparent look of a child who despite all protests is longing for sleep. But where was James? They must wait until he came home so that he could give Joe his present.

Six-thirty, and James had promised to be early. Joe squirmed for his bedtime bottle of milk. Kate cursed James's office and James. She willed him to hurry. Interested speculation in what James had bought dwindled away and was replaced by dread. Dread, because the present-opening should be such a happy little scene – the pyjama-clad Joe shrieking with delight, the fatherly father bending over him and showing him how it worked. As the minutes passed, this little tableau grew gradually more stagey.

In desperation Kate said: 'Come on Joe, let's go into the garden.' The plants needed watering; that might mollify Joe. He could be relied upon to help so long as

Kate first picked up his small plastic watering can. This would make him want it; he would snatch it from her and she could turn aside and stealthily switch on the hose.

For some minutes, blessed peace. This hot summer Kate loved watering her garden, the sun sparkling the spray, the long evening shadows and the golden light, the hiss of the hose and the plants rustling with relief. Joe was quiet. There were two possibilities: he was either obsessively watering one single plant, like pouring quarts of Scotch down the throat of an alcoholic, or he had taken off his slippers and was pouring water into them.

'Never mind, never mind.' Kate picked up Tyne-Tees and gazed into his humourless face. 'I love him really. Honest.' From his shell Tyne-Tees's legs dangled. 'Old torty,' she said.

No doubt she would have continued this conversation had she not seen, at that instant, James standing at the back door. Tactless of her to be actually *holding* the tortoise – hastily she dumped him behind a clump of marigolds. Would James feel honour-bound to bring up the whole business again? Neither of them would care for this.

'Here's Daddy, Joe!' With a quick kick Kate sent his drenched slippers into the flowerbed. She picked up Joe and brought him inside.

'Sorry I'm late, darling. Damned Minister suddenly arrived. Not a word of warning.'

He looked exhausted and in need of a drink. 'Bottle,' whined Joe, in need of one too. Remembering he was irritable, he struggled in Kate's arms.

'Let's go into the sitting-room,' Kate said. 'I'm dying to see what you've bought.'

She poured out the drinks. He held out a parcel; Kate

held her breath. It was tied, touchingly and clumsily, in what looked like office string. Joe looked at Kate and gave it to her.

'No, *you* open it.'

'Mum do. Mum do.'

'Joe do it. Come on, it's your present.' If only James had come home half an hour earlier. 'All right then, I'll just start it.'

She untied the string and passed it back to Joe. He fumbled it open.

'Ah!' Kate cried, truly delighted. 'One of those lovely post-boxes.' She laughed; she had been dreading something lavish and full of batteries, far too advanced and bound to break. Such a suitable present surprised and touched her. She turned to Joe. 'Isn't it gorgeous; just what you wanted.'

'Come along, old boy.' James's voice, jauntier after a gulp of Scotch. 'I'll show you.' He held up the plastic shapes. 'Look, Joe, they go in there. See?' He pointed to the lid of the post-box and slotted the shapes into the appropriate holes. He said to Kate: 'It'll be good for his co-ordination.'

Joe took a shape. Kate, tense, watched. He banged it up and down on the lid of the post-box and looked up for the applause.

'No, Joe. Like this.' James took another shape and posted it through the hole. It clattered down inside the box. 'See? Now you do it.'

He held out a tube shape. Joe took it. 'Into the hole,' said James. Joe pressed it against one of the holes: the triangular one.

'I say, isn't he stupid,' said James.

'He's not! He's just tired. Half an hour ago he was fine.'

'Look, Kate, I said I was sorry. The damned man made us get all the files out. Tariff amendments.' He turned back. 'Now let's try once more.'

Kate drank some gin. Was Joe going to get the hang of it before James got impatient? He had had such a long day. So had Joe. Caught between these two frayed males she thought: hell, so have I.

Joe took his shape, the triangle this time. Feebly he pushed it against this hole and that. James interrupted him. 'For goodness sake let me do it.'

At his tone Joe looked up, a shadow crossing his face. Kate said: 'You're too quick.'

James said: 'Do you know what age this label says? *Eighteen Months Upwards.*'

'He'll learn.' She picked up Joe. She could tell by his rigid legs that he was working himself up to cry; the flimsiest excuse would set him off. 'He's so tired, I'll take him to bed.' At the door she added: 'You just wait. Next week he'll be doing his post-box with his eyes shut.' She smiled.

'Hope so. You see, she said it was just the right age – '

He stopped. Quickly he looked down at his glass.

Kate closed the door very gently behind her; very gently she carried Joe upstairs. No, she told herself. Say it's not true.

It couldn't be true, could it? It was like some terrible parody. She longed to disbelieve it and pretend that he had meant the girl in the shop. The way James had stopped himself, embarrassed, told her that it wasn't.

Maggie Ross, James's secretary, had children; she would know all about suitable presents for suitable ages,

183

wouldn't she? Climbing the stairs Kate cursed her own stupidity, her innocent delight at the post-box and the touching little scene she had created of James, tall and manly in a toyshop, scratching his head and thinking of his son.

Kate stood at the top of the stairs. At the time she had thought it was almost *too* suitable a present; fathers never bought something so very right. And after all, James had said he had had a fantastically busy day. Kate stared at Joe's door.

The depths to which an executive husband could sink, James had sunk. The tender toyshop scene was replaced by James shuffling memos in his office. 'By the way, Maggie, be a dear and just nip out, could you? It's my son's birthday – you know, the eldest one; see if you can find something appropriate.' Then he took out his wallet. 'Here's a couple of quid.'

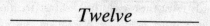

'Tummy buttons,' said Elaine. 'Would you believe it? She thought babies came out of tummy buttons – well, what *she* called tummy buttons. One of my clients, she was.'

'*No*.'

'A nineteen-year-old girl in the swinging seventies.'

'Astonishing, isn't it,' said Jetta. 'I hear that sort of thing too. Had a girl yesterday, been married six years and just acquired a lover. She asked me if she should be taking two Pills a day now.'

Laughter. 'Jetta, *no*.'

Jetta nodded. 'Rather sad, don't you think? More courgettes?'

The Greens were holding a dinner party. Marion would rather be absent; she would prefer to be communing with herself in Alf's room or simply remaining in her den. Nothing, she had found, was more comfortable than listening to dinner party noises and not having to join in. But this time, when asking her if she would like to come, her father had added with an awful roguish twinkle: 'If he can spare you for an evening, that is,' and in the confusion of the moment she had agreed to join them.

So here she sat, concentrating on the food. She wished they were not talking about this sort of thing; she found it disturbing. Her parents and their friends got louder and somehow more hectic on this topic. Still, as long as they did not turn to her she could just sit here and pretend to be invisible.

'Tragic, I know,' said Elaine. 'Heavenly wine, Sam.'

Jetta said: 'Another girl, just about to have a baby, thought she would need an operation before the milk came out.'

'A pin or something? *Jetta*.'

'I had to go through it all step by step.'

Marion's eyes flicked to her mother's chest. Those two confident mounds – she had suckled there. Inside, her stomach moved; she looked away.

Elaine said: 'Sam, isn't it terrible?'

'No. Lovely. Makes one realize how bizarre the real explanation is.' He drained his wine glass. 'Once Marion said something so touching. Remember, Jetta?'

Marion froze. She stared down at her *boeuf bourguignon*.

He said: 'When she was little and we were all in the bus. She looked at Jetta and said in a loud voice: "When did Daddy pass you the seed?" '

Marion kept her eyes on the beige gravy.

Their laughter echoed round the kitchen. She felt her father lean over and ruffle her hair. 'It made me sound so courtly, somehow.'

Marion smoothed down her hair where he had messed it up. How *could* he? She hated him.

Thankfully the conversation went on to something else. She heard them talking about Stockholm; her mother was leaving on Monday. She kept herself bent over her beef. She was seeing Dad more clearly nowadays. Once she had thought he was perfect – when she was young and stupid, that was. It was a chilly feeling, realizing that he was not. It was like the houses in a street being gradually demolished one by one, leaving you standing there.

He was cruel sometimes, he really was. Callous. Could she forget that time when Nick came round, a year ago? Nick was Sharon's brother; she had been so shy asking him to tea without asking Sharon – she had messed about at Sharon's house when he had been there but she had never been with him alone. They were eating fruit, and had quite a friendly little squabble over the last things in the bowl. It was fun; squabbling made them suddenly less shy. Then Dad had said: 'Oh look. Marion's got her eye on Nick's banana.'

She had wanted to die. Still she blushed, thinking of it. She had never gone back to Sharon's house, not until she heard that Nick had left for college.

No, she was noticing lately how moody Dad was and how self-obsessed. Unpredictable. She longed for him to be more boring and more – well, nice. He got so bad-tempered over his book. And how insensitive he was – he who was supposed to be a novelist. Surely they should be all subtle and aware?

Everyone round the table seemed to have forgotten about that seed business. Upstairs they trooped to have their coffee in the sitting-room. Marion made her excuses and escaped back to her den. Like a brimming glass she carried her love for James with her. The more things around her crumbled, the more precious he became. Fragile, perfect, when other things were becoming so coarse.

Marion got ready for bed. Below she heard voices and a burst of laughter, her father's the loudest. A ridiculous pang, she felt, that he could laugh just as loudly when she wasn't there. He had hardly noticed she had gone. Illogical, this, but then not much made sense at the moment.

Ah, but James! She climbed into bed; inviolate in her long-sleeved nightie, she hugged him to her. Her room was silent. It reassured her that beyond the wall there he was. What was he doing – reading a book? Watching TV? Mrs Cooper was a black silhouette at the edge of the picture; she did not like to think about her.

Marion pulled the sheet up to her chin. James shared this bed, this sheet-entwined drowsiness; he shared this room, bathed in the light that filtered through from the street. Outside, the rhythm of the traffic – cars slowing down at the lights, the idling of their engines, the revving-up noises when the lights changed. The shouts and boozy singing when the King's Head closed, the rattling of trains on the raised railway, the doomy wail of the police siren, loud then fading away – he heard this too.

More laughter from downstairs. Marion realized: having James with her meant that she could lie here and actually put a name to Dad's faults. She had not dared to before; now that James was next door; calm, unchanging, she could. She was more adult about Dad now.

It annoyed Marion that she could only feature James in her dozy pre-dream and post-dream time in bed. So far she had never got him into her proper sleeping dreams. These were hopelessly miscast, the starring roles being muscled in on by people laughably inappropriate – the man from the dry cleaners perhaps, with his shiny bald head, or an altered, silly Sharon. Such a waste. At least she could guarantee James her sole attention once she awoke – actually, before she was properly awake. Already in that shifting, stirring time when consciousness is still blurred and loosened – already, then, James was installed.

This was the best moment of the day; particularly today because it was Saturday. No school, no scrambling out of bed and collecting of scattered thoughts. Better than Sunday which already had Monday looming over it.

After Saturday breakfast Marion always went down to the shop to buy her magazines. Today, walking out of her front door and closing it behind her, James also walked out of his. A moment of fluster. Marion hesitated; she set off to the right. He also set off to the right, a few paces behind. She could hear his footsteps.

This was embarrassing. He was just behind her and they were obviously going the same way. Should she turn? Slow down?

No time to think; James was beside her.

'Lovely day,' he said. 'Will the weather ever break?'

'It's lovely and hot,' she said stupidly.

A silence; just the clack of their footsteps. She looked down at her legs, fat and pale. She racked her brains for something to say.

'I like it hot like this,' she said. Half an hour ago she had been in his arms. They had been in a little summerhouse, to be exact, on a wooden bench. Marion blushed.

He said: 'One certainly shouldn't complain. It really is quite remarkable for England, isn't it.'

'Oh yes,' she said. 'Yes.'

Their footsteps clacked on, side by side. She almost wished this meeting could be got over quickly so she could think about it.

'Soon no doubt,' he said, 'someone will be complaining about the *sun*.'

189

'Wouldn't that be funny!' Marion's squeaky laugh startled her.

'Trust the British,' he said.

'Oh yes,' she said. 'Trust them.'

A few more steps and they were at the corner. They paused. Who was going to the left and who was going to the right? The agony of not knowing if you both were or you both weren't. Both, it seemed, were turning to the left.

'You must be off to the newsagents,' said James after a pause. 'So am I.'

They walked along in silence. It was excruciating, trying to think of something to say, no sound but their footsteps. An hour ago they had been talking all the time – that is, between the kisses. Their summerhouse had roses round the windows. Marion, blushing, kept her eyes on the paving stones and the scrunched-up cigarette packets.

At last the newsagents. They went in. With James she stood at the counter.

'Good morning,' said James. 'Marion, what would you like?'

Marion stood transfixed. On the counter, sheaves of magazines. *Stud*, said one. *Knave*, *Climax*.

James turned to the man: 'Do you have *Motor Sport*?'

Of course Marion had seen these magazines before; they were always there. But God they were so glaring and obvious, rows of them – a black stocking top, a piece of thigh.

James's voice. 'Anything for you, Marion?'

Marion could not speak. She stared at them, there was nowhere else to look. Nipples. Glistening red lips. Fingers, oh no, lifting a lacy piece of knicker. She glimpsed a tuft

190

of hair. He was looking at that, he must be. The glossy page was right under his nose.

Marion felt herself shrink away inside. The parts under her clothes, she felt them curl in shame.

In a normal voice James said: 'Oh yes, and could you stop *The Times* from Monday. For seven days.'

'Going away again?' the man asked.

'Just for a week.'

A pause. Marion knew her face must be beetroot. She felt burning and degraded. That parted lace, that tuft – James must be looking at it. Her James.

'Yes?' the man asked.

She could not buy her stupid teenage magazines. Not now, not with James there. She grabbed the nearest thing that had no faces on it and no foul photos.

'*The New Statesman*?' said the man. 'Thirty pence.'

Marion fumbled for her money. 'Please,' said James. 'Let me.' He got there first.

Outside the shop she mumbled: 'Just going, er, this way.' She could not bear, after this, to walk all the way back with James.

She hurried along the road. Her face burned. The pavement thudded past but she saw nothing, only parted legs, creeping hands and slimy rustling leather trousers. To herself she cried: Little summerhouse, little wooden bench!

After a while she got home. Dad met her on the stairs; at her magazine he raised his eyebrows.

'Well hello, Marghanita Laski,' he said. He looked rather bleary this morning.

Marion escaped upstairs. At last, sitting on her bed, she could collect her scattered wits. It took her a while to calm

191

down and realize that James for sure had noticed nothing odd about any of this. Their love had not been shattered into pieces; sitting tranquilly like this she could see it, like one of those delicate amoebas seen under a microscope, merge itself together again into one translucent whole.

And she read her magazine. She ploughed through a whole article on press censorship in Chile and another entitled *Is the Left in Revolt?* James buying it made the words precious; by the end of Saturday morning she knew a good deal about current affairs.

Thirteen

The next day, Sunday, again it dawned hot; again all over England people believed it could not continue. Already perspiring, they emerged from their houses, filling the parks, the benches, the hired deck-chairs. Nut-brown city children ran bare and wild; old ladies rolled down their stockings; dogs lay lifeless in the shade but one twitched when a fly alighted on its nose. Houses became stuffy, doors were left ajar, windows that had not been opened for years were pushed and pulled until they creaked out and let in some air. It was too good to be true, it could not last. Tomorrow the weather would break; next week.

It would not, of course. The gauzy dawns, the perfect days would continue. 1976, summer of the drought. In July there would be water rationing; in August the narrow lanes backing Brinsley Street would look cracked, dun, foreign.

Today though, in June, the grass was still a British green. If someone in the tenements peered through the windows they could have seen the lawns. Some were spread with Sunday newspapers, some with rugs upon which lay bodies. Some were cluttered with luminous plastic paddling pools, ignored by the children who preferred the soggy patches of lawn where the hose had leaked; discarded clothes and plates lay around, which nobody was energetic enough to take back into the houses. In each garden life carried on. Its inhabitants thought themselves private; they adjusted their bikini straps and slapped their children, unaware of next door's presence on the other side of the garden wall. All those next doors, all those parallel needs: food brought out, children brought in, from the frosted back windows the parallel flushing in parallel bathrooms. It looked endearing from up in the flats, those small needs exposed to view.

If anyone, that is, had been there to see. But the afternoon sun slanted on to lino as curled as Alf's had been, worn away to its woven backing. There were pigeon droppings on the windowsills; even in this weather the wallpaper was diseased with damp. Only the net curtains were left, prim remnants like skirts on a corpse for there was nothing living left for them to hide.

If someone had been there, what would they have seen?

Mad Mrs Forsythe sitting at her back door sorting through yellowed newspapers. Why? Only she knew.

Next door the Cooper family dispersed around its garden, Mrs Cooper pale in her bikini, Mr Cooper, fully-dressed and cool, fiddling with the catch of a suitcase. In the next garden the Greens, looking altogether more tanned and hedonistic. Mrs Green lay slender and boyish on a lilo; for an hour the sun could borrow her body – only an hour though, for in her fingers she held a Biro. In Mr Green's fingers was a cigarette, beside him a glass. In shorts he looked monkeyish. He was reading the newspaper.

In the next garden couch grass, thistles and blankets brought out from bedsits. Various people lay about but they were anonymous; they were flat-dwellers and lived different hours. Beyond their unloved rented garden other families, other narrow lawns and shady bushes. Beyond the houses hot, impatient cars queueing at traffic lights, hot bodies throughout the city, glistening faces raised to the sun or turned away this midsummer's eve, this centre of the year – in the country the leafy centre, in London the dusty one.

In the gardens of twenty-three and twenty-one, a sense of waiting, a hesitation in shimmering heat. Tomorrow James would be in Brussels, Jetta in Stockholm; over both sides of the wall hung the impending departures. But beyond this, a sense of things balanced at the equinox, poised.

Poised – before what? Kate was tired, so tired and heavy with sun. Ten minutes' sleep was all she craved. Ten minutes of golden oblivion, undisturbed. She knew she needed to think, but just now all she yearned was sleep. She lay on her stomach, her head resting sideways.

Joe pulled at her hair.

'Shut up.'

He tugged. He wanted to lift up her head and find her buried ear. He was obsessed with ears.

She sighed; she lifted her head and turned it over to the other side. Into her ear Joe put his smug finger.

With her head on this side she could see James. Ruffled, she thought: I wish he'd remove more of his clothes. And I wish he'd stop doing something so useful. Already with his suitcase he looks absent. She closed her eyes.

*

James thought: Not as bad as I'd imagined. Couple of screws here, that'll fix the handle. Then he thought: if Kate's asleep why are her hands clenched?

Sam was reading the book reviews. '*A stunning debut,*' he read. '*A first novel of real substance, leavened by a uniquely wry, sly humour.*' Sam shifted in his deck-chair. '*Rare indeed it is to find a major new talent . . .*'

Itchy with irritation, Sam scratched his thick black hair and turned to the theatre page.

Files, papers, those six case-histories: Jetta thought of the things she must organize before she left. Food for the freezer, instructions for the washing machine. Sam and Marion were such babies; how could they manage without her?

She stretched out her long oiled legs.

It's fate, Sam thought, fate that she's going away. Seven whole days without her. Something must happen now. It will. It must.

'Joe, that *hurts.*'

Kate's voice over the wall. Hoarse with irritation, he loved it still. Kate, Kate.

Kate thought: Seven days. For seven days I needn't feel guilty about anything. I needn't make any meals. I needn't bend over the kitchen sink pulling out tea-leaves and lumps of grease with my fingernails and nobody noticing when I've done it, only when I haven't and the revolting thing silts up.

Startled by her bitterness, Kate opened her eyes. She looked at James. She thought: Have we come to this?

Seven whole days, Marion thought. He said so in the paper shop. Seven times twenty-four hours. I shall make a chart and cross them off.

Sunday drew to a close. In parks and gardens, slanting sunlight; children still playing, their laughter echoing through the leaves as they would echo in a far-off golden age. Shadows lengthened; flinching with sunburn, women reached for their carrier bags. Parents called their children; dogs, revived, danced around and tripped them up. The parks emptied, leaving the grass littered.

Rugs were dragged in across the gardens. Darkness fell. City back-streets, all open windows, frying smells and fire escapes, had a West Side Story air about them, most uncharacteristic. In Brinsley Street the gardens, dark and quiet, returned to themselves – stealthy rustlings, snails leaving silver threads across the lawns. Surrounded by lights and TV noises, their velvet blackness deepened.

Frosted bathrooms glowed briefly then were extinguished. Upstairs windows sprang into life. Then they too went dark. Silence except for the rumble, always the far rumble, of London traffic. In little bedrooms children stirred, sand in their hair. In front bedrooms husbands and wives, all warm limbs and scents of suntan lotion, were making love; even those husbands and wives who seldom did. After all, tomorrow was Monday wasn't it? All briskness and dispersal and battles for the Tube. Anyway it might rain. There might never be another Sunday like this.

Fourteen

'Joe say bye-bye. Bye-bye Daddy. Go on.' Kate held Joe at the doorstep. 'Wave, Joe.' She pumped Joe's arm up and down; the taxi pulled into the traffic. 'Go on, wave.' So many faces she could see, the street was choked with Monday morning cars, but she could not see James's because the taxi window was tinted.

She closed the door. Instead of doing all the things she should be doing Kate went into the sitting-room and sat down. She felt so depressed.

'Your post-box,' she told Joe. 'It was your post-box. I wouldn't mind anything else quite so much if it wasn't for that.'

'Post-box?'

'How could he?'

Joe hurried out of the room. Maybe he had left it in the kitchen. He was mastering the slots now; it really had been a great success.

'Bloody post-box,' Kate said aloud. 'Bloody James.'

No, he was not bloody. He was a good man, a conscientious, kind man; she could see that so clearly it was chilling. Logically she could see all number of nice things about him.

But logic did not help when you had fallen out of love, did it? Kate stared at the dead grate. The door opened and Joe appeared. He had not found the post-box; instead he had discovered a whole tube of Rowntree's Fruit Gums.

In a businesslike way he sat down and started to fumble with the wrapper.

'Joe,' said Kate but without conviction.

When had been the turning point? Or had love just seeped away like water through a leaky drain that nobody had been bothered, lately, to inspect? Seeped away leaving them high and dry. Nothing dramatic – they remained polite, dutiful with one another's bodies, a little more edgy and petty perhaps over the small stupid things that had recently come to loom so large. To an outsider there had been little change – no rows, no tears, no other convenient lover upon whom one could heap the causes.

A grunt of satisfaction; Joe had got the packet open.

'Just one then,' said Kate hopelessly. She returned her gaze to the grate. Subtle and slow the change had been. Only thinking about it like this made her realize it had happened at all. Gradual, the way he no longer noticed what she wore unless its buttonholes were grubby; gradual, the way that at gatherings they no longer caught each other's eye – those swift glances through the talking heads. Painful, so painful thinking of this. When did she realize she no longer found it interesting to sit beside him in a restaurant? Once it had been good simply to be there, his leg against hers, warm together looking at the outside world, their words full of silences, their silences full of words. Nowadays her silences were just calculations about the bill, or worries that he would notice that her asparagus was tinned and start to make a fuss.

Kate sat very still. She heard the clock ticking. When was it that the actual words had changed? When had James's seriousness become James's humourlessness? When, for

199

James, had her charming ineptitudes become irritating ones; when had her voluptuousness changed to simple overweight? Her shape had not altered – James's inner word for it had. When had passion become dexterity?

The clock ticked. There was a busy silence behind her where Joe sat. How could she and James of all people have fallen into the oldest cliché? Other couples might – surely not them. They had started out too aware of this. They had laughed about it with their friends. Not for them the corny old syndrome of housebound wife and hardworking husband, their two lives gradually drifting apart, hers towards children, his towards promotion: two people, once so close, becoming mutually incomprehensible.

'Mummy. Sweet.'

'I don't want one, thank you.' Joe stood in front of her holding out a fruit gum.

Sad. It was so very sad. Not the stuff of high tragedy; it would be less sad if it was. They could do something about it then. But what were they to do about this? What did the thousands – no, millions, of other couples do?

With a sinking feeling Kate realized that they did nothing at all. They did not recognize it. Or at some point they said to themselves: This is marriage after all, isn't it? After the first flush what do you expect? You settle down. Nothing very terrible happens. You jog along; your children, your friends, they all become that little bit more important.

And your husband? Well, you have a certain amount in common – mutual acquaintances, the children . . . and, well, the house, the garden, things like that. What did you expect – to giggle like infants over the fish and chips? Been married six years haven't you? Got to get to work tomorrow. Anyway, mustn't ruin this suit. Much more sensible to bring them home and eat them properly from a plate; then I can catch the Nine O'Clock News.

Kate thought: what does this lead to? Nothing dramatic; a quiet but deadly acceptance of second best, a greater reliance upon one's friends. A chattiness in company; a silence when alone together. A numbness spreading, covering the taste of those early days in the Holland Park flat, him returning on the Central Line, her on the District, the way that pressed against strap-hanging strangers each was longing for the other.

The grate blurred; her eyes filled with tears.

'Sweet.' Joe pressed the fruit gum against her lips.

There was nothing to do but adjust to it. Millions of other people did. Nothing to make a song and dance about, was it? It wasn't as if she was actively unhappy.

In the silent room her sobs startled her. Down her cheeks ran the tears; she did not bother to wipe them, there was no one to see but Joe. He was inspecting her with his cool, clear child's gaze. Still trying to get the fruit gum into her mouth, he was watching her lips, poised.

If only she could blame it on one of them or the other. She could not; they were both at fault. She could stand outside herself and see how boring she was becoming. She had nothing to offer or to talk about any more; no wonder James read his newspaper. She had no respect for her daily occupations simply because no one else did; she did not even earn any money and had the humiliation of asking James for pound notes when it was his birthday.

She blew her nose. Oh James, she thought, what has happened?

Joe watched her mouth, waiting. At the right moment, between the sobs, he pushed it in. She was too weak to

201

resist. Her mouth was thick with tears; inside it, the fruit gum felt rubbery. She started sucking it, obediently. She couldn't do much else, could she?

She recovered of course. She got up, her tongue gluey, wiped her eyes, fetched her cleaning things and started dusting the ornaments along the mantelpiece. Joe took no more notice of her; flicking her duster over a blithe shepherdess, Kate could hear the self-absorbed little humming noise he was making – Joe, the solitary witness of her grief.

Stuffy, so stuffy. Up in his attic Samuel could hardly breathe, this hot sticky Monday afternoon, midsummer's day.

Would you believe it? He was still stuck in the Embassy garden, still at page fifty-one. He had actually got Arabella away from the balustrade. She was standing very near Norton now, his strange, altered Arabella, Kate within her like a ghost, widening her face, messing up her hair, filling her body with that helpless, wondering beauty. Arabella would never push her hair from her face in that way; with painted, meaningful fingers – young girl's fingers – she should be unbuttoning her dress. That was the damned point of this garden scene. Oh Kate, unbuttoning for your child. Through Arabella's spikey mascara it was Kate's candid eyes that gazed at him. *Look, I've got Plasticine under my nails.*

Kate, release me. From its tangle of black letters release my page. Breathe life into this garden, so pasteboard and patrician. Idiotic Embassy with its false fountains. Fill it with night-time living noises; make it real.

Sam sat slumped in his chair; he stared at the criss-crossed page. Next door she was so agonizingly close. If only she lived further away – could he escape her then? But over his shoulder she was gazing, tenderly. She shared these dusty sycamores and behind them the tenement flats, their broken windows glinting in the sun. No stupid Embassy here. She might even be looking at them now. Was she?

How hot he was. Damp with sweat, his shirt stuck to his back. The air like cotton wool filled his mouth and nostrils; he could hardly summon up the energy to shift in his seat. Would this weather never break? He was trapped, suffocating in a cocoon of swaddling heat, bandaged up with words, useless words, page after page of them. Darling Kate, release my book; release my body.

Samuel looked at page fifty-one. He hesitated. Then he snatched up his red Biro and scrawled KATE, in large red letters, across the page. Simply KATE, nothing else, no message. Swiftly he folded up the paper and put it in an envelope. He hesitated, then he wrote her name on the envelope and pushed back his chair.

He did not stop to think. He ran downstairs. He opened his front door, glanced swiftly around and posted the envelope though the door of number twenty-three. Then he hurried back into his own house and shut the door.

He was drenched in sweat. For a moment he stood in his dark hallway. What *had* he done? Appalled, exhilarated, he stood there. He, Samuel Green, was fond of the theatrical gesture, but whenever had he done something quite like this? Would Kate understand?

He was not utterly mad, of course. He was sane enough to know that at this very moment Jetta was on a British Airways flight to Sweden; also that when he had fetched in the milk he had seen James plus suitcase climbing into a taxi. Reassuring, that he had taken this into account when clattering downstairs clutching his envelope.

He knew, too, that this book business was all airy-fairy rubbish, a mere excuse. Bugger his novel. It was not something bloodless and literary that was stirred and confused by Kate, it was the meat of his body. He loved her; he was obsessed by her; it was not just at his typewriter that he thought of her, it was when he was munching toast, brushing his teeth, making love to his wife.

Uncomfortable, Sam shifted on to the other foot. Under the shifting summer sheets he was betraying Jetta, he knew this. For the first time in his marriage it was happening. The body that moved against his belonged to Jetta, but he was caressing Kate, with his hands he was shaping her over the sleek limbs of his wife. He dared not dwell on this – he could just glimpse it, disquietingly, out of the corner of his eye. Eighteen years of marriage and for the first time he was altering towards his wife. There was something about Kate's transparent confusions, her dear burnt nose, that made Jetta appear leathery and smug. Kate's mothering body rendered his wife's – here Sam shifted back on to the other foot – rendered it mannish and barren.

Sam stood in the hall. He said aloud: 'Well something's bound to happen now.' His voice sounded oddly conversational. Too loud. He closed his mouth; Kate's hallway, after all, was adjacent to his.

When would she find it – this afternoon, this evening

Sam's heart stopped beating – was she stooping over it at this very moment?

Soon, thought Sam, we will find out. Ah, but the wait.

There was, in fact, somebody in the next hall. As yet he was not stooping over the envelope; he was sucking a Twiglet. At this stage Joe preferred not to eat them; he liked to suck off the brown bits and lay the Twiglets in a row, pale and slimy, on the floor. He might eat them later. He had found them under the carry-cot mattress, where things tended to accumulate. When he lifted the sheets off the mattress to inspect the bunny pictures he would find all sorts of intriguing stuff to eat – the relics, bluish and furry, of the things he had been given on shopping expeditions when he had started to whine.

Joe looked up and for the first time he noticed something on the doormat. He knew what it was: it was a letter. Letters belonged on the doormat. His parents always laughed, so pleased, when he put letters there.

Joe clambered to his feet and went into the sitting-room. He got up on a chair and looked at his father's open desk. Various stamped and addressed envelopes lay there, written to the Gas Board and Barclaycard Ltd., Northampton. Joe picked them up, climbed down the chair and went back into the hall. He walked over to the doormat and laid the handful of letters with care on top of the original one. Satisfied, he went back to his Twiglets.

His mother was changing Ollie's nappy. When she came downstairs Joe looked up. He removed a glistening Twiglet from his mouth. 'Letters,' he informed her.

She laughed. 'Joe, you idiot!' She put the baby in the

pram and gathered up the letters. 'That reminds me,' she said, putting them into her bag, 'let's post them now, on the way to the shops. Daddy will be furious – well, more disappointed really – if he comes back on Monday and finds I've forgotten.'

So they went out and posted them.

Fifteen

'Should you have another, Dad? I mean, supper's almost ready.'

'For Christ's sake, Marion, stop being pi.' Sam, standing at the drinks cupboard, clattered ice into his glass.

Marion, realizing she had said the wrong thing, jumped up. 'I'll have another one then,' she said brightly.

'Another naughty tonic?'

'Most parents would be pleased,' she said in a moment of spirit.

Sam did not reply; he seemed uninterested in this conversation. He took his drink over to the window and stood looking out at the garden.

'I've made us some sausages,' said Marion. 'You know how we like them and, well, Mum doesn't.'

Sam did not seem to hear. Marion was hurt. She had been so much looking forward to this time together. Without her mother they might be able to recapture some of the old closeness. Before when Jetta had gone abroad it had been fun, the two of them roaming lawless through the house. Not that Mum made laws of course; far from it, she very carefully did not. Why then should it feel so deliciously free when she was away?

'No phone calls?' asked Dad, turning suddenly.

'Weren't you here?'

'I might have been in the bathroom or something. No one knocked on the door?'

'No, I don't think so. Not since I got back from school.'

Sam drained his glass. That was his third whisky. Marion, feeling protective, frowned. He was ruining his health. When Mum was not here she felt altered towards him – cosier, more motherly, tut-tutting with him over his bad habits. He seemed to find that amusing – at least he had once. They had drawn themselves together, sharing meals at which her mother would have looked pained – sausages, tomato ketchup, baked beans, not a lettuce leaf in sight. No ghastly healthy stuff – her mother was the only human being she had ever met who sincerely preferred salads. Over the steaming carbohydrates, Dad and she had been united by their innocent, truanting greed. Sometimes Dad himself had a go at cooking, endearingly aproned, scattering cigarette ash and using about thirty saucepans.

Her father had altered, improved. Without a third person there he had become less unpredictable and less embarrassingly high-spirited. He was a great one for an audience, and without it he subsided into someone quieter and more sympathetic. She was realizing that people are invariably better company on their own. It was lovely; she had had all his attention. He had actually asked her questions about school. Listened to the answers too.

'Just going upstairs,' said Dad. He went to the cupboard and picked up the bottle.

Marion gaped. 'But what about supper?'

'So damned hot and sticky. Couldn't manage anything. Could you?'

'But Dad – '

She stopped. He had left the room; up the stairs his footsteps creaked, pausing at the landing window. What

208

was the matter with him? And why did he keep looking out of the windows in that jumpy way – expecting inspiration was he? Him and his stupid book.

Marion put down her unfinished tonic. She had only asked for it to keep him company. She got up and wandered round the room. Perhaps he would be better tomorrow. They would get into their stride then, herself looking after him and keeping the house nice. Already the sitting-room had improved. In the absence of her mother Marion felt it adjusting to her, settling around her and looking altogether more friendly with its tableful of magazines she had brought down from her den. No tap-tapping heels across the floor making her freeze with guilt. No busy swish of the filing cabinet next to the desk, a swish that said: Of course I don't mind you slumped over *The Generation Game*, darling. Don't you feel, though, that you're putting up some kind of barrier perhaps? We've all got to grow up, you know, and explore all the marvellous relationships that are just opening out . . .

Quiet, empty room . . . with no on here it was almost as good as Alf's. Marion gazed around. Her parents had gone out and explored all right; they had rebelled, what with their coffee bars and duffel coats and Aldermaston Marches. This room had all the right accessories. Why could not she, Marion, be more like this instead of so prim and housewifely? If only she had a desire to plaster her wall with punk rockers; it would make her parents so pleased. Instead her room was painfully neat, with its fringed dressing-table cover and matching bedspread that she had sewn from that pattern in *Woman's Realm*.

Marion stopped in front of the TV. This week anyway she would do exactly what she liked. The pressure was off. And tonight, for a start, she would change into her nice cool nightie and spend the whole evening watching telly, straight through.

Darkness had fallen. Ten-thirty and still the heat was stifling. Kate had had a bath and changed into her thinnest dress, a long Indian muslin thing, white with little bits of embroidery on it. When she had bought it last summer James had said: 'Oughtn't you to wear something under that?' His tone, one of polite enquiry without a trace of lust, had since then effectively consigned it to the back of the cupboard. Tonight though it was so hot. She paused at the mirror. A heavy mother, she wore under its daintily-thonged bodice an enormous nursing bra, but who was there to see?

Returning from the bedroom she stopped for a moment in the attic and gazed at her sleeping babies. At their beauty she was humbled. In his carry-cot lay Oliver, waxen, pure. In the cot lay Joe, stilled at last – his lashes lowered on to his tender cheeks, his thumb, still moist, poised near his mouth. She bent over and smelt his fragrance. Asleep, her children looked so grave; they made the toys scattered around the floor – the luminous duck, the wind-up monkey – look loud and irrelevant. Kate straightened up. Today she felt so odd. That post-box business, her anguish. The slightest thing filled her eyes with tears.

She made her way downstairs. She felt restless and stifled. What should she do – go to sleep? She could not. Usually desperate for slumber, tonight she felt alert and hemmed-in – the four walls of her house, her little world, closed around her. Claustrophobic, housebound housewife. Yes, she knew she had changed. James had married one person and she had become another – hands roughened by washing, mind dulled by the small and insistent needs, ever the same needs, of her babies.

Oh to step outside and wander the streets thoughtfully; shake her head and let in the fresh air. Beyond this house there were other streets, other worlds, aeroplanes taking off and landing. What did she know of this? What could she know, with those dear and fragrant bodies upstairs? Even to open her front door she needed a baby-sitter.

Instead she opened the back door. Even in the garden it was stuffy. The tobacco flowers glowed, palely. Along the top of the wall a cat slid out of sight. Beside her the black shapes of the bushes seemed to be waiting, expectant, this hot midsummer's night.

In his attic Samuel leant forward. He stared out of the window.

She was there. She was wearing something long and pale, it glimmered as she moved. He sat for a moment, watching. Swimmy with whisky he knew, now, that this was exactly what was meant to happen. She had waited until this moment because now was the best time. He knew, she knew; they both did.

Flickering through the foliage, he could see her walking slowly to the end of her garden. Sam's heart turned inside him. How tenderly appropriate, that dress, long and pale. His real Arabella. How she understood! Could such a woman as this be possible?

Not only the dress but the balustrade. She had reached the end of the garden and now she stood on the small, raised, paved area under the sycamores. No balustrade there but something very like it, a trellis.

Sam's heart thumped. Her boldness emboldened him. He stood up; shakily he reached for a cigarette. He gazed at his shrouded typewriter, his empty glass. Now at last it had happened he felt so moved. Kate, Kate.

He left his room and ran swiftly downstairs. From the living-room, TV noises. He crept past, his body cautious, his mind soaring. Inevitable of course: he knew, Kate knew. Inevitable, but still his heart thudded.

Kate leant against the trellis. Around her rose the houses, their chimneys a black jumble, their windows scattered yellow squares. Above them the sky was suffused with an orange city glow. The night was so beautiful, weighty, poised. She could hear the faint rumble of traffic but here in the garden nothing stirred.

Beside her the honeysuckle had been fastened to the trellis by James; he had pinned the clematis to the wall. Patiently he had tied and staked the plants but when did he have time to enjoy them? She would like him here this summer's night to share the scented garden. She missed him – at least she thought she missed him but she also knew he would spoil it. 'Those damned toms,' he would say, sniffing the air. Or: 'Kate, could we possibly keep Joe out of the antirrhinums?'

No, she was yearning beyond her husband. It was that which made her so sad. If only she were not quite so sure what he would say; if only he could be surprising rather than his throat-clearing, all-too-solid self, reducing the infinite down to the finite.

Kate fiddled with the honeysuckle. Eyes blurred, she twisted a stem in her hands. James, is there nothing mysterious left in us? Instead of bickering, could we simply share these flowers, could we sit and breathe in this honeysuckle with its sweet, heavy scent?

Heavy scents, the air was full of fragrance. Roses, honeysuckle, the rising sap, the refreshed grass, the faint sour smell of cats, the scent of a cigarette.

Kate turned round.

'Goodness.' Hurriedly she wiped her eyes. 'Sam.'

He was standing at the end of his garden; he seemed out of breath. The wall was low here. He stood on the other side; she could see his head, deeply shadowed.

'Kate,' he said. 'Kate, I could hardly believe this. It's amazing how right you look.' He paused. 'In that dress.'

'This? It's the coolest thing I could find.'

'It's so exactly right.' His voice sounded odd. Before, she had only ever heard it flippant. He smoked his cigarette in silence, then his shadowed face looked at her. The darkness gave him seriousness. 'It was just an impulse, you see. I'm sorry for making it seem so stagey.'

Stagey? Walking down his own garden? She said: 'You've got every right to do that.'

'God, Kate, that's so sweet. You didn't mind?'

'Of course not.'

'I regretted it the moment I did it.'

What, taking a breath of night air? Puzzled, Kate said: 'Sam, it's nice.' She knew that it was more than nice but she did not say so. The realization shocked her; she stood still.

He said: 'You see, I couldn't go on any longer the way things were. Something had to happen, didn't it? To snap.'

She felt mesmerized by his indistinct face and his glowing

213

cigarette. She was like a rabbit, frozen in the headlights of an oncoming car. Danger; she knew this. What was he getting at? It was not right, and yet at the same time it was perfectly right. If only she could tear herself away, be bright and ordinary. But she was unable to move; she remained standing on the paving stones, rooted by her thumping heart.

He said: 'I suppose you've known all this time.'

She wanted to say: I wish I didn't. They stood for a moment in silence. She heard a roosting bird rustle amongst the leaves and then settle again.

She said, her voice too loud: 'We mustn't talk like this, Sam.' She stood there, the blood thudding. She could not move away.

His voice: 'Kate, please don't stay there. Come nearer.'

She kept her eyes fixed on the trunk of the nearest tree. She thought suddenly: you can stake antirrhinums but you can't stake a sycamore. Then she thought: I must be truly mad, thinking this.

Sam said: 'Come here, Kate, I'll help you over.'

'Over the wall?'

'It's easy. Here's my hand.'

She stared at his outstretched hand; she could not take her eyes off it. She wanted to go over the wall but shouldn't she cling to her trellis? She should.

She took his hand, climbed over the wall and got down beside him. Now in his territory, she felt less dressed.

Her hand remained in his. Helplessly she said: 'It's so odd to be in this garden. I look at it from my window and feel I know it so well.' She paused. 'But now I'm in it, it seems so foreign.'

Like hers it was long and narrow, bordered by

214

flowerbeds. Bushes whose tips could be glimpsed over the wall were now here in their bulky black entirety. The familiar houses with their lighted windows had shifted to the left.

In this garden James had pinned up nothing; no clipping and pruning had he done. Her hand remained in Sam's. Now he could see her face he said: 'Hey, you've been crying.'

She turned away. 'I'm mixed up, that's why.'

'You needn't be, you know.'

She said brightly: 'Look at your garden. I bet you haven't got any half-buried Matchbox cars to stub your toes on.' She chattered on: 'Or flowerless stalks. Joe sees his father dead-heading the flowers and thinks he's so helpful when he goes off and dead-heads all the buds.' She laughed, shakily.

'Kate, why were you crying?'

It must happen. His arm must come round her shoulders. He drew her to him. She stiffened, then she relaxed. She buried her face in his wiry hair and smelt the scent of this man. Embracing James was like clinging to a cliff; Samuel was down there with her, his arms round her, their hair mingling. Could he feel her heart thumping? She could feel his.

She muttered into his hair: 'This must be a mad night. It makes one do unexpected things.'

He moved back and gazed into her face. 'Kate, Kate.'

By now, his kissing her was inevitable. For six years she had known no other breath against her breath, no other warm mouth.

He drew back. 'Kate, does no one ever tell you how beautiful you are, ever?'

215

Truthfully she answered: 'No.'

He kissed her again, she moulded herself into him, their bodies fitted. Again he drew back; he kept on having to inspect her. This close she could see his face clearly; it was so serious, wondering at her. He was tracing around her face with his finger; he ran his finger along her eyebrows, her nose.

'I love your sunburnt nose, my darling Kate.'

'Do you? You can't.'

'I love your delicate, alarmed eyebrows.' Tenderly he pushed her hair, strand by strand, behind her ear. 'Don't frown,' he said.

'This couldn't be right.'

Tenderly, oh so tenderly, he touched her. 'This mouth,' he said. 'Know when I first longed to kiss it?'

'In my outside lavatory.' Of course she knew.

'That ridiculous tortoise.'

'Tyne-Tees.'

'Kate, you're so lovely. So *lovely*. Does no one ever tell you these things?'

'Not for a long time.'

A silence. Sam took her fingers. He gazed at them; he ran his fingers over and around each one. She beseeched the bushes. *James*, she beseeched.

'Kate, remember going into Marks and Spencer?'

'Of course I do.' She looked up at her house. In the attic room, behind drawn curtains her children slept. She felt a dizzy despair. 'I remember every minute.'

'You were so radiant, with your great pram.'

Kate thought: You made that shop for me, you made my streets.

Sam said: 'Did you want me then? At all?'

216

She buried her face in his hair. 'Yes,' she hissed. '*Yes.*'

Upstairs in one of the houses a window closed. They froze.

'I must go,' she said.

'We'll go inside.'

'But Sam – ' Kate looked at him. The name, unsaid, hung in the air.

'It's all right. She's – everyone's away. Marion's watching TV.'

'I must go.' She did not move.

'Kate, come here.'

He took her hand and pressed it against his lips. Then he put it around his waist. 'Come this way.'

'Where?'

Half stumbling, she let herself be led towards his house. They did not go in, however. He led her across the little paved yard and opened the outhouse door. It creaked.

'Sam, this is mad.'

'Close the door.'

He was against her, kissing her throat, her hair. She ran her fingers over his stubbly cheek, over his large endearing nose. The wall rubbed against her dress as she slid to the floor.

A door opened. They heard it quite distinctly.

Her hands froze on the buttons of his shirt. It was not the shed door; it sounded like the back door of the house. It closed and footsteps hurried across the yard. The footsteps stopped. Clinging to Sam, Kate could actually hear someone breathing out there; hoarse, quick breaths. The footsteps set off running down the garden.

Marion had been doing exactly what she said she would, with one small and unexpected variation. No more Ginger Nuts, no more silly tonics; settled in front of the TV, she had beside her a little row of glasses. In each was a specimen drop from the extremely comprehensive selection she had found in the drinks cupboard. First a cautious sniff, then, lips pursed, a tiny sip. She was doing this thing thoroughly; by now she had tried, and rejected with a gasp and a shiver, Johnnie Walker, Booth's Gin, Marsala, Cointreau, and several others whose very aroma had returned them hastily to their bottle. All that remained was Harvey's Bristol Cream Sherry.

Programme after programme she had watched. Leaning forward in her turquoise nylon nightie, she had flipped the channels if anything looked too highbrow. Now at eleven o'clock she was surfeited, her head soggy with images. When the late news came on she could not be bothered to switch to something less demanding.

The newscaster had horn-rimmed spectacles. He was talking about some German terrorist or other, then about the higher than average temperatures. After that he got on to some strike at Heathrow, a go-slow, something like that. Probably she had heard it on the earlier news but since then it had become sedimented over by the subsequent programmes, by *Coronation Street*, women shouting in a wallpapered room, by *Starsky and Hutch*, azure Californian skies and cop sirens, by some frenzied quiz . . .

'. . . *at Heathrow continues*' the man told her. '*Conditions are described as chaotic, with national and international flights suffering delays of up to ten hours . . .*'

It switched to a film, a queue of people shuffled

forward, a close-up of faces, blurring as they turned to the camera.

Marion watched the screen. Poor James, what are you doing? She sniffed the sherry. Not bad, actually; better than the others. She took a tiny, experimental sip. Yes, rather nice.

The camera swung round. A row of seats jammed with people. A nun, bulky in black, a mother with a struggling child, a tall man in shirt sleeves, funny how she saw James everywhere, a woman, a Japanese man, his chest cluttered with cameras . . .

'. . . *temperatures are well into the eighties . . .*'

A tall man in shirt sleeves, brown hair. He was the image of him. In fact, she could have sworn it was James. Silly, just some silly coincidence. That white shirt, something courteous about the tilt of the head. Marion gripped the glass.

'. . . *with the air conditioning broken down and the heat stifling, there are reports of several people fainting . . .*'

But she no longer heard the words. It was James.

Back to the newscaster. Marion stared at his black spectacles. It had been James. She knew it now, she knew it because she recognized the woman. That tanned profile, that blue dress, so oddly familiar. It was her mother.

'*And now, the latest from Headingley.*'

James and her mother, sitting side by side, close together. Very nearly touching.

Marion stared at the screen, at the white figures. She felt sick. No, she thought, not them. Not those two. It *couldn't* be.

It was what they were doing that told it all. James,

all informal with his shirt unbuttoned at the neck. Her mother in her blue dress, leaning up close.

A man caught the ball; a roar from the crowd. Again and again Marion saw that fleeting glimpse – James, his lips parted and her mother gazing tenderly, it appeared, into his mouth. Her mother had a finger actually touching his lips; she was inspecting him with a smile. Who would do that but lovers? Lovers leaving their houses separately, off on some supposed business trip but caught by a strike, by a chance television cameraman, in their shocking moment of intimacy.

Now she thought about it, it all fitted, sickeningly. James in the newsagents – *'Oh, just for seven days.'* Why hadn't she guessed it before? They had so much in common, both so brisk and businesslike, busy professional types bored by their little houses. Seemingly casual conversations over the garden wall, meetings in the street or – who knows – in office hours. A hotel bedroom in some nameless European capital. And who would guess – one husband engrossed in his book, one wife buried in her babies.

James, my James. If only she could cry. But inside she felt scoured out, dry with loss. Her throat was tight. Crouched in front of the TV she rocked back and forth on her heels, clutching her small glass. James, how could you? You and her. She's my mother, don't you see? James, you and *anybody*.

A white-clothed man, bat in hand, walked from the field. His head was bent. Idiot, idiot. Thought he'd been embarrassed, had she, at the newsagents? All those magazines, he was as bad as the rest. Kind, was he? Reliable, did she think? Her perfect man?

Probing fingers, parted legs. The legs of her mother –

220

her mother, walking round the house all bare in her awful liberated way, those patches of skin yellow where her bikini hadn't been, those hairs, not shiny and brown like the ones on her head but coarse and black like Marion's, a great bush. Mounds where Marion had suckled.

Marion clattered downstairs. She needed air, it was stifling in the house. She opened the back door. What were they doing now – gazing at the departure board? Her mother's soft voice: *'James darling, I'm so impatient.'* *'Soon Jaquetta you'll be in my arms.'*

She blundered down the lawn to the end of the garden; she stood under the sycamores. Oh to hurt him, wound him. *'James, it's time for our plane.'*

The sky was a sickly orange. Behind Marion rose the flats, bleak and dark. In those doorways you found meths drinkers propped up.

'I've booked our room again. Our special one.' Marion looked at the houses, a black jumble of roofs, the chimneys pointing like fingers into the suffused, lurid sky. She looked at the Coopers' house. The stairs were lit but the rest of the house was in darkness. The only other light was a globe above the back door. The back door, she could see, was ajar.

'Hurry, darling, our plane.'

Without stopping to think she climbed over the wall and jumped down the other side. For a moment she stood in the brick garden, James's bushes around her, James's wall. Nothing stirred.

Slip-slop went her slippers as she made her way down the lawn. In the little concrete area beside the outhouse she hesitated. James's tools were kept through that door; from her bathroom window she had often watched him

221

carrying his workbench in and out. She opened the door and stepped inside.

No washing machine in here. Instead, rows of saws and hammers, glinting in the light that shone through from the house. Marion's bead was spinning. She touched them one after the other, she fell their cold edges. She picked them up and felt them heavy in her hands as she stood there in this small outhouse just like her own.

James bending over the magazines. *Marion, what would you like? Here, let me. Please.* Let me feel this hammer, let me feel this chisel. With his hand he had touched this wood, clasped this handle. Dad's voice. *Look, Marion's got her eye on James's handle.*

The metal was cool, she laid it against her face. It was stuffy in this little room. So quiet. The handle of the hammer was lovely, shaped wood, warm while the metal was cool. Silence; all she heard was her breathing.

At first she thought it was her breathing. But then she stopped and held her breath. Still she could hear it – a low hum. The murmur of a voice.

Very, very quietly Marion put down the hammer she was holding. She laid it on the window ledge. The voice came through the wall, from her own outhouse. It must be her father, putting in some washing. Murmuring to himself. He often talked when he was alone.

Unnerving, this; swiftly she stepped out through the door and closed it behind her. Her head swam. She looked up at the house; it seemed so strangely deserted. Could Mrs Cooper be out? Had she left the back door open as usual?

Marion had slipped through the door on several previous occasions. She slipped through it again. It was only a small part of her that wondered where Mrs Cooper could be; she could hardly care.

Her slippers flapped against her feet as she climbed up the stairs. The sitting-room was in darkness. She crossed the hall; she gripped the banister. Step by step Marion climbed up towards the bedrooms.

How's my Joe? That large grave hand. *Sleepy boy.*

She knew every stair of this house. She looked up to the next floor, where the banisters curved round out of sight. The stairs creaked as she climbed.

On the top landing she paused. To her left was the children's bedroom. She was panting; it took an effort to hold her breath and to listen. In the silence she heard them stir and sigh. From where she was standing she could see the carry-cot in one corner, the cot against the window. Straight ahead of her lay James's bedroom.

The sweat was trickling down Marion's armpits; her nylon nightie was stuck to her down the sides of her body. James was all around her; how well she knew all his things. Hadn't that foolish Marion been through these cupboards? Hadn't she drooled, inanely, over his fucking photo?

'Fuck him. Fuck him.'

She whispered this. She was not a girl for swearing; it alarmed her, the word whispered from her lips like that. She hated him. He was making her say fuck him, fuck him. He was making her head ache behind her ears. Nice, were you, James?

Will a pound be all right, Marion?

She turned to the left and stepped into the children's room.

223

'It's all right,' whispered Sam. 'It's only Marion. She'll never come in here.'

Cowering in the washing Kate asked: 'Sure?'

'Sure. Look, I'll lock it.'

He clambered to his feet. She watched him fiddling at the door, hunched, his fuzzy head bent. She lay sunk amongst the clothes.

He got down and laid his hands over her breasts; he lowered his head and started kissing her throat and her shoulders. He drew back. 'Kate darling, relax.'

It was with great tenderness that he smoothed back her hair. Her eyes were closed; he kissed each eyelid, a soft, imprinting kiss. She opened her eyes. He was gazing at her, eyebrows quizzical.

'Kate my sweetheart, what's wrong? We're safe here, really. Relax.'

'I can't.' She stared past him; she could see the row of metal knobs on the washing machine.

'Darling, look at me.' He touched her lips. 'Here.' He bent to kiss them, a soft enveloping kiss, his tongue exploring, seeking her out. Warm and persuasive, his mouth.

She lay under him, rigid. Those footsteps had altered it. It was ridiculous, them grappling here like teenagers. I am a mother of two, she thought. With a hand now conscientious she stroked his hair. Suddenly she thought: Is this washing clean or dirty? Are we messing it up?

'Kate.' He took her hand, kissed the fingers and laid them on the remaining buttons of his shirt. It was whisky, she realized, on his breath; that was his scent.

She finished unbuttoning his shirt, for shouldn't she do this? He wanted it; this was no time for second thoughts.

224

To serve was automatic in her: her upbringing had bred it into her and her daily life confirmed it. And heavens didn't she want him, this small, loving, hairy man?

He eased down her dress and stroked the inside of her thighs. He lowered his head. She cradled it; cradling came naturally to her motherly hands. He kissed her belly, then again her hands. Then, lower. Wet tongue, tickling hair.

A noise. She heard it. Kate drew up her legs.

Sam shifted. 'Darling, it's nothing.'

He moved up, he silenced her with his mouth. He held her in his arms, he was inside her now.

'Oh my sweetheart.'

She was sure she had heard it – very faint. Could it be from her own house?

Kate gripped him. The back door, she thought. Tramps, my lost keys. She gripped him tighter.

'Hold me, Kate.'

Kate thought: My babies. I must be mad. Another noise, very faint. Her fingers clenched against his skin. My babies, how could I have left them?

When Joe cried out, it was as if she had been waiting for it.

Jetta moved back; James closed his mouth.

'And it still hurts?' she asked.

'Not much. As long as I keep my tongue away from it.'

'Stiff upper lip,' she smiled, looking at him. 'I can see, James, that you're a solitary person.'

'Am I?'

It was too hot for this psychological stuff but James, his shirt clinging damply, felt hemmed in. There was

225

something relentless and yet hypnotic about this female. He still was not sure whether he was glad or not that he had bumped into her beside the Flight Information desk. He did not have time to decide, what with all those probing questions, those mesmerizing nostrils.

Still, he had to give this to her: she made one think.

'I suppose I am,' he said. 'Solitary, I mean.'

'I feel, James, that you might have been lonely before you married.'

James gazed at the milling crowds, the damp and bothered faces and the squirming children. A few stolid souls had managed to go to sleep. 'I remember when I was living alone in a flat,' he said, 'before I met Katherine. I was making myself an omelette.' Jetta leant forward; he was saying the right thing. This pleased him, for he was a polite man. 'I poured a little oil in the pan – at least I thought it was oil, it was in one of those plastic bottles. When I started scooping the omelette about I realized it had actually been Lime Juice Cordial.' He laughed. 'Do you know? I longed for somebody to be there so I could show it to them, share the joke. It seemed pathetic to be staring at this awful messy frying pan all by oneself.'

'James, that's a very moving story.'

Suddenly James longed for his wife. Looking at Jetta's unruffled, unperspiring face he longed for it to be Kate's; hers would be collapsing into laughter. But then he had never told this story to Kate, had he. He would do so, when he got home.

Jetta stood up. She was just going to the cloakroom, she said. 'Frankly, James, it's painful going into those places.' She picked up her handbag. 'All immigrant labour, you know. Indians from Southall. Paid a pittance.'

226

God it was hot. Surrounded by bothered faces, Jetta's seemed remarkably calm. This gave her a smug look. Through James's mind flashed: Bet you don't give them any tip. He smiled to himself – hadn't he admonished Kate, time and again, for giving too much?

'*Calling all passengers for BE 129 . . .*'

James struggled to his feet. This was his flight.

Sixteen

Marion cowered in the doorway of the newsagent's shop. She was panting, her breath making hoarse rasping noises. So loud, her gasps.

From here she could still see Brinsley Street. Cars flashed by, white headlights, red tail-lights; she wondered if any of them had seen her running along the pavement. A black cluster of men still loitered round the King's Head. No one seemed to have noticed anything.

Should she wait a moment in the doorway or go on? Go on where? She felt dizzy; her head swam. She listened to the rasping noises. What was this body doing? Who was cowering in this doorway, clutching a bundle in its arms? Sensible old Marion?

She caught her breath, she tried to breathe calmly, steadily. Think, Marion. Minutes had passed and no one had followed her. Outside the pub the black knot of men loosened and dispersed. No one walked this way, towards Stamford Place. Despite this, she had not a moment to lose. Soon someone would notice the loss – now, in five minutes, in an hour. Phones would be lifted, police would be called.

Police . . . yes of course there would be police. But not yet. Marion's breath had steadied; she had a moment to gather her thoughts. For the first time she dared to look down. Ollie's blanket was slipping off; she rearranged him in her arms. Surprisingly, he was not crying. He

228

gazed up at her, his face smooth as a doll's in the sodium light.

Quickly Marion looked away. Was it really herself clutching this alien, weighty child? Ollie's eyes, she could feel them, continued their calm inspection. He was surprisingly heavy, his limbs unorganizable, his head large and lolling. How could she prop it up? She did not know how to do this.

Avoiding his eyes she bundled him up in his blanket. Alf's room, of course. There was only one place to go. She would carry Ollie there and they would be safe. No one in her family even knew where Alf lived; it would only take her five minutes to walk. She would not run, just walk, calm as calm. Just an ordinary girl taking an evening stroll, in her arms a sort of parcel.

Ollie slipped; Marion hitched him up. How hot she was! The air was stifling. Her dress stuck to her.

Not her dress. It was only then that she realized what she was wearing.

Marion almost dropped the baby. She pressed herself against the glass of the door; its metal newspaper rack dug into her back. How often had she dreamed of this – standing in a supermarket or posturing on a stage, then looking down and seeing her inadequate clothes, or her body all bare.

But this was no dream. In a moment she would not wake up and say 'Fancy that.' No dream, this heavy weight, this tickling yellow blanket, this transparent nylon nightie clinging to her body.

She clutched Ollie to her chest; in the shop window beside her was a spectral row of girls, their clothes were transparent too. When had she bought those magazines with James? In another century.

She must just walk down the street. After all it was dark; no one would look that closely. What else was there to do? She could not possibly go back and face the person who had been clattering through the back door just as she was escaping through the front. Mrs Cooper, it must have been. Heaven knows what she had been doing, leaving her children like that.

Marion crept out from her doorway and walked down Stamford Place. At the corner she turned into Gifford Road, a line of sleeping terraced houses. A clock struck some hour or other; beyond the buildings a train rattled by. The only emotion Marion felt was a far-off gratefulness towards her body taking her along the pavement, its feet purposeful. Perhaps she would blink and find herself on the sitting-room carpet again with her glass of Bristol Cream.

Ollie, all too real, shifted and squirmed in her arms. She hitched him up. Suddenly fretful, he twisted his head from side to side. Marion fought down panic. A whimper. She had heard it. He was starting to whimper.

She had not meant to take him. Not really. She had just picked him out of the carry-cot to inspect him; hold him for a moment. She had had an impulse of course to rob James, to take something precious from him, but she knew that in a moment the impulse would have passed and she would have put Ollie back. Actually her sensation had been more one of saying goodbye to Ollie, bidding farewell to the whole house. It was Joe that did it, suddenly waking up like that. He must have seen her hunched over in the dark; no wonder he had yelled. It must have scared the wits out of him.

Scared the wits out of her too. The way he cried, rattling

the bars of his cot. Clutching Ollie, fleeing downstairs she had had no time to think. In Alf's room she would collect her thoughts.

The High Street was going to be tricky. Emerging from Gifford Road she hesitated on the pavement. She was lucky: all she could see were a few shadows loitering behind the pillars of Marks and Spencer, the odd staggering drunk. But how wide and exposed the High Street was! Stepping into it was like stepping into an enormous spotlit stage but she could not hurry across, her slippers were so uncomfortable, sliding off her feet at every step.

Heart thudding, she reached the other side and escaped up the alley beside the Odeon. A little gust of wind chilled her damp, transparent nightie and rustled the chip papers in the gutter. In her arms the bundle whimpered, louder now and monotonously.

'Let's keep calm, Ollie,' she whispered, leaning over the yellow blanket. She kept her voice steady. 'Let's, shall we?' Littered glass glinted, watching her. The side of the cinema seemed to stretch a mile, all grilles and vents and doors marked Exit. In one doorway something stirred. Marion averted her eyes and hurried on, slippers flapping.

When she got to Alf's, what then? At least a moment of peace in which to consider her plans. She had not quite sorted them out yet. The first priority was to settle Ollie. Then perhaps she could creep back for some proper clothes and a bottle of milk. He would like some milk; it might stop him whimpering. Somewhere in the kitchen was a little pipette they had used years ago for feeding Shiska's kittens when she had lost interest.

And what about nappies? Already the bundle felt

damp or was that just her sweat? What was she going to do – settle in the room secret from the world and bring up this wriggling infant as her own?

And what about the fact that there was never any milk at home, that she would have to find money for a machine, that this would mean creeping upstairs past Dad's room for her purse, that she had not the faintest idea where there was a milk machine anyway? Ollie would shrivel away. Surely she shouldn't leave him.

She was walking down Alf's street now. She stared up at the passing houses, gaping holes where the windows had been, glinting corrugated iron. Her stomach tightened. Alf's room, her haven. She would feel better once she was in there, safe and sound. She would sort it all out then. There were some biscuits, perhaps she could crumble them up in some water and make a sort of paste, feed Ollie that.

The pavement, unattended to for many months, was uneven and potholey; her slippers were the pink fluffy sort with no backs. She gripped her bundle.

Alf's at last. Clutching Ollie she bent down and rummaged under the brick. Her fingers found the Sainsbury's bag. She straightened up.

It was only then that she looked at his window and realized that something was different.

Behind the curtains, a light glowed.

'Joe darling, Joe my little angel.'

Holding him tightly, Kate staggered through the door to her bed. 'Joe my poppet, it was only a nightmare.'

A swift glance around his room had shown her that everything was all right: nothing disturbed, the furniture just as usual, the shape of the carry-cot over in the corner as it always was. At any other time Kate could have almost relished this whimpering child – in a dreadful way she enjoyed it when he was upset, he clung to her then. Stout and masculine he usually wriggled free from her grasp.

'Come and lie down with Mummy.'

In her panic she had not dressed. In her hand she clutched her white dress and complicated bra. She climbed into bed with her son. Sweet relief flooded her that it had not been worse. Obviously just a bad dream. By the time she had dashed in he had hardly been crying at all, just standing at the bars of his cot and whining, in his mouth his thumb and in his hands his precious blanket. Kate threw up a grateful prayer that her mad neglect, her whole mad night, had not been punished by something more appropriate.

She lay on the bed, Joe cradled in her arms. Into his mouth he inserted his thumb and promptly fell asleep – callously, Kate considered, after all that fuss. What on earth had Samuel thought, lying disarranged amongst the washing? What was he thinking now? Would he be slowly putting on his shirt? Waiting for her? Perhaps she should go down. Tomorrow she must apologize, surely, but could she face him?

She would lie here quietly for a while until she was sure Joe was properly asleep. Pooh Bear was rising and falling rhythmically, but if she moved Joe might stir. She would wait, then go downstairs and make sure she had shut the back door and turned off all the lights. Then she would get back into bed and consider sanely all that had taken place this evening. Now she was safe at the top of her house, away from it all, she could almost pretend that it had not happened. It must have been midsummer madness, mustn't it? But she had not been completely mad; that much she knew.

Before she did that, however, she would just lie here for a moment. The sheets were so cool and welcoming. Her eyelids were so very heavy, her body was so very heavy, her limbs sinking down, sinking into the softness of the bed.

Kate could not stop her eyelids closing. Just for two minutes, she told herself. Two minutes is all I crave. After all that had happened, of course, any feeling person would be sitting up alert and troubled.

Ah but the softness of this bed. Without realizing it she was arranging herself more comfortably. Such a mindless, determined body; there was just one thing that now it craved.

The curtains were made of poor brownish stuff; the light glowed through them. They were not quite closed; through the crack Marion could see something flickering.

There were two people in the room, crouched round a candle. She could hear their voices mumbling.

'Weird things in here,' one of them was saying. Something glinted; he was holding the photo. 'Cast your little eye over this.'

Marion stared at the bent heads. That voice was familiar. So was the pointed nose. The head turned; it was caught in silhouette.

'Must be worth a bob.' The beaky profile bent to inspect it. 'That frame. Sodding silver, innit.'

She knew him. Once he had been in the pub with Ron.

'Not a bad little place,' said the other one. His spectacles flashed as he looked around. 'Sight better than Telemere Road.'

'Yeah, well, couldn't be worse, could it.'

'S'not the fuzz pressure here. Knocking this lot down, aren't they.'

The first one stood up and started poking around. His legs were so thin that his patched jeans looked empty. He picked up first this thing then that, his head cocked sideways.

'Do I detect the feminine touch?' he said.

'Do a nice line in frilly cushions, don't they.'

'A little birdie tells me someone's been here before.' He was holding something against his chest. Marion could not breathe; it was James's shirt. 'Considerate, weren't they. Bit big but it'll do. Austin Reed, no less.'

The other one said: 'Fancy a walnut whip then?'

'You trying to be rude?'

'No, look here, dum-dum.' They bent over Marion's canvas bag. 'It's like a bleeding confectioner's in here.'

The spectacled one put something into his mouth; voice muffled, he called out to the scullery: 'Hey, Pat.'

A short dark man appeared through the door. He said: 'Someone's really tidied up this place.' He sat down and picked up the photo: 'Who's this geezer then?'

'What happens if they come back?'

'Then we'll be one big happy family.'

The man called Pat wore a leather jacket; it caught the light as he bent over; he took out a bed roll. Marion could see, behind him, the shape of a Primus and a pile of carrier bags. 'All in all,' he said, 'for a short doss, I've seen worse.'

235

It was then that Marion realized that she had broken all the fingernails of her left hand, so hard had she been gripping the window ledge. Moving away, she staggered and had to rest for a moment against the wall. She had been clutching Ollie so tightly that her arm ached. For a moment she leant against the wall to calm herself down and let the dizziness pass.

In a while she felt she could move; in a glazed, automatic way she managed to place the paper bag back under the brick. Her body performed this; she remembered nothing of it. From the folds of his blanket Ollie's calm, incurious eyes watched her face and watched her mouth which did not move. Her rather heavy face seemed calm, blank even. Paler? In this sodium light you could not tell, it sucked the colour from a skin, leaving it grey and mask-like.

She was walking now. From his position Ollie could see the empty houses rising and falling to the rhythm of her step. She was hurrying; above him the stars swung to and fro.

The rumble of traffic, bright lights and then quiet again as they left the High Street. Marion's footsteps were muffled thuds, jarring him. Above him Ollie could see TV aerials jerking up and down, he gazed at the rooftops and the jolting stars.

They stopped. Marion looked up and down the street; she appeared to be thinking. Certainly she gripped Ollie more tightly. He let out a squeak. Over him bent her grey face.

She appeared to make up her mind. Ollie's body jolted again; now he could see tall black buildings, a jerking cliff of them, many broken windows. The great black cliffs were

236

close on either side of him, blocking out all but a dancing strip of sky.

At the end of the alley Marion stopped. Ahead of her lay the long back wall of the gardens; behind them rose the sycamores. Against the wall was a pile of rubbish – old packing cases, a tin bath, a broken sink. She tucked Ollie more firmly under her arm and climbed on to a packing case. From here she could see down into the gardens.

She did not know what she had expected. People milling about, torchlight in the gardens? In the windows of the houses, lights and confusion?

Gripping the brick ledge Marion looked down into the Coopers' garden. The one thing she had not expected was that it would look exactly the same.

Ollie squirmed. She hitched him on to her hip and studied the back of the Coopers' house. She stared and stared, searching for some alteration. Nothing had changed: the back door remained ajar, the light up the stairs remained lit. All the rest of the windows, as before, remained in darkness. The back of her own house too was dark, except for the yellow square of her father's attic window.

Marion bundled Ollie under one arm and put her leg over the wall. Even with the bundle it was simple to slip down on to the other side. Thieves, she thought, must find these houses easy. She was in the Coopers' garden now. Holding her breath she crept past the trellis and down the dewy lawn. She reached the back door. She paused and listened. Not a sound, except a thud she recognized as her heart.

Into the house she crept, up the stairs, along the hall and into the darkened sitting-room.

What now? She stood immobile; there was a pulse thumping in her ear. She did not dare go upstairs.

Nobody had closed the curtains; the room lay bathed in the orange light from the street. She gazed round at the dead eye of the television, the waiting chairs. There was only one comfortable place to leave the baby.

Marion laid Ollie on the floor; swiftly she rearranged the cushions on the sofa. Lifting one, something bright caught her eye. A bunch of keys. It must have fallen down a crevice of the sofa. She picked it up and put it on the table. Then she laid Ollie on the sofa in a nest of cushions and wedged him in firmly. With all her body in its damp clinging nightie, she willed him not to cry.

Now she had lain Ollie down, she realized she was terribly tired. Blundering with fatigue, she made her way out of the room, out of the front door. That her father had forgotten to bolt from the inside her own front door, that she could therefore just turn the knob and creep into the safety of her hall, seemed scarcely curious at all. Upon recollection not the slightest bit odd, considering everything else that had happened this strange, strange midsummer's night.

Plough them in, plough them in.

The tortoises were waiting on the ground, rows of them. They did not move though Kate in her dream could hear the plough approaching. As yet it was just a faint rumble . . . how patient the tortoises were. They knew, didn't they, how very good they would be for her garden.

The fact was of course that the bare earth was her garden, rather wider and larger, in truth very much wider and larger . . . all that space, she could see no horizons, and the tortoises waiting, so many brown humps making

238

little mewling noises, she could hear them though the rumblings were getting louder now . . . not just rumblings but bangings too and a man's shout. Good, patient tortoises . . .

It must be a very big plough, it was making such a noise. All those clatters and thumps, she could hardly hear the faint cries, though tortoises don't cry . . . of course, how silly of her not to have seen that they weren't tortoises at all, they were little brown bags, and the yelling inside them, such faint yelling, it was coming from the babies inside, all those babies inside all those little paper bags. They were no longer mewling, now they were yelling as loudly as they could but how very muffled and far away they seemed, and the bangings and rumblings getting louder . . .

At some point before she was entirely conscious Kate knew that the rumblings were the rubbish men. Of course, the rubbish men, making their way slowly down Brinsley Street, throwing their bags into the large and noisy lorry with its chomping teeth. James will be glad, she thought, stirring her legs in the warm sheets. Before she was even awake she realized it, with relief; he was always going on about the go-slows and ringing up the council though he never could find the right department in the phone book . . . Stupid plough, of course it wasn't a plough . . . stupid dream . . . through her half-closed eyes she could see that the sun was already bright though it was still early, the dust-lorry was the only commotion in the silent street . . . a relief, all that rubbish bundled away, pushed into the crunching jaws, one less thing to have to worry James with . . .

Kate drew the sheet up to her chin, so deliciously warm,

so drowsy still . . . sweet relief was stealing through her . . . how horribly human those yells had been. Funny how they didn't stop . . .

Kate sat up. At once she was awake. She pushed back the sheets. Joe lay diagonally across the bed, peacefully asleep. Somewhere the crying was going on and on, faintly. Terrified, muffled screams.

In a moment Kate was stumbling down the stairs, down past the bathroom, past the landing . . . the cries were louder now, hoarse, frightened yells . . . into the hall she ran.

The sitting-room door was ajar; she rushed in. Ollie lay sprawled across the cushions, his blanket on the floor, his face brick red, against his mouth, back and forth, his fists jerking.

It was a full five minutes later, when Kate was lying on the sofa, Ollie pressed against her breast, that she saw on the table the bunch of keys. Over Ollie's wispy scalp they glinted, splayed out from their St Christopher keyring. But though she remained staring at them there was nothing left in her to ask any questions. Not quite yet; not this morning.

Ollie drew back, sated. But her milk still spurted; over his hair and his brow it was scattered, the tiniest of pearls.

_____ *Seventeen* _____

It was a week later that the parcel came and with it a note. The whole breakfast table was full of letters but they belonged to her mother; Jetta had arrived home only the night before and she was sorting through her mail. With the marmalade pushed to one side, the kitchen table resembled a desk.

When Marion unwrapped the clock her mother looked up. 'Darling, what on earth . . .?'

So familiar, that metal face, that square mahogany surround. Marion slit open the accompanying note.

'*My father wished you to have this. He often spoke of you and what pleasure he got from your visits. This is just a little memento.*' The letter, postmarked Hull, was signed: '*Pauline Jenkins (Evans).*'

It was so odd, seeing this clockface here at home; it was like meeting one of the teachers outside the boundaries of school – in the High Street, in a shop. How often had Marion gazed at it, on her early visits, dutifully waiting for the hands to creep round the regulation hour, later surprised at how the time had passed. She turned it round. '*To Harold Alfred Evans. In Grateful Recognition of Forty Years Loyal Service. North Thames Gas Board 1963.*' She had not even known that his first name was Harold.

Marion turned the clock over in her hands. To herself she announced: I shall throw away my Mickey Mouse clock, I shall put this one on the mantelpiece instead. Satisfying,

241

this heavy clock; she ran her hands over its cool face. So Alf had not slipped away completely. She possessed this.

Her parents were talking about the Stockholm conference.

'We've been languishing away here,' said her father. 'Haven't we, Marion? Consoling ourselves with booze.'

'Booze?' Jetta looked alert.

'Marion's into the Bristol Cream. In a big way.'

'*Dad.*'

'Well, a small way. Like a thimbleful. But it's a start.'

'Darling, how amazing.' Jetta smiled at her, really warmly. She laughed, then stifled it with her brown hand. 'Silly, but it's rather a relief.'

Dad said: 'Companionable.'

It had been a companionable week, strangely so. Marion's little glass of sherry had drawn them together those sunlit evenings. Dad had seemed quiet, oddly subdued. At meals they had propped open their books, but he never turned a page. Had he guessed about his wife, suspected something? He had been gentle with Marion; Marion gentle with him, pained for him.

Pained for herself too, of course. She did not think of her mother, she would not look at her. Nor did she dare think of James—not yet. She just closed him away, like closing the last page of her magazine. Instead she had concentrated upon Dad, and upon her own face in the mirror. No more secret eating, no more furtive packets; was it her imagination or were her eyes really larger, her spots fading? She had gone to Boots and bought some eye-liner. Dad said: 'Well hello Liz Taylor.' Was it her imagination or was her stomach no longer so bulgy under its blue skirt?

Her mother said: 'Sam, I was thinking it would be nice

242

to ask the Coopers round. For a barbecue, perhaps. Perfect barbecue weather.'

A silence.

'I thought you'd like that, darling,' she said. 'A neighbourly gesture. You're the one who's always saying how isolated Katherine must be.'

A pause. 'Did I?' Dad seemed to be preoccupied with the Corn Flakes packet. He must be reading '*Fortified with Thiamin and Riboflavin.*'

'Only if you'd like to, darling,' she said. 'It's just that I think James rather took to me – that he feels rather close to me now. Our little chat at the airport – I honestly think he found that rather useful.'

'Dug away at his psyche, did you?'

'Some things I think he found rather liberating to talk about. Painful perhaps.'

'Painful I bet, with that great hole in his gum. Didn't you say he'd just had a tooth out?'

Alf's clock had stopped at ten to three. Marion kept her eyes fixed on the motionless metal hands. She did not dare to breathe.

Dad laughed for the first time in a week. 'Poor sod. Boiled alive in a writhing mass of testy travellers, bleeding great hole in his mouth and then he bumps into you at your most spiritually rapacious.'

'Don't exaggerate, darling. It wasn't bleeding. I inspected it for him; in fact it was healing rather well.'

Ten to three. The hands pointed to the numbers; they pointed them out to Marion as if she were a baby. They said: Fool.

Dad picked up the Corn Flakes packet. 'Listen to these opening instructions.' He lowered his voice. '*Slide finger under flap,*' he murmured in his husky, suggestive voice, '*and move from side to side.*'

Marion did not mind this – in fact, she hardly heard. She looked up into her mother's face, for the first time this morning she met her eye. 'Mum,' she asked. 'What was that you just said?'

'There's something in the bed,' James said. 'I can feel it with my foot.'

Half past eight and they still were not up. Not the usual pattern, this, but James had arrived late the night before and had announced that he was taking the morning off.

Drowsy as she was, Kate could judge that the presence of a foreign object under the sheets had made James less irritable than curious. As he fished for it she remarked: 'Remember when we were first married and always having breakfast in bed? Remember making the bed and finding a whole piece of buttered toast?'

'Aha.' James's hand emerged holding the lid of the post-box. He turned to Joe who had climbed in with them. 'Got the hang of this yet, old chap?'

'Hasn't had a chance,' said Kate. 'Been searching for the top bit for days.'

'Young man,' said James heavily, 'I sincerely hope that you've reached the developmental level expected of you by our neighbouring child authority.'

Kate asked: 'What do you mean?'

'Jetta.'

'Jetta?'

He said patiently: 'Jetta Green. When I met her in the clinic. You know, when we had that coffee together.'

A pause. 'She suggested the post-box?'

'Heavens, I forgot I shouldn't have told you.' He looked at her. 'Why are you smiling? You should be cross.'

'Nothing, nothing.' To hide her blushes, her idiotic mistake, Kate buried her head under the sheet. 'Sweetheart,' she murmured, nuzzling his arm. If she could not apologize to him in person, she could at least press her contrite face into the crook of his elbow.

For a moment they lay there at peace, a bedful of souls warmed by the sun that filtered through the curtains.

'I heard the rubbish men earlier,' said James.

'The go-slow's over,' said Kate. 'They started coming regularly last week.'

'That's a relief. By the way, did I tell you about our neighbouring Tolstoy, Mr Green?'

'What do you mean?'

'Kate, don't jerk like that, you've taken all my sheet.' James pulled it back over his chest. 'You know, Samuel Green. I spoke to him last night. On the doorstep.'

A silence.

'Speak up, Kate. Can't hear.'

'I said: what did you say?'

'Rather embarrassing really. He was just putting out this enormous bag of rubbish. Looked like paper so I said – you know, just for something to say, I was trying to find my door keys and some change for the taxi driver and – '

'What did you say to him?'

'The taxi driver? Oh, Samuel Green you mean. Keep your hair on, Kate, don't stare at me, it wasn't *that* embarrassing. Well, I just said – you know, in a jocular, neighbourly sort of way – *That your masterpiece then?* And do you know what he said?'

A pause. 'What?'

'He said yes. *Yes.* I felt awfully uncomfortable. He said it was rather a relief because really, underneath, he'd always known it wasn't much good. Cardboardy, he said.'

'That was all?'

'I found my keys then. Funny sort of chap. I probably could quite take to him really. Wonder if he'll go back to work.'

There was a silence then. James was thinking of the suggestion he was about to make. Kate was turning over, for the hundredth time, the events of those few night hours a week ago. There was no sense in turning them over: the bizarre facts revolved bumpily round her brain. Nothing could push them flat, settle them into any sensible scheme. The uneventful week since then had distanced them without explaining them. The very oddity of the happenings – the shifting of Ollie, the absence of certain objects – had in some way lifted the guilt from the episode with Samuel. It just made it part of the oddness. It was as if her house were a doll's house and herself a puppet: a large unknown hand had rearranged her, rearranged her things, put her baby in the wrong place, lifted her up and placed her where she did not mean to be. Well, she did not *really* mean to be.

Perhaps indeed the whole thing had been a dream. Suffering as she did from chronic drowsiness, had she just slipped into sleep? As time went by she would look back on the events and see them as gauzier, more unreal: tortoises in rows, a door creaking open into an ivy-twined, fairytale outhouse, a baby found, as in a dream, perfectly unharmed but in the wrong place. Silver keys glinting on a table.

Nonsense: she couldn't get away with that one. There were empty hooks in the hall where the clothes brushes should be, a tide mark on the sitting-room cushions from Ollie's damp occupation, grubby marks on the back of her white dress where she had pressed herself, been pressed against that wall. And what about her feelings when she would come face to face with Sam, as soon she must? No, this could neither be excused nor explained by sleep.

One result of all this was surprising – to James at any rate. In the months ahead it was Kate who became the obsessive one about bolting doors and keeping the house secure – Kate, once so carefree, who never realized that the thief was not the type she had automatically expected him to be. He was not the haunter of alleys past whom she would hurry with her pram experiencing a *frisson* of complacent thankfulness; he was not one of the unfortunates, the dispossessed, against whom James had bolted and barred his home. In the five further years that she lived in Brinsley Street, Kate never did know that the thief came not from without her safe and comfortable little world, but from within.

'You look pensive.' James turned on his side, facing Kate. During the flight from Brussels he had put away the crossword, he had gazed instead at the clouds, turning things over in his mind. Clouds filling his little porthole. He seldom sat, simply, like that; credit must go to Jetta. 'Very pensive.' He pushed back the hair from her forehead. What went on under that creamy skin?

He was about to make his suggestion. A conventional man, it would be a time-honoured solution but who is to despise those? He said: 'What would you say, darling, to a week in Paris?'

Swallowing the question that sprang up about the children Kate cried: 'Yes please.'

247

'We could ask your mother if she would take the babies. Ollie's nearly weaned now, isn't he?'

'James, could we actually have time together? Wander the streets – have nothing else that we ought to be doing?'

'I don't see why not.'

'Make love in the afternoon?' They probably would not. A French room would not change them, it would not solve them. They would need more than that. Still – her eye travelled over the hotel room, exhilaratingly impersonal, its bland decor telling her that she was cut adrift, that she was herself; its little bathroom unscrubbed by her hands. She said: 'Can both our toothpastes be foreign?'

Perhaps whimsical, this was also heartfelt. Kate, so warm, lay back in the soft pillow. Through the curtains the sun seeped into her skin.

For some words to tell James her pleasure without actually putting it into words – that she understood what he was getting at, that she saw how he tried, she remarked: 'It's been a strange summer, James. Different from the other ones.' She smiled. 'It must be the sun. Half past eight and already it's amazingly hot.'

But that was because Joe had got out of bed and switched on the electric blanket. Unseasonable of him, but he liked seeing the little red light come on, didn't he.

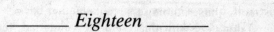

Eighteen

The long hot summer continued. In Gideon Road, where Harold Alfred Evans had lived, the street was closed. Corrugated iron barriers were erected. One Monday in August the men moved in and hammered up a sign: Valori Demolition Ltd.

They gutted the houses and hacked away the floorboards; the crane arrived with its heavy concrete ball. Dust rose, clouds of it – the crane revved, revolving slowly – the ball swung. One thud: the walls creaked, resisting. A second thud: the houses sighed, the walls bowed over, they crumbled. Exposed, the little fireplaces on every floor, the chosen wallpapers. A patchwork of patterns, private ones, they should not be seen.

Above the rubble vistas appeared – the back view of the next terrace, surprised with its dangling washing, the glittering office blocks down on the Marylebone Road. Underneath the railway the row of bricked-in arches where crankshafts were re-ground and cars re-sprayed – for the first time in a century these brick façades caught the evening sun. Where Gideon Road had been, nothing remained – no poignant relic jutting out of the earth. Sold, the photo frame and the silver-topped bottle, to the jewellers next to Tesco; pulverized, the rest, to grey earth hard as concrete. No reminders, no street, just an empty space with lorries parked at all angles and a group of pre-fab huts for the building contractors who at the end of the summer would be moving in (21,000 Square Feet of Office Space and 6 Residential Units).

No, one thing left. In the cab of a lorry lay a clothes brush, quite a classy one with a leather back.

'Take a look at this,' said the young lad, the one who sat in the driving seat. 'It's got initials on and all.'

The older man picked it up. 'Not yours, sunshine.'